Praise for the Aurora Anderson Mystery Series

PAINT THE TOWN DEAD (#2)

"Plenty of charming characters, red herrings, labyrinthine twists and turns and brushes with death before you can even begin to guess whodunit. *Paint the Town Dead* is a cleverly crafted mystery full of secrets and intrigues that kept me guessing till the end."

– Connie Archer, Author of the
Soup Lover's Mystery Series

"Johnson paints characters with a folksy charm that makes them feel like family...Color me a fan!"

– Diane Vallere, Author of
the Material Witness, Style & Error, and Madison Night Mysteries

"Rory is definitely a quirky character; she has the ability to draw the readers in so that they want to follow her through her adventures."

– *Suspense Magazine*

"The plot thickens and becomes more entangled as Rory pursues all and any possible angles [to catch the killer]. Many intriguing complications arise during this search for the truth. An easy to read mystery with an amateur female sleuth who is a very likeable and believable character."

– *LibraryThing*

"Rory finds herself needing to uncover the truth of a friend's shocking death as everyone else seems satisfied with the easy answer. She's willing to risk friendships, and her own life, to chip away to reach the unvarnished truth. Paint the Town Dead is an engaging mystery set amidst a painting convention and showcases the complexity of relationships when a tragedy strikes."

– Christina Freeburn, Author of
Framed to Death

FATAL BRUSHSTROKE (#1)

"Johnson has penned a charming mystery filled with colorful characters, clever plot twists and unexpected surprises that will keep you guessing whodunit right until the end. A rewarding read and a refreshing debut."

—Hannah Dennison, Author of the
Vicky Hill Mysteries and The Honeychurch Hall Mysteries

"Johnson has an assured, steady hand in creating complex plotlines in *Fatal Brushstroke*. Readers will definitely want to revisit Vista Beach in Aurora's next outing of investigating."

– Naomi Hirahara, Edgar Award-Winning Author of
Murder on Bamboo Lane

"A fun and fast-paced romp with plenty of suspense and intrigue, colorful characters, infidelity and family secrets. *Fatal Brushstroke* is sure to please cozy readers, especially those who love crafts mixed with murder."

– Sue Ann Jaffarian, Author of the
Bestselling Ghost of Granny Apples Mystery Series

"Enjoyable, fun and entertaining...Aurora is a strong character you immediately feel like you have known her a lifetime...I love books that keep you reading late into the night and for me this is one of them great books."

– *Shelley's Book Case*

"The strength of the book, as in most good cozy mysteries, lies in the main character...The book really poses the question, within a well-written cozy, is nature or nurture more important in what a person becomes?...This underlying story makes this an interesting choice for book clubs to discuss."

– *Examiner.com*

Paint the Town Dead

**The Aurora Anderson Mystery Series
by Sybil Johnson**

FATAL BRUSHSTROKE (#1)
PAINT THE TOWN DEAD (#2)

Paint the Town Dead

An Aurora Anderson Mystery

Sybil Johnson

HENERY PRESS

PAINT THE TOWN DEAD
An Aurora Anderson Mystery
Part of the Henery Press Mystery Collection

First Edition
Trade paperback edition | December 2015

Henery Press
www.henerypress.com

This is a work of fiction. Any references to historical events, real people, or real locales are used fictitiously. Other names, characters, places, and incidents are the product of the author's imagination, and any resemblance to actual events or locales or persons, living or dead, is entirely coincidental.

ISBN-13: 978-1-943390-33-5

Printed in the United States of America

To my parents, Glen and Mathie,
and my sister, Glenice

ACKNOWLEDGMENTS

Thank you to everyone who joined Rory on her first adventure in *Fatal Brushstroke*. To have people other than my family read and enjoy my work is a dream come true.

Thanks also to my always calm and ever helpful editor, Erin George, for her advice and assistance in making this a better story. And to everyone at Henery Press for their continued support.

To everyone in the mystery community, I value your friendship more than I can say. Special thanks go to Hannah Dennison, for her advice and moral support, and Cynthia Kuhn, for her encouraging words.

A special thanks goes to Project Egypt for the support and friendship you've shown me over the years.

And the biggest thanks of all goes to my husband, Steve, for aiding and abetting me in all of this writerly stuff.

Chapter 1

The rock crashed through the window, barely missing Rory Anderson's head, and slammed into the bookcase behind her. Seconds later, she heard the revving of an engine followed by the squeal of tires as a car sped away.

Rory's heart leapt into her throat. She gaped at the jagged hole in the window in front of her desk and swiveled her chair around to look behind her, where a dozen paperbacks had tumbled out of the bookcase onto the hardwood floor. Nestled among them lay the fist-sized rock that had come close to knocking her out.

Her heart pounding, Rory took several calming breaths and forced herself to sit as still as possible while she listened for suspicious sounds outside. No unusual noises reached her ears. The residents of Seagull Lane appeared to be tucked in for the night, enjoying a peaceful Sunday evening before the workweek started. Once her breathing returned to normal, she cautiously got up from her chair, leaned over her desk, and peered through the damaged window into the darkness beyond. Lights from neighboring houses illuminated enough of her street that she could discern the shapes of cars and trees. A cat crept out of the shadows and crossed her front lawn like a tiger on the prowl. She didn't want to know what the orange tabby was stalking.

Rory's gaze swept her work area from the window past the computer on her desk to the pile of books on the floor. She crossed the room, and tucking her long brown hair behind her ears, bent down to pick up the rock. Wrapped around it was a note. The words on the scrap of pink paper chilled her to the bone: *This is only the beginning. Prepare to pay for your actions. Down with the Akaw!*

Fright turned to puzzlement as the message finally sunk in. Dozens of people had been inside the newly built hotel in the two weeks since it opened. She doubted all of them had been treated to a rock through their window. She *had* written software for the Akaw, but that didn't seem a good enough reason to target her.

Rory carefully placed the rock and note on the desk and wiped off her hands on her jeans. After turning on every light she could find, she took her cell phone out of its charger and called the Vista Beach police department to report the incident. Time dragged on as she waited for a patrol car to arrive. She itched to clean up the mess, but knew the police would want to see an undisturbed scene so, instead, she took photos of the damage for her insurance company.

When ten minutes passed and the normally responsive police were nowhere in sight, she wondered if there'd been a sudden explosion of crime in Vista Beach. Perhaps the influx of visitors common in June was creating more problems than usual for the quiet Los Angeles County beach community.

Rory paced back and forth in the great room that spanned the front of her house, walking from the work area at one end to the living room at the other, periodically glancing outside. She was passing the front door for what must have been the tenth time when a cacophony of yowls and hisses rent the night air. Her stockinged feet slid on the polished hardwood, and she braced herself against a nearby wall to steady herself. As soon as she regained her balance, she poked her head out the door and yelled at the cats to be quiet. Once the warring felines slunk away, she continued her pacing, getting angrier and angrier every time she passed the damaged window, obsessing over the violation of her home and the police department's lack of response. By the time a patrol car pulled into her driveway forty-five minutes later, she was ready to explode.

Light spilled out onto the porch when Rory wrenched the front door open. She suppressed her anger as she watched the uniformed officer traverse the walkway, the beam of his flashlight illuminating the path before him. By the time he stepped onto the porch, she was calm enough to have a civil conversation.

"You called about some vandalism, ma'am?" Officer Yamada said, after introducing himself and apologizing for the delay.

Rory invited the officer inside and pointed to the broken window. He examined the area, then headed outside to look around.

When he returned, she handed over the note for his inspection. "This came through the window wrapped around a rock."

His expression neutral, he stared at the note, not even raising an eyebrow as he read the words on the paper.

"You don't seem very surprised," she said.

"This isn't new to me. I saw an identical note earlier tonight at the home of the chairman of the city council."

"So I wasn't the only one targeted." Rory didn't know whether to find the news comforting or not. "How many others were there?"

"Besides the chairman, two other council members' houses were egged. Those are just the calls I took personally."

No wonder he'd taken so long to get here, Rory thought. "How long has this been going on? The newspaper didn't say anything about vandalism. The only articles I saw were on people complaining about the hotel about, what was it...?" She screwed up her face in concentration. "Something about homeowners near the Akaw claiming construction of the underground parking garage damaged their houses."

"It's been the talk of the department lately. Couldn't tell you if it's true or not. We've had several incidents of vandalism around the city since the hotel opened. The investigation is a top priority for us but, unfortunately, we haven't had much luck so far identifying the culprits."

"How come I haven't heard anything about this?"

"We've been keeping it quiet. Don't want to unnecessarily disturb residents. Do you work for the Akaw?"

"Indirectly. I put together their website and developed an app for guests to use."

The officer jotted something down on his notepad. "An app, huh? My daughter keeps on talking about apps. What does this one do?"

"Gives guests information on the hotel and the city. There's a map of the Akaw, menus for the hotel's restaurant and room service, a list of local attractions, that kind of thing. Users can even order room service and book their next visit right from their phone."

"Sounds useful. Would it be easy for someone to find out you did all this work for the hotel?"

"Pretty easy. My company name and website address is at the bottom of every site I develop. Wouldn't take much research to find out who I was, though I don't know how they'd know where I live. I use a postal box for all of my company correspondence."

The officer cleared his throat. A look of discomfort momentarily appeared on his face. "A lot of people know where you live because of the recent...problem."

When she'd found a body in her garden and been suspected of murder two months before, it was the talk of the town. Between word of mouth and articles in the local newspaper and on blogs, half the residents probably had her address tucked away in the back of their minds by now.

"I'm sorry this happened to you. I know it's troubling. We'll do everything we can to figure out who's responsible." He closed his notebook. "In the meantime, I'll file a report. You can get a copy if you need one for your insurance company."

"What are the chances you'll actually find out who did this?"

"Based on past experience with this kind of thing, not great. But I like to be optimistic. We'll process the note and canvass the neighborhood to see if anyone noticed anything. Maybe we'll get lucky. One of your neighbors could have a security camera. I promise, we'll do our best." Before stepping out the front door, Officer Yamada added, "Be sure to put something over that window. And don't hesitate to call again if something else happens."

After the officer left, Rory wondered whether the police would be able to catch the culprit. If they couldn't find the person who broke her window, she intended to look for the vandal herself. She stared at the photo she'd taken of the note, trying to get some clue as to its author. There wasn't any handwriting to analyze, only a font that could have been printed anywhere. She thought about talking to her neighbors, but one glance at the clock told her most of them wouldn't appreciate being disturbed at this hour. Any questioning would have to wait until morning.

Rory dialed her insurance company's hotline. After spending time on the phone with a representative, she called a twenty-four hour window repair service who promised to send someone right out. While they measured the window and boarded it up, she swept up the broken glass and returned the books to their places.

Too restless to work or go to bed, Rory dug back issues of the weekly newspaper, the *Vista Beach View*, out of the recycling bin and searched for the articles she remembered seeing about the Akaw. She read and reread the two she found for some indication as to who might have targeted her home.

The articles mentioned the contentious debates and endless city council meetings concerning the property that had once housed a private school. When the owners put the large lot up for sale, the city of Vista Beach planned to buy it, but the city council took too long to authorize the funds and the hotel builder swooped in and purchased the land instead. The council approved the hotel project in a close vote, the chairman himself leading the charge. Rory suspected the other council members targeted also voted for approval.

She returned the papers to the recycling bin and tried to figure out what to do next. Now that her anger had worn off, she felt the need to hear a friendly voice, so she speed-dialed a number she called every single day. Two rings later, Elizabeth Dexter answered.

"Hi, Rory," Liz said. "You've got to see this show I'm watching. These people marry someone they've never met. It's like a blind date, only instead of going out to dinner they meet at the altar. Crazy, right?" She launched into a detailed description of the latest reality TV show to catch her eye.

Smiling into her phone, Rory leaned back on the couch, relaxing into its soft cushions. The tension eased from her body as she listened to her best friend's nonstop chatter.

"So what's up with you?" Liz asked after she finished describing all of the episodes she'd seen so far.

Rory took a deep breath and blurted out, "Someone threw a rock through my window."

Without a moment's hesitation, Liz said, "I'll get my jammies and toothbrush and be right over."

A wave of relief washed over Rory. She hadn't realized how on edge she was about sleeping alone in the house that night. Most of the time she liked living by herself, but after the evening's events every creak and groan in the 1,200-square-foot structure made her jump.

Fifteen minutes later, Rory opened her front door to a petite woman, dressed in slacks and a printed blouse, whose head barely reached Rory's shoulders. Her dark brown hair fashioned in a pixie cut, Liz dropped her overnight bag on the hardwood floor and stood on tiptoe to give her friend a hug. "It must have been scary. Are you okay?"

"Much better now that you're here."

Hands on her hips, Liz peered around the room. "How much damage did they do?"

Rory pointed to the boarded up window next to her desk, tracing the path the projectile had taken with her finger. "The rock came through there and hit the bookcase over there. Sailed right past my head. One inch to the left and I'd have been knocked out." She fingered her ear, cringing at the memory of the close call. "I'm still having a hard time believing it wasn't a dream."

"More like a nightmare. On the bright side, no damage was done to your computer, so you haven't lost any work."

"Amen to that." Rory led the way to the rear of the house into the recently remodeled kitchen with its granite countertops and stainless steel appliances.

While Rory put on the tea kettle, Liz settled down at the kitchen table and peered through the window at the dimly lit side yard. She nodded toward the house on the other side of the fence. "I wonder if Granny G saw anything."

"Unfortunately, Mrs. Griswold's on vacation. Alaskan cruise."

"Too bad. She always notices things."

Rory's hyper-vigilant neighbor made it her business to know everything that happened on the block. She had no doubt, had the seventy-five-year-old been home, the police would already have the license plate number of the getaway car and be on their way to arrest the vandal.

Once the tea was ready, Rory cleared off space on the table, pushing a half-finished painting project off to one side. She set two cups filled to the brim on the wooden surface and sat down across from her friend. "Thanks for dropping everything and coming over. I feel better with you here."

Liz laid a hand on Rory's arm and smiled reassuringly. "Anything for my bestie." She wrapped both hands around her cup and sniffed appreciatively. "Mmm, peppermint. Now, what did the police say? Was it Dashing D? Was he the one who came to your rescue?"

An impish grin appeared on her face as she talked about Detective Martin Green, the Vista Beach police officer they'd met two months before when Rory found a body in her garden.

Rory blushed at the mention of the man who had been occupying her dreams more and more often lately. "I'm not a damsel in distress. Okay, maybe I was, a little bit. Anyway, Officer *Yamada* said some city council members' houses were hit as well. There might be others. It seems to be part of a protest against the Akaw." She took her cell phone out of the pocket of her jeans and brought up the photo she'd taken earlier of the note. "This was wrapped around the rock."

Liz studied the phone's display and whistled. "The pink paper's a nice touch. I'll have to ask my contact at the police station how many houses were hit. Lots of people work at the hotel, but I doubt most of them live in the city. The owner doesn't even live here. Rumor has it, he's up north somewhere."

Rory didn't question how her friend knew this tidbit. As a real estate agent, Liz never knew where her next sale or client would come from so she kept her ear to the ground, taking special note of any information relating to houses and plots of land within the city.

Rory put her elbow on the table and leaned her cheek against her hand. "It just makes me mad they hit my place. I wrote some code, that's all. There's no reason to threaten me or damage my home."

"You put together the website for the convention, too, and that's at the Akaw," Liz said, referring to the decorative painting convention they were scheduled to attend in the coming week. "That gives you two connections to the hotel. Besides, you're an easy target. Some people in town still have issues with you even after you were exonerated."

Rory didn't like to think that was true, but every once in a while she noticed covert glances cast in her direction as she walked around town. "I wonder if Ian's house was hit. He manages the hotel."

"Ian Blalock, right? He doesn't live in town. Bought a place in…Hawthorne, I think. Cheaper."

Rory hoped the vandals were too lazy to drive the short distance inland and the man's home had been spared. "I hope he's okay. He seems like a nice guy. What else do you know about him?"

"You worked on the hotel's website. Didn't you talk?"

"Only about business, not his personal life. He doesn't wear a wedding ring, that's about all I know."

Liz gave Rory her best you-never-learn-anything-useful look. "Been in the hotel business for years. Like you said, he's single with a college-aged son. Moved here from Oregon or Washington, something like that." She took a sip of her tea. "Plus, he has the hots for Nixie," she continued, mentioning the name of the convention organizer and founder of the Ocean Painting Society.

"I hope all this nonsense doesn't ruin the convention for everyone. Nixie put tons of work into it."

"She's got a lot riding on it. It's the only thing she's got going since she was laid off from that event coordinating job. I'm looking forward to it. Your mom's going to be on the trade show floor, right?"

Rory's mother, owner of Arika's Scrap 'n Paint, a combination tole painting and scrapbooking supply store in town, was renting space on the trade show floor for the upcoming convention.

"That reminds me. Could you help set up the booth on Tuesday? I'm not sure what time yet."

"Sure, I can do that. Just let me know when to be there." Liz glanced at her watch. "We should probably get to bed. I've got an early showing tomorrow."

While Liz made herself at home in the guest bedroom, Rory did a final tour of the house, making sure every window and door was locked. By the time goodnights were said, she felt calmer and in more control. Within minutes of her head hitting the pillow, she fell fast asleep.

Chapter 2

Rory spent most of the following day getting the window replaced. In between dealing with the insurance adjuster and the window company, she spoke to her neighbors about the vandalism but, contrary to Officer Yamada's hopes, no one had seen anything useful. Although some of the houses on the block boasted security cameras, none of them were trained on the street. She gave up on investigating the incident for now and returned to her own house to oversee the work. By the time afternoon rolled around, a new window was in place and her home returned to normal.

At five, Rory put on her nicest khakis and blouse and headed to the Akaw to pick up her childhood friend, Jasmine Halliday, for dinner at the Andersons. She was only two blocks from the hotel when a red Ferrari whipped around the corner, half in its lane, half in hers. She swung her steering wheel to the right and slammed on her brakes, narrowly missing the car as it drove past, her own sedan coming within inches of hitting a parked car. She tried to catch a glimpse of the driver, but all she saw was a red blur. Her hands shaking, she continued on to her destination. By the time she reached the hotel, she'd recovered from the near accident.

As soon as she entered the Akaw, located steps away from the ocean, Rory felt as if she'd been transported to Hawaii. Between the tropical plants scattered around the lobby and the hotel staff dressed in Aloha shirts and Hawaiian-print dresses, she could have been in any hotel on one of the islands.

She'd taken only half a dozen steps when a brunette in a floral-printed summer dress rose from a padded bamboo chair and picked her way across the lobby, her graceful movements betraying her years of ballet training.

Rory was reaching out to hug her friend when Jasmine's head fell forward, her eyes fluttered shut and her knees buckled. Rory eased the young woman to the ground as she slumped to the floor like a marionette whose puppeteer had dropped its strings. After making sure Jasmine's body was positioned so she could breathe properly, Rory sat down on a nearby sofa to watch over her friend and wait for her to recover.

She'd barely settled down onto the loveseat upholstered in a fabric reminiscent of Hawaii when a well-groomed man with a closely cropped beard hurried toward them. "Rory, is everything okay? Is there anything I can do?"

Rory pushed her long hair behind her ears and smiled in what she hoped was a reassuring manner at the hotel's manager. "Don't worry, Ian, she'll be fine in a minute or two."

The man studied Jasmine where she lay on the hardwood floor. Her eyes were closed, and her chest moved up and down in a regular rhythm. "She looks okay, I guess. Are you sure I shouldn't call 911?" He drew a cell phone out of the inside pocket of his suit.

"Please don't. It's not an emergency. Jasmine just needs a minute or two to recover."

"Oh, is this...? I see. My staff told me she would be staying with us. Narcolepsy, is it?"

Rory's face registered surprise that anyone from the hotel knew of her friend's health issues. Jasmine generally told as few people as possible about her condition. "I didn't realize you knew."

"Her husband phoned. Wanted to inform us since she's staying with us during the OPS convention." For the next six days, two hundred decorative painters would descend on the hotel for the Ocean Painting Society's inaugural convention.

"How much did Peter tell you?"

"The basics. Plus, he gave me a list of her medications in case there was an...issue." His gaze strayed back to where Jasmine still lay as motionless as a mannequin. "Should we move her somewhere more comfortable?"

"No need, I'm fine." Almost as quickly as she collapsed, Jasmine recovered, slowly rising to her feet and settling down on the sofa next to Rory. "Thanks for your concern." She frowned. "Did my husband really call you?"

"You could hear me?" Ian said.

"Every word, I just couldn't respond."

Sympathy written all over his face, he said, "Your husband didn't really give me any instructions on how to deal with...this. Does it happen often? How should I tell my staff to handle it?"

"I don't expect it to happen much at all. But, if it does, just make sure I can breathe and no one touches me. I prefer to be left alone when I'm in that state. I usually recover very quickly. If you have questions, Rory knows what to do. She's been there from the beginning."

Rory cast her mind back to the day of Jasmine's first cataplectic attack when they were both fourteen. Jasmine had won a dance contest and had been super excited. Then her legs turned to rubber and she collapsed, unable to move or respond for several minutes. A few weeks later she received the diagnosis that changed her life.

After Jasmine assured him she was fine, the hotel manager headed toward the front desk.

Rory looked with concern at her friend. "I thought your cataplexy was under control."

"I don't have as many attacks as I used to, but they haven't completely gone away. The new medicine *is* helping. I didn't take my second dose last night. Didn't hear the alarm. That's probably why it happened." Jasmine glanced around the lobby as if checking to see if anyone noticed her collapse. "I wish Peter hadn't called. It's embarrassing."

"You have nothing to be embarrassed about. You can't help your condition. And Peter's just worried about you." Rory stood up. "Are you ready to go? My parents are expecting us."

"Let me just make sure I have my medicine. I don't like to leave it in the hotel room. Don't want it to get stolen." She rummaged around in her shoulder bag. "Found it. Let's go."

As Rory drove toward her parents' home, Jasmine said, "Thanks for picking me up. It saved Peter the trip."

"No problem. Why did you decide to stay at the hotel for the convention, anyway? You don't live that far away."

"It's more convenient. Peter doesn't have to drive me there every day."

Rory had forgotten her friend had never applied for a driver's license, too afraid her condition would cause an accident. "I would've been happy to pick you up. We don't live that far from each other."

"That's too much of a bother. Besides, this way I can take a nap when I get tired."

"How are you guys settling in? It's quite a change from Riverside, isn't it? Hard to believe it's already been over a year since I moved here. I missed you guys."

"We missed you too, and your parents. It's been an adjustment, but I think we're going to really like it here. The weather's a lot different, that's for sure. I miss some of my old haunts, but you and Brandy live nearby, so that's good. The Four Musketeers, together again. It'll be just like high school."

Rory smiled and patted Jasmine's hand. "I'm looking forward to it. What about your bookkeeping clients? Were you able to keep any of them?"

"Most of them. These days with the internet, it's easy to work from a distance. Oh, I forgot to thank you for recommending me to Nixie."

"You got the job doing the convention books? That's great." The convention organizer started out doing her own accounting, but a few weeks ago she found the task so overwhelming she'd looked around for someone to help.

"I wish she'd hired me sooner. The books were a mess."

On the rest of the short drive, they talked about the upcoming convention. When they walked through the front door into the Andersons' home, the heady aroma of meatloaf and gravy greeted them. Familiar voices drifted into the entryway from the living room.

"...she'd be here before us," a male voice said.

"She's with Rory. She's fine," a female replied.

When Rory and Jasmine entered the living room, they found a slender young man pacing in front of the fireplace while a striking woman, hair styled in a buzz cut, sat on a nearby couch.

"Here they are now." Brandy Whitaker stood up and rushed over to give Rory a big hug. "It's been so long since I've seen you! I've missed you."

"Me too," Rory said.

A look of relief came over Peter Halliday's face. He hurried over to kiss his wife. Placing his hands on her shoulders, he looked with concern into her eyes. "Everything okay?"

"Sorry we're late," was all she said before turning to Brandy with a grin on her face. "What? Don't I get a hug too?"

Brandy enveloped her friend in her arms. "Of course, but I see you all the time."

"How did practice go? Are you all ready for the competition?" Jasmine asked.

"Brandy and I are in a ballroom dancing competition on Thursday at the local elementary school. Argentine tango. We were at our final practice session," Peter explained to Rory. "The competition's all day Thursday. I'm lucky my boss let me take the rest of the week off." Jasmine's husband was an accountant for a small firm in a nearby town. The job paid the bills, but his heart belonged to dance. "We would love it if you could stop by some time when you're not in class. We'll let you know when we're scheduled to compete."

"Sounds good." Rory turned to her friend and said, without thinking, "Remember that time you and Peter demonstrated the waltz in junior high? You two were really good, even then. Do you enter competitions together too?"

As soon as the words left her mouth, she wanted to kick herself. An awkward silence fell over the group. She felt her face heat up and mumbled an apology. "Sorry, I didn't think. Forget I said anything."

Jasmine gently touched Rory on the arm. "It's okay. Your comment just tells me that you think of me as normal. That makes me happy. I'm content with simply dancing around the house these days."

Peter looked at his wife and said, "I bet there are other people with your condition who go out and dance. You should give it a try. You don't have to compete. Just go to a dance club with me some time."

Brandy nodded her encouragement. "You should think about it. You move so beautifully."

Jasmine tightened her lips. "Not in public," she said in a tone that indicated the subject was closed.

Arika Anderson poked her head around the kitchen doorway. "I thought I heard new voices. Dinner will be ready soon." When she spotted Jasmine, Rory's mother entered the living room and gave her a bear hug. "So nice to see you, dear. It's been a long time." She studied the young woman. "You're looking a little thin. What you need is a good hearty meal."

Jasmine had always been on the slim side, but Rory had to admit she now appeared to be on the verge of being excessively thin.

"You know how much I love your cooking. I've missed it."

Rory had lost count of the number of dinners her mother had prepared for her friends over the years. She smiled at the thought of their all being around the table once again.

"Could you give me a hand?" Arika said to her daughter.

Rory followed her mother into the kitchen where Arika put her to work mashing the potatoes. "Is Dad working late again?"

Her mother nodded. "He's disappointed he's missing everyone, but now that they've all moved to town, there'll be plenty more opportunities."

"I was hoping he would be here so I could tell you both something. He'll have to hear it from you. You'll never guess what happened last night."

"Someone threw a rock through your window," Arika said in a matter-of-fact tone of voice, without looking up from taking the meatloaf out of the oven.

Rory stopped mid-mash and stared at her mother in disbelief. "How...? Not *Detective Green*?"

"He stopped by the store today. He's worried about you. He heard about the rock and wanted to know how you're doing."

"Why didn't he just ask me?"

"Maybe he feels like he can't."

Her mother must be mistaken. Rory didn't understand why the detective should feel she was unapproachable. The few times she'd seen him at Arika's Scrap 'n Paint, their conversations had been comfortable, centering around painting and her job. As far as she remembered, she hadn't been standoffish. Convinced she would never understand men, Rory shrugged her shoulders, put the finished potatoes aside and began spooning gravy into a serving dish.

"You should call him some time. He's a good man."

Liquid splattered all over the side of the gravy boat and onto the granite countertop. Rory wiped up the mess and gaped at her mother. She wasn't used to Arika getting involved in her love life, let alone giving a man her seal of approval. Rory shook her head and went back to work.

"The delivery company picked up all the boxes this evening. Everything should be on the trade show floor by early tomorrow. We should be able to start setting up the booth around eleven. Will you still be able to help?" Arika said.

"I'll be there. Liz said she would help too. I'll let her know what time."

"Good. Too bad she couldn't make it tonight." Arika sliced the meatloaf and placed it on a serving platter. "Is Jasmine okay? She seems a little...off."

"She had one of her attacks at the hotel."

Arika patted her daughter's arm. "She's lucky you were there." She ran her eyes over all of the serving dishes. "That's it. I think we're ready. Help me take this out to the dining room. Let's eat before it gets cold."

Once everything was on the table and Rory's mother said grace, the five of them dug in. Conversation soon turned to the painting convention.

"Thanks for hosting the meet and greet, Mrs. Anderson," Jasmine said. "Aunt Viveca is looking forward to it."

"It's Sunday afternoon, right? Aren't you usually closed then?" Brandy asked.

"I don't mind opening for a special event now and then," Arika said. "I'm always happy to introduce someone to the local tole painting community. Or, in this case, reintroduce, I guess. I'm glad Viveca is teaching again. I never understood why she stopped."

"It was right around the time my mom, you know..."

Arika nodded her head in sympathy. "I remember. Your mother was a lovely woman, God rest her soul."

When Jasmine was barely sixteen, her mother died of cancer. Rory remembered the hours both Jasmine and her aunt spent at the hospital during the long illness.

"Your aunt's booth is across from mine. VivEco, right?" Arika said. "What kind of company is it?"

Jasmine nodded. "That's right. They manufacture eco-friendly painting supplies. Sealers, varnishes, that kind of thing. I'll be working at the booth off and on. They're good products. You should consider carrying them in your store."

"I'll be sure to check them out." Arika gestured from their empty plates to the half-full serving dishes. "Eat, everyone. Don't be shy. There's plenty to go around." She turned to Brandy who was sitting next to her. "How's *your* aunt doing, Brandy? Any improvement?"

"Afraid not. We're looking into long-term care facilities for her, but they're so expensive."

Arika squeezed the young woman's hand. "You're good to put your life on hold and move to town to take care of her like this. I'm sure she appreciates it."

"I'd do anything for her. She's like a second mother to me."

After they'd cleared away the dishes and spooned out the ice cream, Peter raised his glass. "A toast. To old friends being together again."

Rory clinked glasses with everyone else and smiled, looking forward to spending as much time as possible with her childhood friends.

Tuesday morning, Rory drove toward downtown Vista Beach and rounded the corner onto Driftwood Lane straight into trouble. Protesters lined the sidewalk in front of the Akaw, blocking all its entrances. A group of at least a dozen men and women shouted at passing cars, waving picket signs that read "Down with the Akaw!" and "Fix Our Homes!" As Rory slowed down, then slammed on her brakes to avoid hitting a couple of new additions who ran across the street in front of her, she wondered which one of them was responsible for the damage to her window.

As she inched her way forward toward the entrance to the hotel's underground parking structure, Ian Blalock hurried toward the group. The driver of the Mercedes in front of Rory honked his horn as he tried to maneuver between the people into the structure. One middle-aged protester, a man in a red t-shirt and jeans, pounded on the car's windshield while others surrounded the Mercedes, preventing it from going any further. Quickly realizing the crowd had no intention of allowing anyone to park in the structure, Rory continued down the street to look for a temporary parking space in the nearby neighborhood. As she rounded the corner, she glanced in her rearview mirror. Two patrol cars raced to the scene.

Five minutes later and less than a quarter mile away, she found a street with plenty of parking. As she eased her sedan into a space, she noticed a sign stuck in the lawn of a nearby home. At first she thought it was an election sign someone forgot to take down, but then she noticed the slogan: "No Hotel Parking!" She peered through the windshield at the street parking sign in front of her. Other than the two hours reserved for street sweeping the following day, no restrictions were mentioned.

Satisfied she'd parked legally, Rory grabbed her painting supplies out of the trunk of her car, slung her bag over one shoulder and headed toward the Akaw. She'd taken only a few steps when a young woman with a fuchsia streak in her black hair, a nose ring and vibrant eye makeup fell into step beside her. Dressed in low-rise jeans and a midriff top that showed off her belly button ring, Veronica Justice puffed as she tried to keep up with Rory's long strides.

"Just the person I wanted to talk to," the reporter for the *View* said in a raspy voice.

She should have known the news about the vandalism would spread quickly, Rory thought. "Hi, Veronica. So you heard. Did the police tell you?"

"The police? Why would they be involved?" The thirty-year-old stared at Rory, a puzzled look on her face.

"I called them. Wouldn't you?"

"You called them on your *friend*?"

Rory stopped in the middle of the sidewalk and gaped at the reporter. "Wait, what are you talking about?"

"What are *you* talking about?"

Rory took a deep breath. "Okay, let's start over. Exactly what did you want to see me about?"

"Your friend, the one who had the attack at the Akaw. I thought it would make a nice human interest story. Not too many people know much about narcolepsy."

"Jasmine? She's a very private person. I don't think she'd want me to talk to you about her."

"Maybe she wants to educate people about her problem. You'd be helping her do that."

Rory had never considered that possibility. An article explaining her friend's condition and what she dealt with on a day-to-day basis could be a good thing. "I might be willing if Jasmine says it's okay." She started walking once again toward the hotel.

Veronica trotted after her. "Wait up. I'll mention it to her at the convention. You'll see, she'll jump at the chance to tell her story."

Rory slowed down enough so the reporter could walk beside her without having to run. "You're attending, then?"

"I'm doing a feature on it for the paper. Taking a couple beginning classes. Thought I'd get a better view of it that way. More of an inside piece, if you get my drift. I'll also put some pics up on VBC and tweet during the convention." Veronica had started Vista Beach Confidential before she began writing for the newspaper. The blog covered happenings around the city and often included photographs of local events.

Rory pointed to more of the "No Hotel Parking!" signs that stuck out of lawns and flowerbeds from over half of the houses they passed.

"What are all these signs about? Are they part of the protests? I don't remember your mentioning them in your articles."

"All part of the issues with the Akaw. People are parking on the street like we just did instead of in the hotel's underground parking structure."

"We didn't have much choice. The protesters were blocking the entrance."

"True, but lots of other people are parking here to avoid the fees," Veronica said.

"No wonder people are upset."

"And then there's all the noise and trucks blocking driveways during the construction phase. That didn't make people happy, either."

Rory cast a sympathetic glance at the houses they passed. She knew how annoying construction could be. Six days a week for the past five months, she'd awakened to the pounding of hammers, whining of saws, and beeping of trucks backing up while a house on her block was being remodeled.

As they stood on the other side of the narrow street from the hotel and waited to cross at the light, Rory looked at the hotel's parking entrance where protesters were crowded around two uniformed officers and the hotel manager. One officer was talking to a man with a goatee and a tattoo on his neck who seemed to be in charge of the group. Rory counted three dozen men and women listening to the conversation.

"All of their homes couldn't have been damaged, could they?" Rory said.

"I'm sure some are residents who thought the hotel shouldn't have been built in the first place." Veronica pulled a camera out of one of the two tote bags slung over her shoulder and took several shots of the now departing protesters. Three of them, when they noticed the camera pointed in their direction, waved signs and chanted. "Some of them probably wanted the city to build that park they'd originally talked about putting in." She lowered her voice. "I don't have any proof but, between you and me, I think money changed hands."

When the light turned green, they crossed the street and headed toward the Akaw, its entrance now free of protesters. A small group stayed behind, quietly sitting in the courtyard in front of the building, half-heartedly waving signs. The two women walked through automatic doors into a lobby lit by a combination of strategically placed skylights and overhead lighting and headed toward the convention office. A banner reading "Ocean Painting Society invites you to Join the Painting Wave" hung near the entrance to the Manhattan ballroom.

They joined the well-mannered line of women snaking out of the room and down the hallway toward the lobby. Everyone chattered companionably as they all waited for their turn to pick up their convention packets. The line moved steadily forward. Rory and Veronica were steps away from the doorway when the commotion started.

Chapter 3

"No need to be snippy, young man. Mind your manners!"

A hush fell over the crowd as everyone's attention was riveted to the drama playing out before them. From her position near the doorway, Rory looked over the heads of the people in front of her into the ballroom reserved for the convention office. Inside, two teenagers sat on folding chairs behind a long table, handing out registration packets and convention brochures. An older woman in a red tailored suit and matching fedora stood in front of one of the teens, waving her cane at the young man who stared back through eyes encircled by black guyliner, a bored expression on his face. With his half-black, half-blond spiky hair, he looked a bit like a young male version of Cruella de Vil.

Veronica stood in front of Rory and craned her neck, trying to find out what the fuss was all about. "What do you see?"

"Maybelline is having words with someone at the check-in desk."

"Maybelline?"

"Sorry, I forgot you don't know everyone. Maybelline Winkelman. Retired high school principal at VB High. Believe me, you don't want to cross her."

Rory met the woman years ago in a painting class and enjoyed talking with her. During her career as a principal, Maybelline had been a strict disciplinarian, but the majority of her students adored her, inviting her to weddings and christenings years after they'd left high school.

The older woman continued in a ringing voice that carried out the door and down the hallway. "Pick it up and apologize right now." She thumped her bejeweled cane on the ground for emphasis. Every time it hit the floor, its tip lit up.

The young man leaned across the table and pointed at the ground. "Pick it up yourself, Granny. It's right there beside you."

Rory stepped out of line and moved to one side so she could see what the teenager was pointing at. A driver's license lay on the carpet next to Maybelline's feet. The eighty-year-old remained stubbornly independent and could paint up a storm, but she had her limitations. Bending down to pick anything off the ground was no longer something she could easily do.

Rory started forward, intending to pick up the license herself, but a woman at the front of the line beat her to it. As the woman bent down, Maybelline lifted her cane, preventing the Good Samaritan from reaching the fallen item. "Thank you, but leave it, please." She peered at the name tag pinned to the teen's black t-shirt. "I want Gordon, here, to get it for me. He needs to learn to respect his elders."

The woman who had tried to help took a long look at Maybelline's determined face and straightened up, leaving the license on the floor.

"Like hell I will." Gordon sat back in his chair, folded his arms in front of his chest and glared at the former principal defiantly.

The scent of a combination of jasmine and gardenia wafted down the hallway toward them. A plus-sized woman exuding a slightly frazzled air rushed past the line and squeezed through the doorway into the crowded office, coming to rest next to Maybelline's side. "What seems to be the problem?" Nixie Mohr said after she recovered her breath.

"This young man is being very rude. He threw it at me and now he won't pick it up."

It took several minutes for Nixie to sort out the problem.

Apparently, Gordon had tossed Maybelline's license on the table only to have it skitter across the surface onto the floor.

"I'm so sorry. Gordon, pick up the license and apologize to Mrs. Winkelman."

"I don't even want to be here, Mom. It's your stupid convention."

In a low voice and with a smile on her face she said, "I'm paying you and you'll be as polite as all of my other employees are."

Gordon Mohr stared at his mother defiantly for a moment, then grudgingly moved around the table, grabbed the license and handed it to Maybelline. "Here."

"Gordon," his mother said, a warning note in her voice.

"I'm sorry," he said to the older woman in a tone that clearly indicated he wasn't. "I've got to pee." He shouldered his way through the doorway and headed down the hall in the general direction of the restrooms. As he walked past, Rory caught a glimpse of a silver earring shaped like a skull in his left ear.

"Sorry about that. Teenagers," Nixie said to Maybelline. "Did you get your packet?"

Maybelline nodded her thanks and stuffed her license in her wallet. Registration packet in one hand, cane in the other, she headed out the door. People murmured words of support as she passed by.

Nixie took over her son's spot and started processing registrants as if nothing had happened.

"Nixie's son wasn't very polite, was he? I wonder if losing his father had something to do with it," Veronica said as the line moved forward.

"Probably. He's only sixteen. Hard to lose a parent at that age," Rory said.

"It was sudden, wasn't it? I heard she woke up one morning and found her husband sitting in a chair, dead of a massive heart attack."

Rory's heart went out to the woman. "I can't imagine what she went through. She didn't even have a chance to call for help." She nodded toward the girl at the table who was motioning with her hand, indicating she was ready for the next person in line. "You're up."

Veronica headed over to the teenager while Rory stepped up to where Nixie was now free. She handed the woman her ID, but the convention organizer waved it away.

"No need, Rory, I know who you are." She riffled through the box of packets, alphabetically sorted by last name, until she found the right one.

Rory took the packet and plastic badge holder Nixie handed her. "Thanks. Is Gordon okay?"

"He's hanging in there. As you can imagine, it's not been easy for either of us. I'm at my wit's end. I don't know what to do with him."

"I'm sorry to hear that."

"I shouldn't be bothering you with this. It'll all work out in the end, I'm sure." Nixie squared her shoulders and smiled. "I think you're all set. Is there anything else I can do for you? I'm selling aprons to protect your clothes during class." She plucked a white apron with the conference logo emblazoned on it off of a neat stack beside her on the table.

Rory patted her tote bag. "Thanks, but I've got one right in here."

Convention materials in hand, Rory made her way to the lobby and sat down on an empty chair, her body sinking into the soft cushion. With her back to the front entrance, she inspected her packet, which contained a list of her classes, a badge insert with her name and hometown printed on it, and a ticket for each class she'd signed up for. Satisfied nothing was missing, she pinned her badge to her t-shirt, stuffed the rest into her tote bag, and checked the time on her cell phone. Half an hour before she was needed on the trade show floor. She was studying the convention schedule when a shadow fell over her. Rory looked up to discover Maybelline Winkelman standing in front of her, smiling.

A twinkle in her eye, Maybelline extended her hand. In it was a forest green hexagonal box. "I brought you something from my last trip to Seattle. I know how much you love them."

Rory gasped in delight. "Frangos! Thanks so much!" Her mouth watered at the thought of the scrumptious mint chocolates. She gestured toward the empty chair beside her. "Sit down and have one with me."

Maybelline motioned toward the front door with her cane. "I'm heading out for a walk. You're welcome to come with me."

"I wish I could. I'm supposed to meet my mother at her booth soon."

An explosion of giggles directed their attention to a conversation area across the lobby where Gordon was sitting on a chair with a teenage girl on his lap. Rory guessed the young man wasn't planning on returning to work anytime soon.

Maybelline sighed and shook her head. "I saw a lot of kids like him when I was working. All could-care-less on the outside, but hurting deeply on the inside. I heard his father passed away recently."

Rory nodded. "Six months ago."

"Very sad, but that still doesn't excuse his behavior." Maybelline readjusted the hat on her head. "I'll be off. Say hello to your mother for me," she said before heading out into the sunshine.

No sooner had the woman left when Liz and Veronica sat down in the empty chairs flanking Rory. She tore the plastic wrap off the box of chocolates Maybelline had given her and offered a Frango to each one of them.

Veronica popped her chocolate in her mouth whole, while Liz nibbled on hers.

"When are we supposed to help with the booth?" Liz said to Rory between bites.

Rory checked the time once again. "We should leave in ten minutes or so."

Moments later, the automatic doors whooshed open. Liz glanced over at the hotel entrance. "Dashing D's here," she said in a low voice.

"Where?" Rory asked.

Liz nodded toward the sliding glass doors. "He just walked in."

Rory twisted around in her seat. Her heart skipped a beat when she caught sight of the muscular detective who stood nearby, his handsome face scanning the crowd.

"Do you think there's been a murder?" Veronica whispered in a tone of suppressed excitement.

"I hope not." Rory shuddered at the thought. She would be happy if she never saw another body in her life. Visions of arms sticking out of the dirt still plagued her dreams.

The detective caught sight of the three of them and headed in their direction, whistling as he walked.

"Ms. Anderson, Ms. Justice, Ms. Dexter," he said.

"I didn't expect to see you at the convention," Rory said.

"Or is there a body?" Veronica withdrew a pen and small pad of paper from the large tote bag that served as her purse.

The detective's lips twitched. "Not that I know of. I just came to meet my girlfriend for coffee. She's attending the convention."

An unexpected wave of disappointment washed over Rory.

Liz looked at her friend in surprise and mouthed "girlfriend?" behind her hand so the detective wouldn't see. Rory shrugged. In all her conversations with the man, he'd never mentioned a significant other. She doubted her mother knew either. Arika would never have suggested Rory call him if she knew he was taken.

He nodded toward the hallway that led to the ballrooms. "There she is now. Let me go get her. I'll introduce you."

The three watched as the man made his way over to a petite woman with delicate features and curly dark hair that framed her face. Rory felt gangly and uncoordinated as she watched the woman walk gracefully forward. The detective gave her a peck on the cheek before guiding her toward the group waiting to meet her. A pang of jealousy pierced Rory's heart as they walked hand in hand across the lobby.

"Melosia Ortega, meet Aurora, sorry, Rory, Anderson, Liz Dexter and Veronica Justice. Veronica's a reporter for the *View*.

Watch what you say around her." He said the last jokingly, but his eyes betrayed his seriousness.

Melosia shook each of their hands. "You can call me Mel. So nice to meet you. I understand you're all attending the convention, too."

"Mel here has family in Riverside," Detective Green said. "Maybe you know some of them, Rory."

Before Rory had a chance to reply, the detective's girlfriend said, "It's a big place. I'm sure she doesn't know them."

"Have you two known each other long?" Liz asked.

"For years, but we lost touch for a while." Mel looked at her boyfriend as if asking permission to say more. "You could say this is the second time around for us."

Rory and Liz exchanged curious glances.

Even though Rory itched to know why the two had broken up the first time, she opted for a less intrusive line of questioning. "Have you been painting long?"

"I just started. Martin gave me a certificate for a class at Arika's Scrap 'n Paint here in town and I got hooked. Do you know it?" Mel said.

"That's my mother's store," Rory said.

"I love that place. I wasn't sure I could handle classes here at the convention, but your mom thought I should give it a try."

So her mother *had* met the detective's girlfriend, Rory thought. She put *ask mom about Mel* on top of her mental to-do list, then pushed the thought to the back of her brain. "The important thing is to enjoy yourself. It's not a contest. You'll do fine. What classes are you taking?" She studied the class list Mel handed her. "Liz, she's taking your strokework class tomorrow."

"Good," Liz said. "Rory's helping out so we'll both be there. We'll make sure you know what's going on."

Rory's cell phone quacked, reminding her it was time to head to the trade show floor. "Sorry, we've got to go. Nice meeting you, Mel. See you later, Detective, Veronica."

Uncharacteristically silent during the conversation, Veronica now whipped out her notepad and began grilling Detective Green's girlfriend as Rory and Liz walked down the hallway leading to the ballrooms.

When the two young women arrived at the space reserved for Arika's Scrap 'n Paint, Rory's mother was taping the booth diagram to the open-shelving unit positioned across its front. Forty booths, selling painting supplies and other items of interest to decorative painters, filled the Hermosa ballroom floor. The Scrap 'n Paint booth was located halfway down the first aisle of the trade show floor in direct line of sight of the entrance.

Rory's gaze swept the double-sized booth from the interlocking foam tiles in a checkerboard pattern of blue and black that covered the floor to the tables and racks lining the edges. "Looks like you have all the display cases set up. What do you want us to do?"

"Start with the pattern packets. They're over there." Arika gestured toward a cluster of cardboard boxes at the back of the booth.

Before she started working, Rory drew her mother aside so Liz couldn't hear. In a low voice, she said, "I met Detective Green's girlfriend just now. Did you know?"

"Yes. Melosia. Lovely girl. Very promising painter."

"If you knew, why did you tell me to call him?"

"You misunderstood me. I never said you should go out with him. I just thought you could be friends. Never hurts to have one on the police force." Arika raised her voice so Liz could hear. "I'm missing some supplies. You girls put together what you can. I'm going to find Nixie and see if she knows where they are."

Liz set to work hanging the pattern packets on wire racks while Rory sat on the padded floor and unpacked a box. They'd finished setting up half the booth when a wave of excitement rippled across the trade show floor. Muted cries of "she's here" preceded a flamboyantly dressed woman, at least six feet tall, as she swept inside the door and down the aisle. In her red cape and spiked heels, she looked more like she belonged on a runway than on the trade show floor. She waved and smiled at everyone she passed. Everything about her seemed perfect: perfect hair, perfect clothes, perfect makeup.

Rory tugged self-consciously on the t-shirt and jeans she was wearing. "Viveca's here." She pointed toward the woman who was entering the VivEco booth across the aisle.

"She's so beautiful. That's an Armani cape she's wearing. Cost a bundle." Liz looked wistfully at the woman. "Wish I'd remembered to bring that pattern book for her to sign."

"You'll get a chance at the meet and greet. Who's that with her?" Rory nodded to the slim gray-haired man in a white short-sleeved shirt and black pants who was helping Viveca Forster off with her cape.

"Her new husband, I think."

"He seems a bit..."

"...older? About twenty years, from what I hear."

"Do you want to meet her? I'll introduce you."

Liz could barely contain her excitement as Rory led the way across the aisle. Wearing a sleeveless dress that hugged her figure and accentuated her long legs, Viveca stood next to a table, studying a piece of paper, while her husband unpacked a box on the other side of the booth.

"Ms. Ca...sorry, Forster? I don't know if you remember me, but we met years ago. I'm a friend of Jasmine's. Rory Anderson."

The statuesque blonde in five-inch heels frowned for a moment as if she were having trouble placing the name, then her face cleared.

"Of course, Aurora. It's been years! And please, call me Viveca." She held Rory gently by the shoulders and studied her. "Let me look at you. So tall, and such beautiful eyes. You haven't changed a bit." She frowned. "Except...what happened to that lovely blonde hair you used to have? This mousy brown color isn't nearly as becoming."

Rory didn't want to explain to the woman how tired she was of dumb blonde jokes and how people treated her more seriously as a brunette, important in the male-dominated field she was in. Instead, she introduced Viveca to her friend who was grinning from ear to ear.

Liz's words tumbled out. "I'm a huge fan of yours! I have all of your old pattern books. I was so happy to hear you'd be here."

"That's very kind of you. I appreciate it. Always happy to hear from a fan, especially since I've been out of the business for over a decade." Viveca plucked a brochure out of a nearby box. "I'll be giving a series of seminars in the fall. I hope you'll consider attending."

Liz eagerly took the brochure, looking as if the woman had handed her the keys to a multi-million dollar home.

Viveca turned to Rory and said, "Tell me what you've been up to recently."

Jasmine's aunt nodded her head and smiled as Rory briefly told the woman what she'd been doing since high school. When Rory mentioned her freelance programming business, Viveca glanced at the young woman's clothes as if to say "that explains the casual attire."

"It's nice to see you both. So glad to meet you, Liz. Don't forget about those seminars I'm teaching. Now if you'll excuse me, I must get back to work." Viveca picked up the piece of paper she'd been looking at earlier and frowned. "Maybe you can help me with something. We're missing some boxes. Were they delivered to your booth by mistake?"

"I don't think so, but let me check," Rory said.

The three of them examined every unpacked box in the Scrap 'n Paint booth, finally coming across one in the far corner that belonged to VivEco.

Viveca tut-tutted. "This convention is not as well-run as the ones I attended years ago." She raised her voice, directing her attention toward the booth across the way. "Hully! I found one of them, but the other's still missing. You'll have to go looking for it." She headed back to her own booth. Glancing over her shoulder, she said, "Could you bring that over here, Aurora?" She pointed an elegant finger with a long nail covered in crimson polish at an empty table.

Rory hauled the box across the aisle and placed it in the designated spot.

"Hully, this is Jasmine's friend, Aurora. They went to school together. Aurora, this is my husband, Hulbert."

Hulbert Forster shook Rory's hand. "Any friend of Jasmine's is a friend of mine." He glanced across the aisle at the Scrap 'n Paint booth. "Aurora, I don't recall seeing your store on our client list. Perhaps you'll consider stocking our products."

Before she could explain she wasn't responsible for store purchases, he handed her a product brochure and business card. Rory took the proffered items and promised to give them to her mother when she returned.

"I'm going to see if I can find that other box." Hulbert laid the clipboard down and headed out on his quest.

After a few more minutes of chit-chat, Rory crossed the aisle once again and started helping Liz put two-ounce bottles of acrylic paint in a wire rack. They were shoving the last of the boxes under a table when Nixie and Arika approached the booth. Steps behind them, a burly young man wheeled a dolly with two boxes on it.

"You found them," Rory said. "Where were they?"

"I'm so sorry for the inconvenience," the convention organizer said. "They were on the loading dock. Someone had mixed them in with hotel supplies. Where would you like us to put them?"

Arika pointed to a spot on the floor near the small table set up as a cashier's station. The young man unloaded the boxes and, after a nod of dismissal from Nixie, headed out the entrance with his dolly.

"I'm beginning to regret having the convention here," Nixie said. "It's been nothing but problems. Granted, this is my first time putting together a painting convention, but not all the issues have been mine. I'm much better organized than the hotel is. And did you hear? The hotel event coordinator up and quit. Just like that. Couldn't deal with all of the controversy surrounding the Akaw.

Very unprofessional, if you ask me. In my old job, I would never have done that, no matter how I felt. Still, they did give me a good deal. What's that old adage? You get what you pay for."

Nixie drew a pad of paper and a diagram of the layout of the trade show floor out of her jacket pocket. She took a deep breath as if gearing herself up for the task ahead. "Well, I'd better get to it. I have my cell on. If you have any more problems, text me." She squared her shoulders and headed down the aisle.

Arika surveyed the booth. "This is shaping up nicely. You girls have done a great job."

Rory's cell phone quacked, telling her it was time to leave for the special event she and Liz had signed up for. "I hate to go, but we've got a class. Unless you need us to stay...?"

Arika gestured with her hands in a shooing motion. "Go, both of you, have fun. I could use your help tonight, though."

"I'll be here." Rory was looking forward to working at the booth during the early shopping opportunity from six to nine that evening when those already registered for the convention could shop before the trade show floor officially opened to the public the next day.

Talking excitedly about the class they were about to attend, Rory and Liz slung their tote bags full of supplies over their shoulders and headed out the ballroom door.

Chapter 4

Between the special event and working at the Scrap 'n Paint booth, the rest of Tuesday flew by. Rory tumbled into bed that evening exhausted but happy. The excitement of the day had banished all thoughts from her head of the rock that crashed through her window and the threatening note attached to it.

The next day, when Rory entered the Zuma ballroom twenty minutes before Liz's class was scheduled to begin, half of the thirty spaces were already filled. Six long tables covered with white plastic tablecloths were set up in two columns, chairs facing the front where Liz stood talking with one of the students. The room buzzed with excitement as convention attendees set up their workspaces and waited for the basic strokework class to begin.

A puzzled look on her face, Jasmine sat in the back row, her painting supplies spread out before her. Painted on a roller bag that sat at her feet were the word "Jaz" and the star-shaped flowers the woman was named after.

As soon as she spotted her friend, Rory walked over to say hi. "Everything okay?"

Her long hair hid her face as Jasmine stuffed a yellow folder into her bag. "Nothing that can't wait. Do you have time to talk later?"

"Sure, after class." Rory looked to the front of the classroom where Liz was unpacking the boxes of supplies recently delivered to the room. "I'd better go and help set up. Catch you later."

Rory spent the next ten minutes distributing bottles of paint, heart-shaped wood pieces, and plastic sleeves filled with instructions to each student while Liz tested out the projection system she planned on using. Mel soon arrived and settled down in the only spot left in the front row.

When all of the students were seated and Rory had picked up all the class tickets, Liz began teaching, starting by going over the rudiments of the comma stroke.

"Take out your number eight round brush." She held the brush in the air so everyone could see and reviewed the proper way to load paint. "We're going to practice the strokes before we apply them to the wood. Each of you should have tracing paper to practice on. For a comma stroke, push down and come up on the tip. Push down and come up on the tip." Liz demonstrated as she talked.

Rory was walking around, seeing if anyone needed any help, when a loud ringing accompanied by a series of shrill beeps shook the air, the harsh sounds reverberating throughout the ballroom.

Everyone in the class stopped what they were doing and looked up as the fire alarm continued to sound.

"Okay, everyone," Liz said loud enough she could be heard above the ringing of the alarm. "Stay calm and go out the nearest exit. Leave your supplies at your place. They'll be safe here in the room."

Rory helped usher everyone out the door, joining the throng heading toward the hotel entrance where Detective Green stood, making sure everyone left the building in an orderly fashion. Off to one side of the lobby, Ian gave orders to his staff. When Rory and Liz passed by the front desk, they heard the clerk talking on the phone in a calm voice. "...front desk calling. The fire alarm is sounding at this time. It's not known the exact extent of the emergency. However..."

They were almost at the exit when Rory spotted Veronica hiding behind a pillar near the hotel manager, taking notes. She motioned for Veronica to follow them toward the door, but the reporter shook her head, indicating she planned on staying where she was.

Once they were outside, Rory and Liz joined the other guests milling around the courtyard in front of the Akaw. Hotel staff kept everyone fifty feet away from the entrance, creating a safety zone and leaving space for emergency personnel to enter when they arrived. People gathered in small groups, talking and periodically casting worried looks at the hotel.

Rory did a double take and nodded toward a woman with a camera, smaller than a pack of playing cards, strapped around her head. "Is that Stella Nygaard with the head cam?" She'd barely recognized the woman they had met at the Creative Painting convention in Las Vegas a few months before. She'd lost several dress sizes since they saw her last.

Liz looked in the direction Rory had indicated. "That's Stella all right. She's filming the convention for her painting chapter in Minnesota. She promised to show me some of the footage later. I might even get a chance to play around with the camera."

"Sounds like fun." Rory's gaze swept the crowd. "I don't see my mom. I think she was on the trade show floor. There's an exit on the side of the building. Let's head that direction and see if we can find her."

They were making their way through the crowd when a fire truck pulled up, its siren sounding and lights flashing. The hotel manager and Detective Green met the firefighters at the entrance. After a short discussion, the group headed inside. Someone silenced the alarm and, twenty minutes later, the fire department declared the building safe for re-entry, informing everyone it was only a false alarm.

After all of the excitement, it took time for the students in Liz's class to return to their stations and settle down. Once they did, everyone worked on their strokes and, as soon as they'd gained confidence in their abilities, applied them to the project. Rory walked around the room to see if anyone needed any help. Once or twice she noticed Jasmine nodding off. Liz was explaining the last step when murmurs coming from the back of the class reached Rory's ears. When she walked over to see what the fuss was about, she found Jasmine slumped over her project, her hair resting in the wet paint on her palette paper.

Rory assumed her friend was in the midst of another cataplectic attack but, when she moved Jasmine's hair out of the paint, she sensed something was different and very, very wrong. She bent over and studied her friend's face, then straightened up and said in a hushed voice, "I don't think she's breathing."

Chapter 5

A stunned silence fell over the classroom as Liz stopped teaching and everyone realized something was wrong. Hushed cries of "Did she say she's not breathing?" and "Is she okay?" ran through the ballroom.

Rory was going over in her mind the emergency procedures she'd learned as a Girl Scout when Mel stepped forward and said in a soothing voice, "Okay, everyone. Stay calm. I'm a paramedic."

They all cleared a path for the woman to get to Jasmine and waited anxiously for her assessment. "She's breathing." Mel pointed toward Rory and a woman standing next to her. "You and you, help me get her on the floor. Quickly now."

Supporting her head and neck, the three women carefully lowered Jasmine onto the carpet. Mel checked to make sure nothing was blocking Jasmine's airway, then turned to Rory and Liz and said, "Liz, call 911. Rory, do you know if she has any medical conditions? Is she on any medications that you know of?"

"She has narcolepsy." Rory tried to remember what her friend told her about the prescription drugs she took, but nothing came to mind. "She takes several medicines, but I don't know anything about them. Wait, Ian might have the details."

Mel nodded her head, indicating she understood. "See if you can find him. And let the hotel staff know what's going on and make sure the ambulance crew knows where to go when they arrive."

Relieved to have something useful to do, Rory sprinted out the door and down the hallway toward the convention office. Inside, she found the hotel manager quietly talking with Nixie as he massaged her shoulders. By the time she explained the situation to them, the paramedics were entering the front door of the hotel. Rory led them to the ballroom, Nixie and Ian following closely on their heels.

After bringing the ambulance crew up to date, Mel stepped aside and kept everyone back while they worked. As soon as the paramedics wheeled Jasmine out the door with Ian close behind them, Nixie moved to the front of the room, held up her hand and addressed the class. Everyone turned startled faces toward the convention organizer. "This is all very upsetting. All we can do is hope she's okay." She consulted her watch. "There's still half an hour left in the class. Liz tells me she's gone over all the steps with you. I know many of you are too upset to continue painting, but anyone who wishes to work on their project is welcome to stay. Liz will be here to assist you."

After Nixie left the ballroom, the students returned to their seats. Half the class cleaned up their work spaces and packed up their belongings. The other half bent down over their projects, not saying a word as they painted.

Rory stood by Jasmine's station, not quite believing what had happened. She knew the basics of her friend's condition, but had never thought of it as life-threatening.

Liz walked over and gave her a reassuring hug. "I'm sorry about Jasmine. I'm sure they'll do everything they can."

Rory sank down onto a nearby chair as a thought suddenly struck her. "Peter. How am I going to tell Peter?"

"I'll call him if you want."

"No, I should do it." With a heavy heart, Rory picked up her cell phone and dialed, explaining to Peter what happened and where the paramedics took his wife. After she promised to meet him at the hospital and ended the call, she stared at the painting supplies spread out on the table before her. "Could you put everything in her bag? I'd do it myself, but I need to get to the hospital as soon as I can."

"Sure, I can do that. I'll stick the bag in the convention office. Someone can pick it up later." Liz grabbed Jasmine's purse off the floor and handed it to her. "Here, take this with you. They might need something from it." She pushed her gently toward the door. "Go, Peter needs you."

Rory smiled her thanks. She was heading toward the ballroom entrance when the door flew open and Veronica raced inside.

As soon as she spotted Rory, the reporter headed in her direction. Veronica thrust a digital recorder into the young woman's face and said, "Is it true? Did someone die?"

Rory batted the recorder away. "Please shut that off. You shouldn't be asking questions right now. This isn't a news story, it's someone's life we're talking about." She continued out the door. Veronica followed her, practically nipping at her heels. The reporter peppered Rory with questions as they walked down the hall, but soon gave up when she realized she wasn't going to get any answers.

The atmosphere in the hotel was unnaturally quiet. Word had spread that an attendee had collapsed in class and been taken away in an ambulance. As Rory made her way to the Hermosa ballroom to see if Viveca wanted to go to the hospital with her, a number of people stopped her and asked about Jasmine, but there was little she could tell them.

On the trade show floor, she found a group of women clustered around the VivEco booth, blocking the aisle. Rory eased her way through the crowd to where Arika and Nixie were consoling Jasmine's aunt while Hulbert and his employees dealt with the few customers who were interested in purchasing products.

When Rory entered the booth, the convention organizer drew her aside. "Have you heard anything?" she said in a low voice.

Rory shook her head. "I'm headed to the hospital now. I thought maybe Viveca would want to go with me."

"I asked her, but she says no. From what I gather, hospitals hold too many bad memories for her. I'm going to take Viveca to Ian's office. It's nice and private. She can wait for news there without all *this* going on." Nixie inclined her head toward the crowd that was growing by the minute. "When you hear something, go straight there." She went over to where the distraught woman sat, staring off into space. She leaned down and said gently, "Viveca, why don't we go to the manager's office now? Rory will let us know the minute she hears anything."

"What about the booth?" Viveca said in a voice barely above a whisper.

"The girls and I can manage," Hulbert said, gesturing toward the two employees standing off to one side.

Viveca turned a tear-stained face toward her husband. "I need you with me, Hully."

"I'll help out," Arika said. "We'll be just fine. No need for you to worry about anything."

While Nixie led Jasmine's family to the hotel manager's office, Rory headed toward her car for the short drive to the hospital.

Chapter 6

The ER wasn't the chaotic scene Rory expected. No one rushed around like they did on television. Everyone spoke in hushed tones, if they spoke at all. An almost oppressive silence pervaded the waiting area where barely a quarter of the chairs were filled, most by people waiting for word on their loved ones. A muffled "clear" came from behind double doors that shielded the room's occupants from the patient examination area.

Rory headed toward the reception desk but, when she spotted Peter sitting by himself in a far corner of the room, changed course and joined him.

"Any news?" she said as she sat down in the chair beside him.

Tension written all over his face, Peter looked up and shook his head. "Not yet. Thanks for coming."

"I brought her purse." Rory set the shoulder bag down on the floor between the two of them. "We thought you might need her ID or insurance card."

He nodded in acknowledgement, then put his elbows on his knees and buried his head in his hands.

Rory patted his shoulder, wishing she knew how to comfort him. "They're doing everything they can. Do you need me to call anyone? Are you hungry? I can get you some food. There must be vending machines around here somewhere." She scanned the room for an alcove or hallway that might house a coffee or snack machine.

Peter sat up and gave Rory a ghost of a smile. "It's okay. I don't need anything right now. It's enough that you're here."

They sat in silence, each thinking their own thoughts. Every time someone in a white coat came from behind the double doors, their bodies tensed and they both sat up straighter, slumping back down in their seats when no one headed in their direction.

"What's taking so long?" Peter finally said.

"I don't know. Let me go and see what I can find out." Rory was halfway out of her chair when a petite woman in a white coat headed toward them. From the strained look on the doctor's face, Rory knew the worst had happened. She sank back down into her chair and touched her friend's arm. "Peter," she said softly.

"Mr. Halliday?" the doctor said. Peter started to stand up, but she indicated he should remain seated, then sat down in a chair facing them. After introducing herself, Dr. Kendrick cleared her throat and said, "I'm very sorry. We did everything we could, but I'm afraid we were unable to save your wife."

A sob erupted from Peter's mouth. "She's...dead?"

"I'm afraid so." A sympathetic expression on her face, the doctor looked at them both, patiently waiting for them to absorb the news.

A single tear trickled down Rory's face. She squared her shoulders and wiped it away, then asked the question Jasmine's husband seemed unable to put into words. "What happened?"

"We believe she overdosed on one of her medications, Xyrem, sodium oxybate."

"Xyrem? What's that?" Rory said.

"In Jasmine's case, it was helping with her cataplexy."

"So she screwed up?" Peter said.

A blank expression settled over the doctor's face. "How was she feeling recently? Any signs of depression?"

"Suicide?" Rory looked over at Peter who stared down at his hands and shook his head.

Jasmine had suffered occasional bouts of depression over the years, but she generally handled her medical condition with a positive attitude. "No, I don't believe it. She would never do that," Rory finally said.

"Do you have her medicine?" the doctor asked. "Someone will want to examine it."

"I think she kept it in her purse." Rory rummaged through Jasmine's shoulder bag, but didn't find any medicine inside. "That's odd, I could've sworn she said she kept it with her. She must have left it in the hotel room."

The doctor nodded her understanding and stood up. "I know this is hard to take in. If either of you have any more questions feel free to stop by. If I'm available, I'll do my best to answer them."

"Can I see her?" Peter asked.

"Just give us a few minutes. I'll have someone come out and get you."

The double doors were closing behind the doctor when Brandy entered the emergency room and headed toward them. She took one look at their faces and said in a trembling voice, "She's gone?"

Rory stood up, drew her friend to one side and related what Doctor Kendrick told them.

"An accidental overdose? Are they sure?"

"As sure as they can be at this point." Rory looked over at Peter who was clutching his wife's purse to his chest, then lowered her voice and said to Brandy, "I need to tell Viveca what happened. I don't think it's the kind of news that should be given over the phone. She's back at the hotel. Could you stay with Peter and make sure he gets home all right?"

"Of course," Brandy said, her voice stronger. She sank down onto the chair beside Peter and put her arm around the grieving man's shoulder.

Her heart aching, Rory drove back to the Akaw.

Rory spent the evening in her parents' comforting presence, then went home and cried herself to sleep. When she woke up the following morning, gloom hung over the city, as if the sky, too, mourned Jasmine's passing. Rory longed to bury her head under the covers and stay there all day, but her concern over Peter's wellbeing got her out of bed and dressed in record time. After calling to make sure he was awake and taking visitors, she headed out the door.

One short stop later, she pulled up in front of a single-story stucco house on the northern edge of the city. She rang the bell several times before Peter finally answered, looking as tired as Rory felt.

Still in his pajamas and robe with his hair sticking up all over his head and stubble on his face, he appeared as if he'd just rolled out of bed. From the dark circles under his eyes, Rory suspected he hadn't slept a wink.

"I brought breakfast. Bagels from that place you like around the corner." She held up a paper bag. "And I got you coffee. Couldn't remember how you took it so it's black. I hope that's okay."

"Come on in." Peter turned around and headed toward the rear of the house. Rory closed the front door behind her and followed him into the kitchen.

"Sorry about the mess." He motioned toward the boxes that lined the hallway. "Been here two weeks and we still haven't gotten around to unpacking everything. You know how that goes. We were planning on working on it after the convention."

He took coffee creamer out of the refrigerator and sat down on a stool in front of the kitchen island while Rory placed the food in front of him.

A few bites of bagel and sips of coffee later, he said, "Thanks for the food. Didn't feel like having dinner last night. I didn't realize how hungry I was." Peter stared at her as if seeing her for the first time. "That looks familiar. The necklace. Did Jaz paint it?"

Rory fingered the heart-shaped necklace she wore. A rose painted in varying shades of pink graced its center. "That's right. She sent it to me for my birthday. Seemed right to wear it today." She blinked several times before regaining her composure, then motioned toward the pile of dirty dishes in the sink. "Do you mind?"

"Go ahead." He ate in silence while she began washing the mound of plates and cups.

She was halfway finished when Peter said, "That detective was here. The one you told me about. He found her medicine."

Her hands still in the soapy water, she looked over her shoulder. "Detective Green? Where did he find it?"

"In Jasmine's hotel room, just like you thought. They're checking it right now to make sure there's nothing wrong with it."

"You're talking about the one she overdosed on? What's the name of it again?"

"Xyrem. X-y-r-e-m."

Rory tucked the information away in the back of her brain.

"I just don't get it." He set his coffee on the counter. "I don't see how she could have overdosed. She was so careful about her medication. She had to go through a special program before her doctor would prescribe it for her. They made sure she understood everything about the drug—its dangers, what she could and could not do—everything. And I always double-checked to make sure she didn't screw up."

Rory put the last dish in the drainer and wiped her hands on a kitchen towel. She turned around and leaned against the counter. "But she was staying at the hotel by herself. Maybe without you there…"

"She might have missed one or two doses recently, but she never, ever took too much. It wasn't an accidental overdose. I'm sure of it." His chin jutted out in defiance.

"And what about…the other?" Rory said in a soft voice, staring down at the towel in her hands, not daring to look in the man's eyes.

"Suicide? You said it yourself, she would never do that. She was able to do so much more lately." Peter shook his head, clutching the piece of bagel he was holding so tightly an avalanche of crumbs dropped onto the island. "This medication was a godsend. Her cataplexy was under better control. She was getting out more. And she was excited about the convention. No, there *must* be something wrong with her medication."

Rory was inclined to agree with him. The Jasmine she knew always followed her doctor's orders and took any medicines exactly as prescribed. "I guess we'll have to see what the police find out." She hung the towel on the rack and returned the coffee creamer to the refrigerator, noting how little food it contained. She made a mental note to buy some groceries and drop them off later. She turned to look at him in concern. "Is there anything I can do for you?"

Peter looked up from his coffee. "Could you check in with the police and see what they have to say? You've dealt with that detective before when he investigated that woman's death, the one you found in your garden. He might tell you more than he would me."

Rory doubted Detective Green would tell her more about an active investigation than he would the victim's family, but if it made her friend happy, she was willing to try. "Sure, if it'll make you feel better."

"Could you do something else for me?"

"Anything."

He held out a hotel key card with the Akaw logo on it. "Pack up Jaz's things in the hotel room. I can't face going up there and seeing all her stuff just...waiting for her. It's paid for through Sunday, so there's no rush. You can even use the room if you want."

"What about the police?"

"They told me they're done with it. They've taken everything they need."

"I'll take care of it." She grabbed a felt-tip pen off the counter and wrote the room number on the back of her hand. As she prepared to leave, she said, "Are you sure you'll be okay by yourself?"

"Don't worry. I'm already feeling better thanks to you. Brandy said she'd come over later."

Rory studied his face for a moment, looking for some assurance he would be okay on his own. The lost look she'd seen on it when she arrived had disappeared. A little food and some conversation had done him a world of good.

She promised to check on him later. Before heading to the convention, she sat in her car and called her mother. Once she assured Arika that Peter was okay, Rory drove to the hotel, hoping Detective Green would be there with some answers.

Chapter 7

Rory exited the parking garage elevator into the hotel lobby less than fifteen minutes later. When she passed by the hallway leading to the restrooms, the stench of rotten eggs filled her nostrils. She was on her way to report the problem to the front desk when Ian and a man in gray coveralls hurried past her into the men's bathroom.

Moments later, Rory sank down into an empty chair next to Liz who was finishing up a call on her cell. As soon as she hung up, she turned to Rory and said, "I'm so sorry about Jasmine. She seemed sweet. Last night on the phone you said something about an accidental overdose?"

"That's what they think right now. The police are still looking into it. But I don't know. Something tells me there's more to it."

"How's Peter doing? Have you seen him?"

"Just came from his place. He's hanging in there. The police stopped by before I got there."

"Dashing D? What did he have to say?"

Rory told her friend about her conversation with Jasmine's husband.

"What's this medicine she overdosed on? Xy-what?"

"Xyrem. I don't really know much about it. Let's see." Rory drew her smartphone out of her pocket and a few screen taps later she had some answers. "It's a liquid. It says here it's a form of GHB."

"The date rape drug?" Liz said. "Doctors prescribe that?"

"Apparently it helps with cataplexy. According to this, it's a Schedule III controlled substance." Rory scrolled through a few more pages. "Wow, talk about being tightly regulated. You can only get it from a central pharmacy. And you have to go through a special program to make sure you know how to use it. Peter said something about that today. How Jasmine had learned all about the drug's dangers and the do's and don'ts." She frowned. "This doesn't make sense. It says here that she was supposed to take her first dose at night before she went to bed and that it takes effect in five to ten minutes. Then another dose two and a half to four hours later. But that's still hours before she died." She looked through other website pages, but a lot of the information required more medical knowledge than she possessed. "I don't understand half of this."

"Maybe that ER doc can answer your questions," Liz said.

"Maybe."

Liz nodded toward the entrance to the Wave bar which, at this time of day, was more coffee house than tavern. "Isn't that Dashing D?"

Rory's heart fluttered at the sight of the man entering the bar. She shoved the feeling to the back of her mind and stood up. "Let's go and see what he has to say. I promised Peter I'd find out the latest." She tucked her cell phone in the front pocket of her jeans and led the way to the Wave. With its rattan chairs and pots filled with exotic-looking plants, the place reminded Rory of a tropical paradise. She soon spotted the detective at a table in the middle of the floor with Mel, talking and sipping coffee.

Rory and Liz wended their way through the tables toward them. As they approached the couple, they heard Mel say, "That's all I remember. The paramedics took it from there."

Detective Green jotted something down in a notebook and looked up at the new arrivals. "You must have read my mind. I was just going to look for you two. Have a seat." He indicated the empty chairs at the table. Rory sat down next to the detective with Liz on the other side of her.

"I'm very sorry about your friend." He reached over as if to place a comforting hand on Rory's arm, then glanced over at his girlfriend and seemed to think better of it. Instead, his hand closed around his cup, and he took a sip of coffee. "Mel here was just telling me about what happened in class. Tell me what you two saw." He looked at Rory. "You go first. Start with the moment you entered the room."

She cast her mind back to the day before, describing everything in as much detail as she could. "Then there was the fire alarm. Everybody left their stuff at their places and left the ballroom as fast as possible."

"What about her medicine? What do you know about that?" the detective asked.

"That was a little odd," Rory said. "She told me the other day she planned on carrying it with her. Didn't want to leave it in her room because she was afraid it would be stolen. So I was surprised when I didn't find it in her purse. I heard you found it in her hotel room."

"You talked to her husband, then?"

"Just came from his house. I wanted to make sure he was okay."

"What about her purse? Did Jasmine take hers with her during the fire alarm?" he continued.

"I guess so. I don't really notice that kind of thing. I don't carry one myself." She turned toward Liz. "Do you remember?"

Liz frowned in concentration. "Sorry, I don't. I was too busy making sure everyone got out okay. But it was on the floor by her seat after she collapsed. You took it to the hospital with you."

Rory nodded. "That's right. I gave it to Peter. I thought he might need it."

"What about her demeanor yesterday?" Detective Green asked. "Did she seem her usual self?"

"I guess." Rory thought back to when she'd last seen her friend. "You know, there was something. She seemed a little out of sorts at the beginning of class. I asked her about it, but she said it wasn't important, she'd speak to me after class. I have no idea what she wanted to talk about."

He plied both of them with questions that they answered as best they could. As the conversation went on, Rory realized how she could be of help to the police.

"I can track Jasmine's movements the day or two before she died if that would help. People might talk to me when they won't talk to you," she said to the detective.

"No investigating by you—" His steely gaze landed on each of the women at the table. "—or anyone else. Leave it to me. Do you understand?"

They all nodded, but Rory silently vowed to find out what she could. She told herself he didn't really mean it when he said she shouldn't ask questions. She was sure he would appreciate the information once he had it. Besides, she might discover something he wouldn't be able to find out otherwise.

Detective Green ended the interview with a request for the list of students in the class. Liz was digging it out of her purse when Rory said to him, "Has the police lab had a chance to check out her medication yet?"

He stared at her as if deciding how much to tell her. "We're still processing the bottle. We should know something soon." He cocked his head. "She was a friend of yours. What do you think happened?"

"It wasn't an accident and definitely not suicide. I feel it in here." Rory pressed her hand against her heart. "She was too excited about attending the convention and moving to town."

"Really?"

Rory narrowed her eyes. "What aren't you saying?"

"Ask her husband," was all he said before bending over to study the class list Liz placed on the table.

As she tried to puzzle out what the man meant, Rory's gaze swept the bar. The only other customers were a black-haired woman sitting on a stool at the counter talking with the bartender, her back to them, and someone at a table in a corner so dark Rory couldn't tell who it was. As Rory watched, the waitress carried a glass of white wine to the customer and returned to the bar with an empty glass.

Rory was squinting her eyes, trying to make out who the unknown person was, when Ian approached them. "Detective, could I speak with you a moment, please?" He nodded toward an empty table. "In private."

"Excuse me, ladies. Thank you for your time. Let me know if you think of anything else." The detective stuffed the class list into his jacket pocket, then leaned forward and said, "Remember what I said. No investigating." After those words of warning, he stood up and walked over to join the hotel manager at a table far enough away they couldn't hear what the two men were saying.

"What do you think they're talking about?" Liz said.

Rory strained to hear the conversation, but couldn't make out a single word. Not for the first time, she wished she knew how to read lips. "Ian doesn't look happy, whatever it is," she finally said. "Maybe he's asking about Jasmine's death. Can't be good for business to have someone collapse in your hotel."

"It's something hotels and motels have to deal with all the time," Mel said. "I've dealt with a lot of emergencies at them for work."

Rory nodded her head. Given the sheer number and variety of people who stayed in hotels, there were bound to be all sorts of accidents and medical issues that required a paramedic's attention. She turned to Mel. "You said you know the paramedics who treated Jasmine. Could you introduce me to them? I'd like to ask them some questions. I want to make sure Peter has all the facts."

"Sure." Mel jotted down two names and a phone number on a cocktail napkin. "The fire station's only a few blocks away. Let them know I sent you. But I'm not sure they'll be able to tell you anything you haven't already heard." She glanced at the clock above the bar. "I need to get to class. Let me know if I can be of any more help."

As Mel passed by the table where the hotel manager and detective sat, the men stood up and shook hands. The detective and his girlfriend exited the bar together while Ian headed toward the table in the corner.

Rory stuffed the napkin in the pocket of her jeans. The next time she left the hotel, she planned on stopping by the fire station to see if the paramedics who treated Jasmine were on duty.

"I wonder what Ian wanted to talk to Dashing D about," Liz said.

The woman at the counter shifted in her seat, revealing a fuchsia streak in her black hair.

"I know how we can find out." Rory nodded toward Veronica who stood up, took a final sip of her soda, and placed a bill on the counter. "She was practically falling out of her chair trying to hear what the two of them were saying."

As the woman turned toward them, Rory motioned the reporter over to the table. For once, Veronica's quest for the next big story might come in handy.

Chapter 8

As soon as Veronica settled down into the chair Detective Green had recently occupied, Rory got straight to the point. "What did you hear?"

The reporter fingered her nose ring and stared at each one of them in turn as if deciding how much to reveal. "I'll tell you what I heard if you tell me about your friend, the one who died."

Rory considered the reporter's request. She would probably write an article anyway. At least this way, Rory would have a chance to make sure people knew what a good person Jasmine was and that she was more than her medical condition. "Deal, but I get to see what you write before it gets published."

Veronica nodded in agreement, then leaned in and said in a conspiratorial whisper, "Sabotage. That's what they were talking about."

Rory stared at the reporter in disbelief. She'd expected to hear something about Jasmine's death and Ian being worried about the bad publicity it would cause, not this. "The alarm?" she finally said.

"And the bathroom. Someone placed a stink bomb in the men's room."

That would explain the horrible smell she noticed earlier, Rory thought. "Any idea who put it there? Or when?"

"It was on some sort of timer. Ian thinks the protesters are responsible, but that detective didn't seem as convinced. He said he was keeping an open mind until they know more."

"But he's investigating?" Rory asked.

Veronica nodded. "Ian's handing hotel security footage over to the police, but I don't know how much help it'll be. There aren't any cameras in the restrooms."

"There might be in the hallway. Maybe they can get something from that." Rory tried to visualize the area. She couldn't remember seeing any cameras, but they might be hidden in a plant or behind a decoration. "I wonder if the same person who planted the stink bomb also threw the rock through my window. Have you heard anything?" she said to Veronica.

The reporter shrugged in a noncommittal gesture. Rory suspected any news would end up in the paper or on Vista Beach Confidential long before it made its way to them. She made a mental note to periodically check the blog over the next few days.

Veronica sat back in her chair. "Okay, I've told you everything I know. Tell me about Jasmine. You were childhood friends, right?"

Rory was gathering her thoughts, deciding where to begin, when the sound of loud voices reached their ears. Everyone in the bar turned to stare at a table in the corner where Ian was arguing with a woman Rory now recognized as the convention organizer.

When a waitress approached the table with another glass of wine, the hotel manager waved her away. He stood up and grabbed a partially empty glass off the table. "I'm cutting you off. It's for your own good."

Ian brought the glass over to the bartender and repeated his instructions. Nixie stood up and, a little unsteadily, headed toward the lobby. She was concentrating so hard on putting one foot in front of the other, she didn't notice the group of women staring at her. As soon as Nixie passed by their table, Veronica left the bar, mumbling something about looking after the tipsy woman.

"Do you think Nixie will be okay?" Rory asked.

"Veronica can handle it. She has a lot of experience with drunks," Liz said.

Rory stared at her friend, a question in her eyes, and waited for her to elaborate.

Liz's face turned red. "I shouldn't have said anything. Her parents were alcoholics. I'm not sure she wants anyone to know."

Rory mimed zipping her lips shut with one hand and fingered the hotel key in the front pocket of her jeans with the other. "Let's go upstairs. I promised Peter I'd pack up Jasmine's things. She was staying here for the convention." She looked at the back of her hand where she'd written down the number. "Room 643."

They exited the elevator on the top floor and headed down the hallway, smiling at the maid pushing her cart toward the service elevator. When they found the room they were looking for, Rory drew the key card out of her pocket. She was about to insert the card in the lock when Liz tugged on Rory's arm. "Wait. Do you hear something?"

Rory pressed her ear against the door and listened. A faint sound reminiscent of a drawer sliding open came from behind the locked door. "Someone's inside." She slipped the key card in the lock and turned the handle.

Chapter 9

Rory cautiously pushed open the hotel room door. A short hallway led to the main area of the room where she could make out a flat screen TV, a low dresser, and a neatly made up king-size bed flanked by twin night stands. The room appeared empty, but noises came from somewhere inside. She motioned Liz forward. They crept down the short hallway and peeked around the corner. Light streamed through the half-open bathroom door. From their position at the end of the hallway, neither of them could see who was inside, but whoever was there was making little attempt to keep quiet.

Rory looked around for something they could use to defend themselves. She pointed toward the bolster pillows on the bed and Liz nodded. They each picked one up and, as quietly as possible, crept forward.

Liz pointed her index and middle fingers at her own eyes then at the bathroom door, then repeated the motion.

Rory whispered, "What does that mean?"

"I have no idea," Liz whispered back. "But they always do it on TV shows."

Rory stood on one side of the half-open bathroom door, Liz the other. Just as Rory was about to kick it open, the intruder came through the door.

Veronica jumped and squeaked her surprise when she saw the two of them brandishing their makeshift weapons. "Give a girl a little warning. You scared the pants off of me."

Rory lowered her pillow. "What are you doing in here? I thought you were taking care of Nixie."

"She's in the hotel manager's office. I thought it was the best place for her. He's plying her with coffee. What are you two doing in here?"

"Peter wanted me to pack up Jasmine's things. What's your excuse?"

"Just doing my job. Your friend's death seems a little suspicious to me so I thought I'd take a look around." Veronica repositioned the two tote bags on her shoulder.

"How did you get in?" Rory's eyes narrowed. "How did you even know which room was hers?"

The reporter nodded at Rory's left hand. "You told me yourself."

Rory looked down at the back of her hand where she'd written the hotel room number in felt-tip pen. She guessed it didn't take much of an imagination to figure out what the number meant. She frowned. "How did you say you got in? You don't have a key, do you?"

Veronica grinned. "I have my ways."

Remembering the maid they passed in the hallway, Rory suspected the reporter had charmed her way inside the room.

"Do you think you could put that bolster down?" Veronica pointed to the pillow Liz was still holding threateningly in the air. "You're making me nervous."

Rory and Liz both returned their pillows to the bed, then Rory said to the snooping reporter, "How much of the room did you search? Did you find anything?"

"Not really. Maybe you'll have better luck." Veronica waggled her fingers in a goodbye gesture and turned toward the exit.

The woman was almost at the door when Rory spotted an empty five-by-seven picture frame on one of the nightstands. "Wait! Did you steal a photo?"

Veronica backtracked and drew a picture out of one of the tote bags slung across her shoulder. "It's just a picture of Jasmine and her husband. I was going to scan it in and post it on my blog. I don't know what you're getting all tweaked out about. I was planning on returning it later."

Rory grabbed the five-by-seven out of the reporter's hand. "If you want something like this, don't just take it, ask her husband. I'm sure he'll be happy to give you one."

Veronica grumbled all the way down the hallway.

Once the door closed behind the woman, Rory returned the picture to the frame, then surveyed the room. "We should conduct our own search while we pack up Jasmine's things. Why don't you take the bathroom, and I'll look around in here. Maybe Veronica and the police missed something."

While Liz explored the bathroom, Rory checked out the bed area. A quick inspection of the nightstand drawers revealed nothing of interest. She opened the closet door, dragged the suitcase and carry-on she found out onto the bed, and checked the pockets in the empty luggage. The only things she uncovered were a small lime green TSA lock and a nail file. Once she was sure the suitcase and carry-on were completely empty, she started putting items into them. She carefully folded Jasmine's clothes, placing the picture frame on top of them in the suitcase, then checked everywhere she could think of—the floor of the closet, the dresser drawers, between the box spring and mattress, under the bed. When she spotted the in-room safe in the corner of the closet, she thought for a moment she'd struck pay dirt. But, when she went to examine it, the safe's door swung open, revealing the emptiness within.

Rory was finishing her sweep of the room when Liz emerged from the bathroom with a makeup bag and bottles of lotion. "Found a bunch of makeup and beauty products. Nothing unusual. Where should I put these?"

"In the carry-on." Rory pointed to the purple bag on the bed beside her.

After Liz packed the bathroom items, she turned to Rory and said, "The bathroom's clear. Didn't see anything suspicious."

"Did you look everywhere? Even the toilet tank?"

"First place I looked. That's where I'd hide something if I didn't want anyone to find it."

"That's it, then." Rory surveyed the room one last time. "I think that's all we can do. I'll let Peter know everything's packed and see what he wants me to do with it all." She exchanged a series of texts with Jasmine's husband, who thanked her and told her to leave everything in the room for now. After stashing the suitcase and carry-on in the closet, they left, locking the hotel door securely behind them, and parted ways in the lobby.

Rory headed toward her next class, but when she stepped inside the ballroom and stared at the group patiently waiting for the Rosemaling class to begin, she knew she was too preoccupied to stay. She collected the pattern packet and painting surface and immediately left the ballroom along with two other students who had the same idea.

After making sure she wasn't needed on the trade show floor, she drove out of the hotel parking lot and headed toward Peter's house to check on him, stopping off at a grocery store along the way. When she rang the bell, Peter answered looking more human than he had earlier that day. He still had dark circles under his eyes, but he'd showered, shaved and dressed.

"Aren't you supposed to be at the convention?" he asked.

"Doesn't seem as much fun since...you know."

"What's this?" He nodded toward the grocery bag Rory held in her arms.

"Brought you a few things. I noticed you didn't have much food in the refrigerator. I've got frozen dinners, a barbecued chicken, and fruit."

Peter took the bag from her and motioned Rory inside. "Thanks. We were just on our way out."

She followed him into the kitchen where she found Brandy putting away her own groceries.

"Guess we had the same idea," Rory said to her friend.

"Between the two of you, I won't starve, that's for sure." Peter set the grocery bag he was holding down on the kitchen island and gave each of them a grateful smile. "We were just heading out to make some...arrangements."

"Have they finished the autopsy, then?" Rory asked in a subdued voice, a little surprised the coroner had finished so quickly.

Brandy closed the refrigerator door. "No. Peter just wanted to start the process so we'd be ready when they release her. Neither of us have ever done this before."

Rory nodded in sympathy. She dreaded the time when she would have to make similar arrangements for someone she loved. "I can go along if you want. Provide moral support."

Peter shook his head. "We're okay. Besides, afterwards, we're going to run through our routines one last time before tonight."

"Tonight?" Rory looked at the two of them, puzzled.

"The tango competition."

"You didn't drop out?" Rory said in surprise.

"We were going to," Brandy said. "But Peter wanted to continue. For Jasmine."

"She did enjoy seeing you dance." Rory cleared her throat. "I talked to Detective Green. He was asking about our class. I thought I'd help him track her movements Tuesday and Wednesday."

"Why? I thought it was an accidental overdose," Brandy said.

"The police haven't confirmed that yet. They're still testing her medicine," Rory replied.

"It's okay. If it helps the police figure out what happened..." Peter stared down at the granite countertop as if collecting his thoughts. "Of course you know about Monday evening. She checked into the hotel that night right before dinner, so I don't know much about where she was Tuesday or Wednesday. She called me during your class yesterday, told me about the fire alarm. Tuesday evening she worked the trade show floor. You probably saw her there. Before that she had a meeting with Nixie."

"About the books for the convention?"

"That's right. Nixie wanted to go over a few things. Jasmine called me before the meeting."

"Oh?" Rory said. "How was she?"

"Excited about working in the booth. Did the detective have anything else to say?"

"Not really. It's what he didn't say that bothers me."

"What do you mean?" Peter asked, a confused expression on his face.

"I was sure he was holding something back. When I asked him about it, he told me to ask *you*, Peter. Do either of you know what he meant by that?" Rory looked from Peter to Brandy and back again.

The two of them shared a look that made Rory wonder if they were hiding something. Finally, Brandy said, "You'd better tell her."

"Tell me what?"

With his finger, Peter traced a square on the countertop. "Jaz tried to commit suicide once. Pills."

Rory's legs wobbled, and she braced herself against the kitchen island. "When was this?"

"A year ago," he said. "That would make it a couple months after you moved here."

"Why didn't anyone tell me?"

"We didn't want to bother you. You'd just found out about your birth parents. We figured you had enough to deal with," Brandy said.

When Rory learned her birth parents were serial arsonists responsible for numerous fires and a few deaths around Vista Beach, she'd mentioned her discovery to them, but hadn't expected her childhood friends to keep her out of the loop because of it. "I wish you'd told me." She looked at Peter. "Jasmine had been dealing with her condition for almost fifteen years. Why, all of a sudden, did she try suicide?"

Peter stared down at the granite countertop. "We were going through a rough patch. Her condition wasn't easy to live with for either of us. One day she found it to be too much, I guess."

"The doctor in the ER asked about suicide. Why didn't you say anything?" Rory asked.

"That was all in the past. It has nothing to do with this. She went into therapy and was doing so much better. Our marriage was good. The new medication was working. Her cataplexy was under better control, and she didn't nod off as often as she used to. There's no way she'd try to kill herself again."

Rory turned to Brandy. "What do you think?"

Without a moment's hesitation, the young woman said, "I don't think she'd do that. She was too excited about the convention and moving here."

Peter looked at the two of them. "I wonder how the police found out about her suicide attempt. I never told them."

Brandy's mouth dropped open. "I didn't tell them because I thought you had. Why didn't you? That's something they should know."

Peter's face turned red. "I was protecting her memory. She never wanted anyone to know. She felt so embarrassed about it. Guess that was stupid of me to keep it from the police."

Brandy patted his arm. "Understandable under the circumstances. They know now, that's what's important." She glanced at the clock on the wall. "We'd better get going. We have that appointment. Peter, why don't you put away the rest of the groceries, and I'll walk Rory out."

As soon as they were outside with the front door closed behind them, Brandy turned to her friend, a sad look on her face.

"I wish Jasmine were still here. I miss her already. You've talked with the detective in charge of her case. What do you think happened?"

"She was too careful about her medication. I can't believe it was an accidental overdose. There's something wrong about her death," Rory said.

"Maybe the pharmacy screwed up and it was just a horrible accident."

"Maybe."

"Whatever it is, I hope the police come to a conclusion soon. Not knowing is killing Peter."

"What about you? How are you doing? It seems stressful enough taking care of your aunt, and now this."

"It's not easy, but nothing compared to what Peter's going through."

"If you ever need a break and want me to stay with your aunt, let me know."

"My mom and I have it covered, but thanks." Brandy waved goodbye and walked over to where Peter was locking the front door.

Rory headed to her car. Before she'd talked to her friends, she would have sworn Jasmine would never try to commit suicide. She still wasn't convinced that's what happened this time. Jasmine deserved the benefit of the doubt. Rory hadn't been there for her when she needed her before. She intended to be there now.

Rory put her car in gear and headed back to the hospital to learn as much as she could about the medication her friend had overdosed on.

Chapter 10

As soon as she entered the ER, Rory's body tensed. She had to fight the urge to run back to her car and drive as far away and as fast as possible. After a few deep breaths, she pushed the bad memories to the back of her mind and stood in line at the reception desk. She relayed her request to talk with the doctor who had treated her friend, then settled down in a chair, flipping through a celebrity magazine to pass the time. She'd almost given up when Dr. Kendrick came through the double doors and walked toward her.

"You wanted to see me?" The light of recognition dawned in the woman's eyes. "You were here yesterday, weren't you? Your friend, Ms....Halliday, was it? I'm so sorry for your loss."

"Thanks. I was wondering if you had time to answer a few questions. I'm trying to understand what happened."

The doctor glanced at her watch. "I have a few minutes." She looked around as if searching for somewhere more private to talk. "Let's go over here." She moved over to the side of the room, as close to the wall and as far away from people as possible. "This will have to do. Now, what did you want to know?"

"I was reading online about this medicine she took, Xyrem. I understand it's a form of GHB."

The doctor gave an almost imperceptible wince at the word "online," but didn't chastise Rory for conducting medical research on the internet. "That's right."

"From what I understand, she took her medicine at night. If she took too much the night before she died, could that have caused her collapse the following day? Hours after she had taken it?"

"As you're probably aware, absorption of any medication depends on a lot of factors. But, in my opinion, she would have shown problems long before she was brought in. She probably wouldn't even have woken up. That's assuming she took it when she was told to, of course. She might have missed a dose and taken it later during the day even though she wasn't supposed to. People aren't always smart when it comes to medication. For the one your friend was on, most people fall asleep within five to ten minutes of taking it."

That confirmed what she read online, Rory thought. "What about the medicine itself? Could there be something wrong with it?"

"Doubtful, but it's a possibility. If that's what happened, the police will figure it out." Dr. Kendrick touched Rory on the arm in a sympathetic gesture. "I'm really sorry about your friend. I know you want a definitive answer, but I'm not sure anything I can say will give you the closure you're looking for. Is there anything else I can help you with?"

"I think that's it. Thanks for your time, Doctor. I appreciate it."

The doctor gave Rory a pat on the arm and a reassuring smile, then headed back through the double doors.

Rory leaned against the wall and closed her eyes, thinking about what Doctor Kendrick had said. If the effects were felt so soon, Jasmine must have taken the medicine during class or right before she returned to the ballroom after the all-clear for the fire alarm was given. Rory couldn't remember seeing her take anything, but she wasn't watching her every move. Since they'd found no medication in Jasmine's shoulder bag, she must have taken it outside of the classroom. Rory added *find out where Jasmine was during fire alarm* to her mental to-do list.

She drove back to the hotel, stopping off at the fire station to talk with the paramedics who treated her friend. They willingly answered her questions, but could tell her nothing she didn't already know. Less than ten minutes after that, she walked into the lobby of the Akaw. Almost as soon as she stepped inside, Ian rushed over to her.

"Finally! Where have you been?" he said. "I've called and texted for the last hour."

Rory checked her phone, but didn't see any texts or missed calls from his number. "I didn't get any of them. Sorry. I'm here now, what's going on?"

"No one can get to the hotel website. People are complaining."

She entered the website address into her phone's browser, hoping it was a temporary glitch and the site was once again available. But that hope was crushed moments later when she discovered it was still inaccessible. She opened her mouth to explain what she thought the problem was, but he held up his hand and stopped her from talking.

"Before you start spouting all kinds of technical jargon, let me say that I don't care *what* the problem is. Just fix it. All I care about is guests and potential customers being able to access the site."

"I'll get right on it."

Rory spent time on the phone with the website's hosting provider, dealing with the issue. By the time they resolved the problem, only five minutes remained before the silk painting class she'd signed up for was scheduled to begin. She settled into the seat Liz saved for her, put on her apron and set out her supplies.

Her friend looked at her inquiringly. "I almost gave up on you. Where have you been?"

Rory nodded toward the front where the teacher was poised to begin. "I'll tell you after class," she whispered.

As she painted, her mind drifted off so often, she lost track of how many times she needed to ask Liz what they were doing. By the time the teacher had covered every step, Rory's project was only halfway done, but she didn't have the patience to stay in the room and finish it.

"That looks nice." Rory nodded at the silk scarf covered in

poppies and butterflies her friend had painted. "Mine's a lost cause. Let's go."

The two of them packed up their supplies and headed to the lobby, where they found a quiet corner to talk. Rory quickly brought her friend up to date on the website problems and the information she'd obtained from the emergency room doctor.

"Ian's pretty mad at me," Rory said.

"The website stuff wasn't your fault. Didn't you say it was a, what did you call it, denial of something or other?"

"Denial-of-service attack. Doesn't really matter if it was my fault or not, I'm a convenient person to blame."

"Remind me what that is again."

"In this case, the Akaw's website was flooded with requests from multiple computers, so many that the server couldn't handle it. The result, no one could access the hotel's website."

Liz whistled. "So no one could book a room or find out about the hotel, right? Sounds like a protest to me."

"The protesters could have organized it. Wouldn't be hard to do."

"They certainly seem to have it out for both you and the Akaw."

Liz glanced over at a nearby table where a hotel employee was setting out newspapers for guests to read. She walked over to the display of papers and brought back a copy of that day's *Vista Beach View*, scanning the front page as she made her way back across the lobby.

"Look at this." Liz pointed to a headline below the fold on the front page. "Veronica wrote about the convention. She mentions VivEco and even put in some pictures." She handed the paper to Rory who skimmed the article.

The piece featured a short account of the first days of the OPS convention, including a photo of Stella Nygaard modeling her camera and another of Viveca striking a pose on the trade show floor with the name of her booth prominently displayed in the background. In the interview with Viveca that appeared alongside her photo, the woman talked about her former career as a painting teacher, and how, when she'd decided to return to the business after eleven years, she'd started the eco-friendly painting product company with her new husband's help.

"What's this?" Rory pointed to an article above the fold on the protesters plaguing the Akaw. "It says here the group protesting denies setting off the alarm the other day."

"Of course they're going to say that. They don't want to get in trouble."

Rory summarized the rest of the article for her friend. A confidential source told Veronica hotel security footage showed a member of the Akaw's maintenance staff pulling the alarm. All of the staff had been questioned, but no one had taken responsibility for the act of sabotage. "I wonder who the confidential source is."

"I'll ask Veronica the next time I see her," Liz said. "What does it say about the stink bomb? Do the protesters deny doing that too?"

"No, they take credit for it. Sound a bit proud of it, actually. Seems odd, doesn't it? That they'd take credit for one and not the other."

"Maybe all this new information will help the police figure out who threw that rock through your window."

"I doubt it. It's just a bunch of anonymous statements. They can't arrest everyone." Rory's thoughts turned back to the alarm. "I wonder if someone was masquerading as a janitor. That's what I would do. Wouldn't be hard to put on some coveralls over your clothes, set off the alarm, take off the coveralls and blend in with the rest of the crowd exiting the hotel. But you'd have to get rid of them somehow." She turned the problem over in her mind. "They could have put them in the hotel garbage. If the trash hasn't come, they might still be there. I wonder if anyone's thought to look through it." She placed the newspaper on the table between their two chairs.

"Maybe Dashing D knows."

After a moment of thought, Rory dialed the detective's

number. He listened patiently to her theory about the protesters and the coveralls. "Interesting," he said after she finished.

"So you'll look into it?"

"We'll add it to our list of things to investigate. While I have you on the phone, I thought you'd like to know that we've closed your friend's case. We've determined it was an accidental overdose."

"What about her medicine? Did you analyze it?"

"It checked out. Nothing suspicious about it. The concentration is fine and the amount left in it is consistent with an overdose."

Rory opened her mouth to ask a question, but before she could say a word, the detective said, "No fingerprints on the bottle other than your friend's, either."

"So that's it? You're not going to investigate anymore?"

"We've done everything we can. As far as we can tell, there's nothing suspicious about her death. Unless new evidence comes to light, the case is closed."

Rory hung up and puzzled over the news. With everything she'd learned about the medication, she didn't see how her friend could have overdosed. If bad medication wasn't the culprit, then the only other conclusion she could come to was someone had dosed Jasmine with Xyrem. She couldn't let that person get away with it. If the police weren't going to investigate, she would.

"Did I hear right?" Liz said. "The investigation's over?"

Rory relayed everything the detective had told her to her friend.

"We need new evidence so he'll reopen the case. We've got to think like the police. Phone records. Email messages. Alibis. Means, motive, opportunity." Rory ticked the last three items off on her fingers.

"We won't be able to get access to phone records and emails, but we can look into alibis and motives," Liz said. "We need suspects. Who would want to kill her? You know if the police were investigating, the first person they'd look at is Peter."

"From everything I've heard, the spouse *is* the prime suspect. He did have easy access to her medication. But he loved her, why would he want her dead?"

"He might have wanted out of the marriage. Must be hard being a spouse of someone with her condition."

Peter had said as much when she talked to him earlier, Rory thought. "There is such a thing as divorce."

"Maybe he thought he'd look like the bad guy, divorcing someone who had a medical condition she had little control over. Or he'd taken a boatload of life insurance out on her," Liz continued.

"There must be other possibilities." Rory frowned in concentration. "But right now I can't think of a single one."

"Looking at where she went since she arrived at the hotel might help. Didn't you talk about tracing her movements?"

"That's right. Let's see." Using the memo app on her cell phone, Rory took notes as she talked. "She checked into the hotel on Monday. We had dinner at my parents that evening. Tuesday she had a meeting with Nixie right before she worked on the trade show floor that night."

"Anything unusual happen there?"

Rory cast her mind back to the early shopping opportunity, trying to remember everything she'd seen and heard. "Not that I noticed, but I wasn't working with her. I was in my mom's booth and she was across the aisle at VivEco. It was pretty busy. We talked a few times, joked around. If anything unusual happened, I didn't see it."

"Okay, what about Wednesday?"

They both remained silent for a minute, each picturing the awful moment when Jasmine collapsed in class.

"She called Peter during the alarm and told him about it," Rory said, breaking the silence. "That's about all I know. I'm not sure what classes she was signed up for. We should probably find that out." She'd just typed *Jasmine, class schedule* in the app when her cell phone quacked. She stared down at its display. "Mom wants to know if I can help in the VivEco booth. I'll see what Viveca and Hulbert know." She quickly texted back she'd be right there, said goodbye to Liz and, taking the newspaper with her, headed to the trade show floor.

Chapter 11

When Rory reached the VivEco booth, she found Hulbert working by himself. Half a dozen customers stood around, clamoring for attention. She stowed her painting bag under a nearby table and, after a few instructions, started ringing up purchases while he answered questions. When the bottles in the display racks had dwindled and there was a lull in business, she helped him replenish the supplies. She reached in one of the boxes underneath the table and brought out bottles of varnish with a blue label.

"Not those," Hulbert said. "We had some problems with the manufacturing process. Didn't realize what happened until we got here and someone complained. Get the others, the ones with the green label."

As they restocked the shelves, Rory asked, "How's Viveca doing?"

"As well as can be expected. To tell you the truth, I'm a little worried about her. Jasmine was like a daughter to her."

"They became close after Jasmine's mother died." Rory tried to pull one of the cardboard boxes out from under another table, but it was so heavy she couldn't make it budge.

Hulbert easily maneuvered the box into the open where they could get at its contents.

Rory smiled gratefully at him. "Viveca was very supportive of Jasmine. She always appreciated that."

"No one ever talks about the father. What was he like?"

"He's still around. Jasmine doesn't—didn't—see him very often. He was embarrassed by her condition. Didn't want her to go anywhere, do anything. Didn't even want her to go to school. Her mother—and, afterwards, Viveca—encouraged her to live as normal a life as possible."

"That explains a lot," Hulbert said. "Has anyone called him to tell him the news?"

"I assumed Viveca had."

"I'll ask her when she gets back. She's being interviewed by the press right now. She should be here soon."

Rory took the copy of the *View* out of her tote bag and handed it to him. "Did you see this article? There's a nice picture of Viveca in front of the booth."

Hulbert skimmed the paper, then placed it on a nearby table and returned to his work. "Nice bit of publicity for the company, too. She'll be pleased. The interview she's doing now is for an online painting blog."

"I wish I'd been able to spend more time with Jasmine that last day. I hope Viveca got to see her."

Hulbert shoved a box underneath a table and brought out another one. "Jasmine worked the booth in the morning, before she went to class. Seemed worried."

"Oh? What about?"

"Something to do with convention finances, I think. She did the books, you know. Doesn't matter, anyway. It was all just a horrible accident. That's what the police told us." He lowered his voice. "Everyone's relieved they ruled it an accident. The life insurance won't pay off if she committed suicide, you know. And Peter could use the money."

"Why do you say that?"

Hulbert looked confused. "He had to get a second job to make ends meet. I thought you knew. Some sort of maintenance work, I think."

"Where?"

"Here, at the hotel."

"Are you sure? Maintenance work isn't exactly his cup of tea. If he needs more money, why doesn't he pick up more accounting work?"

"I never thought of that. When I saw him dressed in coveralls going into one of the ballrooms, I assumed he was working here and was too embarrassed to tell anyone about it."

"When was this?"

"That last day, during the alarm. He was going into the Zuma ballroom. That's where Jasmine had her class, right? I thought he was checking to make sure she got out safely."

"And you're positive it was him?"

"I only saw him from a distance, but it sure looked like Peter to me."

"You know, there was an article in the *View* about the protesters." Rory picked up the paper to refresh her memory. "It says here the man who pulled the alarm was wearing coveralls. They saw him on the security video. Couldn't see his face, it was obscured by a ball cap. Was Peter wearing one?"

"You don't think he set off the alarm, do you? Why would he do that? That doesn't make sense."

"I don't know. It could have been one of the protesters. Maybe the police will find some evidence when they dig through the hotel trash. Whoever pulled the alarm might have dumped the coveralls."

"I hope it wasn't Peter." Hulbert glanced at his Rolex. "Thanks for your help. I've got some workers coming, but they won't be here for half an hour. Can you stay?"

"No problem."

Before he could say anything else, a woman entered the booth and asked about the advantages of the eco-friendly products. While he gave his sales spiel, Rory continued to ring up purchases. As she worked, part of her mind wondered why Peter felt the need to take on a second job and if he'd been the one to set off the alarm.

Rory and Hulbert were kept busy until Viveca returned to the booth. As soon as he saw her, the man's face lit up and he reached under a table, producing a single red rose, which he presented to his wife.

"Oh, Hully," Viveca said and smiled for what Rory suspected was the first time since her niece's death.

While the two employees that followed Viveca into the booth started working, the painting teacher turned to the younger woman and said, "Thank you. I appreciate your being here. Be sure to keep track of your hours. We'll pay you."

Rory waved away the offer. "No need. I'm glad I can help. I heard the news about the investigation being over."

"Thank God. They'll be releasing her body soon, and we can finally have a service for her."

"Let me know if there's anything I can do to help."

After saying goodbye to everyone in the VivEco booth, Rory gathered her things and headed off the trade show floor toward the convention office to see what Nixie had to say about her meeting with Jasmine. Outside the Manhattan ballroom, she found an impromptu shrine to her friend. Bouquets of flowers, pictures, and painted pieces clustered around the legs of the memo board that stood outside the ballroom entrance.

As Rory bent down to study a collage of photographs, she heard raised voices coming from the other side of the partially open door. Moments later, a teenager about Liz's height in a camisole and tight-fitting jeans yanked open the door. "You need to do the right thing," the girl said to Nixie before brushing by Rory and heading down the hallway.

When Rory entered the ballroom, the overpowering smell of a floral perfume filled the air as if someone had spilled an entire bottle on the carpet.

"Hi, Rory, what can I do for you?" Nixie said.

Rory cleared her throat. She hated this part of running a business. "I haven't received payment for my last invoice yet for the convention's website. I was wondering if you got it. I mailed it a month ago."

Elbows on the table, Nixie put her head in her hands and

groaned. "I thought Jasmine took care of that. Let me see if I can find that invoice." She was looking through a stack of folders when her cell rang. "Sorry, I've got to take this. I'll be right with you." Nixie pressed her phone to her ear, frowning at whatever the caller had to say. After she hung up, she looked up at Rory and said, "There are no trash cans in any of the classrooms. Can you believe it? All of the students have to fill their painting buckets in the bathroom. And there's nothing to dump the dirty water into. The cans were there when I checked the rooms earlier today. Apparently, someone from the hotel hauled them off without replacing them. It's one problem after the other with this place. Getting the kinks worked out, I suppose. Could you—"

Before the woman could finish her sentence, Gordon walked into the office, his head buried in his own cell phone.

"Never mind, Rory. I have to take care of this problem first, then I'll write that check for you. I'll get it to you as soon as I can. If you need to talk to me about anything else, I'll be back later. Otherwise, Gordon will be happy to help you." Nixie gestured to her son who was now sitting on a chair behind the table, his thumbs working overtime on his phone's display. She turned to him and said, "I've got to take care of something, so stay in the office. When I get back, we have to talk about that girl you've been dating."

Nixie's son barely glanced up. Rory walked out the door with the convention organizer. As she passed the memorial, she stopped to place the necklace she was wearing around the photograph of Jasmine at the display's center. She pressed her middle and index fingers to her lips, then touched them to the photograph.

Overcome by emotion, Rory headed outside for some fresh air.

As soon as she reached the sidewalk, she encountered the man with a goatee and tattoo on his neck she'd seen leading the protesters the day she couldn't get into the parking garage. His presence reminded her of the damage to her window. He tried to give her a flyer, but she waved it away.

"Why should I support a group that threw a rock through my window?" Rory said.

For a moment, the man was taken aback by her comment, but he soon rallied. "We had nothing to do with any rocks being thrown or houses being egged. None of us in the group does anything that causes damage. We're just trying to get the word out about how unfair the owner and builder of the hotel have been."

While they talked, passersby stopped and listened to the conversation. Before long, a sizeable group had gathered around the two of them. The man took the opportunity to hand out flyers to all of the bystanders.

"What about the stink bomb? I read in today's *View* that was your group," Rory said.

"That was different. We didn't hurt anything. Just making a point. The hotel has been stinking up our lives, so we stunk up theirs."

"What about the guests of the Akaw? That wasn't exactly pleasant for them. They didn't do anything."

"Collateral damage. All of the protests would go away if the hotel's owner would take some responsibility. Houses were damaged and many people who've lived in this city for years can't afford to repair them. Many of those are senior citizens who've contributed to Vista Beach for decades." The man's voice grew louder and more strident, attracting even more pedestrians.

The press of the crowd around the two of them made Rory nervous. "You're not taking responsibility for the false alarm the other day," she continued. "People could have panicked and been hurt trying to get out of the building."

The man shook his head. "That wasn't us." In a much softer voice, he mumbled what sounded to her like "wish we'd thought of it." In a tone that carried down the block, he continued his tirade against the hotel, addressing the crowd instead of her.

Rory grew angrier and angrier. Before she said something she regretted, she shouldered her way through the group and walked around the building, trying to vent her frustration at not being able to get the protesters to take responsibility for the damage to her property and others. Before long, she found herself at the loading dock where two giant metal beasts stood side by side, lids closed, a faint stench emanating from each one.

She stared at the dumpsters and wondered if her theory was correct and the person who had pulled the alarm had thrown the coveralls in the trash. By the time the police got around to looking into it, the garbage would probably have been hauled away. Maybe if she found them herself, there would be some evidence on the clothing that would point to a specific person, someone who could tell the police the name of the individual who had thrown the rock through her window.

Chapter 12

Rory peered around the area to make sure no one was nearby to prevent her from rummaging through the trash. The roll-up door on the loading dock was closed and the place appeared to be deserted. She wrinkled her nose in displeasure, not looking forward to the task at hand. She dug her cell and keys out of the pocket of her jeans and tucked them inside her tote bag, hiding it in a corner behind some empty boxes.

She approached the first dumpster and opened one side of the lid, then the other. A thin layer of half-eaten food, soiled diapers, and miscellaneous trash covered its bottom. One glance inside and she knew the container held nothing of interest.

When she lifted the lid on the second one, the smell of rotting garbage assaulted her nostrils. Flies flew out of the dumpster and buzzed around her head. Rory brushed off the ones that touched down on her hair then, with both hands flailing in the air, batted the rest of them out of the way before looking inside. The dumpster appeared half full, a mixture of discarded food, packaging materials, and various other items thrown out by their owners. At the top of the heap was a pair of new-looking tennis shoes, but no coveralls or anything that resembled a janitor's uniform lay in sight.

Rory leaned over the edge and reached inside, moving the topmost layer around, trying to see what was below it. She winced in pain as her arm scraped against something rough. When she pulled it out, she discovered a three-inch long scratch on her forearm. Not wanting to injure herself further, she walked around the area looking for a pole or something similar to use in her search. Finding an old broom handle leaning against a wall, she used it to move the contents of the dumpster around.

When nothing interesting came to light, she ditched the broom handle, dragged a wooden crate she found nearby to the side of the metal container, climbed up on the crate and leaned over. She dug around, getting excited when she saw a bit of gray cloth near the bottom. She stretched her arm as far as it would go, tottering on the edge of the metal beast, bracing herself with her other hand. Just as her reaching hand closed around the gray material in triumph, she heard footsteps behind her. When she turned her head, all she saw was a plank of wood, coming straight at her. Before she could raise her hand to defend herself or cry out, it slammed into her head and she plunged headfirst into the dumpster. Somebody pushed her face into the trash so she couldn't see. She struggled to breathe as her assailant rummaged around in the garbage beside her. Then, suddenly, her head was released and she gasped for air.

Before she could lift herself up, the dumpster's lid slammed shut, imprisoning her in darkness. Moments later, she heard the squeaking of wheels and felt the metal container moving. She pushed herself to the top and peeked out from under one half of the lid only to find herself rolling down the incline toward the street below, straight into the path of a garbage truck.

Rory scrambled to get out of the trash container but, as the dumpster gained momentum, she was thrown back into the garbage. Finally giving up, she crouched down in a corner, and in approved airline fashion, buried her head in her knees, covered the back of her neck with her hands and braced for impact. Moments later, the container crashed into something solid, shuddered and came to a stop.

Once she was sure the dumpster was no longer moving, she slowly stood up. As she flung back the lid and emerged from the container like the Loch Ness monster rising from the deep, she came face-to-face with a garbage collector. Their eyes locked for a moment, then the man emitted a string of words in Spanish. Rory didn't know much of the language, but she guessed some of what he said would not be acceptable to utter in polite company.

Rory hastened to assure him she was okay, then looked around for the gray cloth she'd been reaching for, but it was nowhere in sight. Whoever had hit her over the head must have taken it with them.

With as much dignity as she could muster, she clambered out of the trash container, the garbage collector helping her to the ground.

"What happened?" he said, a note of concern in his voice. "Are you okay?"

"I'm fine. Nothing to worry about." Rory brushed off wet paper towels that clung to her jeans, then waved her thanks at the astonished man and, ignoring the curious looks of the pedestrians she passed, headed up the incline back to the hotel. When she reached the loading dock, she grabbed her tote bag from its hiding place and pulled a bottle of antibacterial gel out of the bag. She slathered her hands and the cut on her arm with the gel before continuing on her way.

Feeling as if she wasn't front door material, she entered the hotel grounds through a gate that led into the side courtyard, hoping to see as few people as possible before she cleaned herself up. As she slipped through the iron gate, she heard the hotel manager's voice. His back to her, Ian paced the empty courtyard while talking on a cell phone. She squeezed into an area between the stucco wall surrounding the hotel grounds and a collection of bushes and trees. Peeking through the leaves of one of the plants, she constantly adjusted her position so she remained out of sight every time he got close to her hiding spot.

"I *am* taking this seriously. I know you're not joking...Yes, I know bad online reviews can crush a business. I've seen it happen...You'll take them down if we promise to pay for the repairs to the houses?...And what about the lawsuit?...I see. What guarantee do I have it'll go away too?"

A faint breeze blew in over the wall surrounding the courtyard, sending dust and flower petals in her direction. Rory felt a tickle in her nose. She pinched it closed, trying to suppress the sneeze she knew was coming, but all she managed to do was muffle the sound that erupted moments later. Afraid the man had heard the noise, she stood as still as possible, but he continued pacing and talking, seemingly unaware of her presence. She brushed a few petals out of her hair while she quietly continued to listen to the conversation.

"That's extortion. I could call the police on you...Fine, no lawyers...I'll think about it and get back to you."

Ian ended the call, then stood stock still, staring straight at the spot where Rory was hiding. For a moment, she feared he'd spotted her. She breathed a sigh of relief when he ran a hand through his hair and headed back inside.

Rory played with a leaf on the plant in front of her and thought about the problems at the Akaw: protests outside the hotel, a false alarm, a stink bomb in the men's restroom, an attack on its website, and now bad online reviews. From the little she'd heard, she guessed Ian was planning on recommending to the hotel's owner they bypass the lawyers and agree to the caller's requests.

When she stepped out into the open moments later, a deep voice behind her said, "Is there some reason you're skulking behind a plant?"

Rory turned to discover Detective Green standing in the courtyard, an amused expression on his face. "I wasn't skulking."

"Uh-huh." He sniffed the air and stared pointedly at a stain on her jeans. "What *have* you been up to?"

"I could ask you the same thing. Why are you sneaking into the hotel from the side door and not the front?"

"Someone reported a suspicious character lurking around the back of the hotel. Know anything about that?" His gaze bore into hers, silently encouraging her to confess.

She stared down at her tennis shoes, unsure what to say.

"You have something..." When she looked up, he gestured toward her hair. "May I?"

Rory nodded her consent. The detective reached up and removed stray petals from her hair, his hand lingering for a fraction of a second longer than necessary, making her blush.

The detective cleared his throat and stepped back. "Now, are you going to tell me what you were doing behind the plant?"

"I may have...overheard Ian talking on the phone. Someone's blackmailing the hotel. At least, that's what it sounded like to me."

He stared at her, waiting for her to continue with her story.

As accurately as possible, Rory related as much of the conversation as she'd overheard to the detective.

He looked off into the distance as if absorbing everything she'd told him. When she raised her arm to push her long hair behind her ears, he pointed at the scratch on the inside of her forearm.

"What happened to you?" he said.

She searched her mind for an explanation that would satisfy the policeman. The only thing she could come up with didn't even sound convincing to her own ears. "I just scraped it on the gate."

"You sure about that?" he said, giving her the opportunity to come clean.

"I'm sure."

He studied her face for a moment, then gently placed his hand in the small of her back and pushed her toward the hotel entrance. "Leave the police work to me. Now, go clean yourself up and go to your convention. You smell like you've been rolling in garbage."

With that, he walked back through the side gate. Rory made her way into the Akaw and bought a t-shirt and sweats in the hotel gift shop. Several convention goers she encountered asked what happened, but she laughed it off and headed toward Jasmine's room to take a shower and make herself presentable once more.

Chapter 13

Less than an hour later, Rory was scrubbed clean with her dirty clothes put into the care of the hotel laundry. Inside the Manhattan ballroom, she found Nixie sitting alone at a table, staring at a laptop screen, loose papers spread out next to the computer.

"You're here about that check, aren't you? I'm so sorry, I forgot all about it."

"No problem. I'm actually here to talk to you about something else," Rory said. "Or is this a bad time?"

"I'm not sure there is a good time right now." Nixie waved her hand at the papers. "What's worrisome are these accounts. I can't make sense out of them. I was never really good at the financial side of things. Jasmine tried to teach me, but I'm afraid it didn't stick. Hold on, I'll be right with you. Let me just find this one receipt." The convention organizer searched through several pieces of paper and, not finding what she wanted, opened a three-ring binder, revealing a well-worn photograph tucked in its inside pocket.

Rory moved to one side and twisted her head so she could make out who was in the picture. Taken at a table in a restaurant, Nixie sat next to an older version of the young girl she'd seen coming out of the office earlier that day. Rory was about to ask about the photo when the woman closed the binder, looked up at her and said, "Now, what can I do for you?"

"I'm retracing Jasmine's steps the days before her death. I understand you had a meeting with her on Tuesday?"

"Why do you want to know? Didn't the police declare it an accidental overdose?"

"I'm just trying to fill in the blanks for Peter."

Nixie nodded her head in sympathy. "Poor guy. He has so much to deal with right now. I know exactly how he feels. That was me six months ago. I remember wanting to know everything about my husband's last few days." She took several deep breaths. "Let's see, you wanted to know about Tuesday. Jasmine and I had a meeting. Five-ish. We went over the books. Or Jasmine tried to go over them with me."

"How did she seem?"

"Seem?" Nixie looked puzzled. "Other than a little frustrated with me, she seemed fine. Her usual self. Why?"

"I was just wondering if you noticed anything different about her."

Nixie sat back in her chair and tilted her head. "She did seem a little worried that day. She told me she thought her husband was keeping something from her."

"Did she have any idea what?"

"I'm afraid not, but..." Nixie stared off into the distance as if trying to decide whether to reveal something she knew. "You've heard the rumors, right?"

"What rumors?"

The convention organizer lowered her voice. "About Peter. He's under invest—No, it's not right. They're just rumors. That's what I told Jasmine. Forget I said anything."

Rory stared at her, unsure what to make of the woman's comments. "Are you saying Peter's under investigation for something to do with work? Where did you hear this?"

"Rumors, just rumors." Nixie waved her hand at her laptop. "I wish Jasmine were here. I've gone over everything twice. Something's just not right."

"Have you asked Peter? He's a CPA, maybe he can help."

"Doesn't seem right to bug him right now. Don't worry, I'll figure it out."

If Jasmine's husband was under some sort of investigation, Rory could see why the woman wouldn't want him looking at her books. It might also explain his getting a second job in maintenance instead of accounting, though she hadn't confirmed that yet. She made a mental note to ask Peter the next time she saw him.

Nixie looked pointedly at her computer screen. "Now, if you'll excuse me. I must get back to this."

Rory waved goodbye and headed toward the lobby. As she walked down the hallway, she wondered what Peter had been keeping from his wife. They always appeared to have a good relationship and seemed to be honest with each other, but maybe something changed recently. If he were in trouble for something he'd done at work, he might have wanted to keep that from Jasmine so he wouldn't worry her. Or maybe he took an extra job to pay off a debt his wife didn't know about. Of course, even if he was under investigation, that didn't mean he'd actually done anything wrong. She knew about baseless accusations and how damaging they could be all too well.

Moments later, Rory found Liz outside a nearby ballroom talking with one of the other convention attendees. As soon as she spotted her friend, Liz excused herself and hurried over.

"Where've you been? I thought you'd look in on my class, but you didn't. Is everything okay?"

"Sorry, something came up." Rory readjusted her tote bag on her shoulder.

Liz pointed to the bandage on her friend's arm. "What happened? And you weren't wearing those clothes earlier. What's going on?" She placed her hands on her hips. "Have you been sleuthing without me?"

"I was searching through the hotel's dumpsters, looking for those coveralls I was talking about, and someone smacked me on the side of the head, that's all. I'm fine." Rory pushed her concerns to the back of her mind. She squared her shoulders and did her best to appear calm so she wouldn't worry her friend, but thinking about the incident still frightened her.

"That's all? Someone hit you on the head and you say 'that's all?' Are you okay? Did you tell the police?" The questions came rapid-fire out of Liz's mouth.

"I saw Detective Green right afterwards," Rory said, not bothering to mention that she hadn't told the man about her adventures in dumpster diving. "I didn't see much, anyway."

Liz peered at Rory anxiously. "Do you need me to take you to see the doctor?"

Rory shook her head. When it began to pound, she immediately regretted the action. "Other than a slight headache, I feel fine."

"Okay, but if you feel queasy, you tell me right away. That could be an indication of something serious."

Rory nodded in agreement, glad she had a friend who was so concerned about her.

Since neither of them had found time for lunch, the two young women headed toward the El Porto ballroom where convention attendees could buy quick meals and snacks. As soon as they settled down at a table, Liz said, "So, what did you find out?"

Rory told her friend about how she'd almost had her hand on what she thought was important evidence when someone hit her over the head and spirited it away. She touched the tender spot on the side of her head and winced at the memory.

"Are you sure your falling into the trash container didn't just bury it further in the garbage?"

"I felt someone rummaging around and taking something."

"You didn't even get a peek at whoever it was?"

"I was facedown in garbage. Didn't have a chance to see much of anything."

Liz wrinkled her petite nose in disgust. "Eww! I'm glad that wasn't me."

"Doesn't matter anymore. The trash is gone now. But there's something else." Rory brought her friend up to date on the phone conversation she'd overheard between Ian and the mystery caller, as well as what Hulbert had said about seeing Peter on Wednesday.

"Have you asked Peter about being in the hotel?" Liz said. "Seems suspicious he was wearing coveralls."

"We still don't know it was him," Rory said. "He and Brandy are competing this evening. I thought I'd talk to him afterwards."

"You're putting it off, aren't you?"

"I'm a little afraid of what he's going to say."

They were trying to decide what to do next when Veronica walked up to their table. Speaking into a digital recorder, she said, "What do you have to say about the Akaw's handling of Jasmine Halliday's death?" She thrust the tiny device in front of Rory's face and waited for an answer.

"No comment," was Rory's immediate reply.

"Can you at least confirm what you said on Facebook?"

Rory had no idea what the reporter was talking about. She hadn't logged into her account since the convention started, and even if she had, she didn't think anything she wrote would be newsworthy. "What are you talking about?"

Veronica pushed the OFF button on her recorder and stuck it in her tote bag. "Look at the convention's Facebook page and you'll see what I'm talking about."

"Why?"

"Just look."

Rory directed her phone's browser to the page she'd set up for the convention and read, with growing horror, what she'd supposedly confided to the person who posted the comment.

"I never said that! I never said the management of the Akaw was too slow to act when Jasmine collapsed." Her mouth hung open in disbelief. "I would never say anything against one of my clients. And I certainly wouldn't say it's their fault she died. The hotel did nothing wrong."

"That's horrible," Liz said.

Rory took note of the name of the individual who had posted the lie then deleted the post from the convention's page, hoping she'd taken it down before anyone who worked at the hotel noticed it.

"Sorry, no story," she said to Veronica.

For a moment, the reporter seemed disappointed, then her face lit up. "There's always a story. Just not the angle I was looking at." With that cryptic comment, Veronica scribbled something down on a notepad and walked out of the ballroom with a smile on her face.

"What do you think that was about?" Liz said.

"I have no idea. I'm not sure I want to know." Rory looked through the rest of the entries to make sure there weren't any other time bombs. She smiled at a photo her mother had posted of her and Jasmine clowning around on the trade show floor the night of the early shopping opportunity. Her smile faded when she realized less than twenty-four hours later her friend would be dead.

Before she shut down her browser, she checked out the page of the person who had posted the lie. Most of it was blank: no posts on the timeline, no picture of who the page belonged to, no friends. Even the name was so common, she found over twenty versions of it on the site. She wondered if this was yet another effort by the protesters to stir the pot and do more damage to the hotel's reputation.

While Rory was looking at the page, trying to get a hint as to who had put it together, Liz peered down at her own phone. "Who's this with Nixie's son?" She held out the display to Rory. "She's in a lot of photos with him."

"I don't know her name, but I saw her with him in the lobby the other day." Rory cast her mind back to the first day of the convention when she'd seen the teenage girl making out with Gordon. "Come to think of it, I saw her coming out of the convention office when I went to see Nixie. They were arguing about something."

"She sure gets around. Isn't that her talking to Jasmine?"

Rory peered at her friend's phone. In the background of a photo of a group of convention goers in the lobby, the teenager stood next to Jasmine, an earnest expression on the girl's face. "Sure looks like it."

A short time later, they were heading toward the lobby restrooms when Gordon walked toward them. He peered at Rory's badge and handed her an envelope. "Here. Mom wanted me to give this to you."

In the envelope, Rory found a check for the amount due to her. "Thank her for me."

As he turned to go, she said, "Who's that girl I saw with you the other day in the lobby?"

The teen looked at her as if to say you need to be more specific.

"Brown hair, petite."

His face turned sour. "Oh, her. Just a girl I hung out with for a while. Mom asked you to grill me, didn't she? Well, you can tell her she has nothing to worry about. We're not going out anymore. Tempest was just using me."

At least now she had a name to go with the face, Rory thought. "Your mother didn't send me. I saw Tempest with a friend of mine. Just wondered what they were talking about."

The teen shrugged. "You'll have to ask her yourself."

Rory opened her mouth to ask how she could get in touch with the girl when a voice behind them said, "Tell them, tell them what your mother did."

Chapter 14

Rory stared at the young girl from the photograph who stood behind Gordon, arms akimbo, an angry expression on her face. Hard to believe this was the same girl who'd been making out with Nixie's son only two days before.

"What are you talking about?" Rory looked from Tempest to Gordon and back again. "What did Nixie do?"

"You have no proof," Gordon said to the young girl, ignoring Rory's question. "No way my mom stole that money. You just don't want to believe your mother did it."

"Face it. Your mom's a lush. Probably doesn't know what she's doing half the time, anyway. You told me you don't have much money. That your mom can't always pay the bills. You know she probably drinks away most of it."

"I told you that in confidence." Gordon raised his hand as if to strike the girl.

Rory stepped between the two angry teens, ready to intervene if circumstances warranted, but the tense moment soon passed. The young man took a deep breath, lowered his arm and stepped back.

"Calm down. What's going on?" Rory said in what she hoped was a soothing voice.

"My mom's in prison and I'm stuck in a foster home. All because of *his* mother." Tempest stabbed a finger at Gordon's chest.

"She embezzled from the company she worked for and blamed it on *my* mom. All I want is for Nixie to admit to what she did so I can get my life back. I've tried to convince him, but he won't believe me. He needs 'proof.'" Tempest air-quoted the last word.

If Tempest had accused Nixie of the crime to her son's face, no wonder they were no longer going out, Rory thought.

"My mother would never, ever do that," Gordon insisted. "I told you before, I won't try to convince my mom to confess to something she didn't do." He stormed off and headed toward the hotel exit.

"Is that true? What you said about Nixie?" Liz asked Tempest after Gordon left.

The girl nodded. "I warned that woman, the one who does the bookkeeping for the convention. Told her what Nixie had done."

"When was this?" Rory asked.

"Monday, late afternoon. She was sitting in the lobby waiting for someone. She got all upset at me. Didn't believe me, either."

That must have been right before she picked Jasmine up for dinner, Rory thought. Her friend hadn't mentioned the encounter to her, but she had a cataplectic attack not long after hearing the news. Strong emotions often brought one on. She wondered if Jasmine had asked Nixie about the girl's accusations at her meeting the following day.

Happy to have someone finally listening to her, Tempest told them all she knew about the crime. After she finished her tale, she thanked them for hearing her out and left the hotel.

"We need to talk with Nixie," Liz said.

"I think we should confirm Tempest's story first. She could be making it all up. Nixie does carry around a photo of a woman who looks a lot like Tempest. I bet it's her mother. So they must know each other. There might be articles in the paper about the case. Let's walk over to the library and see what we can find out."

When they walked into the imposing glass and steel building that housed the city's library, light streamed through the windows onto the shelves and tables set throughout the one-story structure.

Rory and Liz wended their way through the stacks to the metal shelf containing paper copies of the *Vista Beach View*, disappointed when they discovered the library only kept the last two months in hardcopy. The librarian at the reference desk directed them to the newspaper website where they could find the back issues they were looking for.

With Liz looking over her shoulder, Rory settled down at one of the library's computers and searched the archives for information on the embezzling case. Before long, she found articles on the arrest and trial of Tempest's mother.

After they looked at everything she could find, Rory sat back in her chair and pondered what she'd read. "Tempest's story checks out, but that doesn't mean Nixie did it. We don't even know if she worked at the company. But if Nixie did and Jasmine asked her about it..." she whispered, not wanting to disturb the older man working on the computer next to hers.

"Do you think Nixie could have killed Jasmine?" Liz whispered back.

Without lifting his eyes from the screen, the man scooted his chair closer to them.

"Maybe." Rory sneaked a peek at her neighbor who had now stopped typing and was avidly listening to their conversation. "Let's walk back to the hotel. We can talk about it on the way."

She cleared the browser's history and closed the window. Neither of them said a word until they were out on the street.

"So what do we do now?" Liz said.

"We need to ask Nixie about where she worked. If it's not the same company as in the articles, we'll just drop it."

With renewed vigor, the two headed into the Akaw to see what the woman had to say, but by the time they reached the convention office, Gordon was the only one there and the convention organizer was nowhere in the hotel.

Putting off the interview until later, the two young women parted in the lobby. Liz went to a class while Rory headed down to the beach to think.

The overcast skies had burned off, revealing bright sunshine that beat down on row upon row of sun worshippers stretched out on colorful towels.

Rory took off her tennis shoes and socks, rolled up her jeans and stepped out onto the hot sand. Squeals of delight drifted toward her on a breeze as she walked along the beach, parallel to the water, until she reached an unoccupied swing set the city had set up not far from the nearby walkway. Dropping her shoes down on the sand beside her, Rory settled down onto a swing facing the water and contemplated the ocean as she gently swung back and forth in time with the waves.

She was mulling over everything she'd learned that day when she sensed someone beside her. She looked up to find Detective Green standing with one hand on the empty swing next to hers. "May I?"

After Rory nodded her agreement, he sat down on the U-shaped seat. Neither one looking at the other, they both swung back and forth, side by side, in companionable silence.

"How's the convention going?" the man finally said.

"Fine. Any leads on the person who threw the rock through my window? Someone's still investigating, right?"

"Unless someone confesses, we'll probably never know."

"What about Jasmine's death?"

He stilled his swing and stared at her quizzically. "That was an accidental overdose. You know we closed the case. Why are you asking me about it?"

Rory placed her bare feet on the sand to stop the swing's momentum and looked directly into his eyes, daring him to contradict her. "You're wrong. That's not what happened." Before he could bring it up, she said, "And I'm not talking suicide."

"There's no evidence it was anything other than an unfortunate accident. What makes you so sure it was anything else?"

"First, how did she take her medicine when it was found in her hotel room, not in her purse? She had to have taken it shortly before she collapsed. Within five or ten minutes. How do you explain that?"

"Simple. She went up to her room before she returned to class. That trip wouldn't take very long."

"Where's your proof?"

"She was spotted entering the elevator right after the all-clear was given."

The information took Rory by surprise. She mulled it over for a minute. "That doesn't mean she went to her room. Does the hotel security footage show her actually going inside her room?"

"There aren't any cameras on the guest room floors."

Rory stared at him in disbelief. "Why not? It's a brand-new hotel."

The detective shrugged. "Not my department. You'll have to ask someone from the hotel that."

"What about the ones in the elevator? I've seen them. Could you tell what floor she got off on?"

"The top floor. That's where her room is, so it stands to reason that was her destination. What else have you got? What about motive? Why would someone kill your friend? As far as I can tell she's lived a pretty blameless life. No arrests. No legal problems. Not even a parking ticket."

"What about Peter? He had access to her medicine, knew her class schedule, and was even seen in the hotel the day she died, going into the classroom. Then there's the life insurance. That's means, motive, and opportunity. Isn't that what you guys are always talking about?"

"I thought he was a friend of yours."

"I didn't say he did it. I said he could have. I'm just using him as an example. There might be others we don't know about. I've barely started looking into it."

Detective Green's brow furrowed, and his face darkened. "I told you. No investigating. You know what happened last time. I don't want to have to worry about you."

Rory basked in a moment of unexpected pleasure at his

concern. "I thought you didn't believe she was murdered."

"I still don't. Some people don't like anyone getting into their business. People can be unpredictable. You never know who you'll upset." The detective stared at the ocean. "Is that all you've got?"

Rory thought about mentioning Nixie's alleged embezzling, but decided against it. She didn't have any proof yet. Detective Green wouldn't believe her unless she had something concrete. Plus, she wanted to give the woman a chance to tell her side of the story first.

"Listen." He stood up and laid his hand on her shoulder. "I'd lock you up if I thought it would keep you safe, but something tells me you'd find a way to get in trouble, even then. Promise me, whatever you get up to, you'll be careful."

Before she could answer, someone behind them cleared their throat. As one, the two of them turned toward the sound. Clad in a sundress and carrying flip-flops, Brandy stood in the sand nearby.

Detective Green removed his hand from Rory's shoulder, then nodded at the two of them and headed across the beach toward the nearby walkway.

"What was that about?" Brandy sat down on the swing the detective had been sitting in moments before.

"I was just trying to convince him to reopen Jasmine's case."

"What did he say?"

Rory shook her head. "I think if we found more evidence he'd reconsider. Did you see Jasmine the day she died?"

Brandy looked down at her feet and sighed. "No, I didn't see her. I wish I had." She took a deep breath. "I'd feel better. Closure, you know?"

"I know what you mean. Are you and Peter still dancing tonight?"

"I came to give you our schedule. We were hoping you could make it."

After telling Rory the where and when, Brandy headed home. A dozen swings later, Rory gave one last wistful look at the ocean before walking back to the hotel. She checked in with her mother and, after retrieving her now-clean clothes from the hotel laundry, went in search of Liz. The two ate an early dinner in the hotel restaurant, keeping their conversation focused on decorative painting and away from murder.

Later that evening, Rory walked the four blocks to Vista Beach Elementary to see Brandy and Peter compete in the finals of the dance competition they'd entered. The gymnasium where the contest was taking place pulsed with excitement as she stepped inside. The judges sat at a long table on one side of the floor with bleachers opposite them reserved for family and friends of the contestants.

Relieved to see she wasn't out of place in her V-neck t-shirt and jeans, Rory settled into a spot in the bleachers moments before the emcee took the floor, announcing the start of the final phase of the competition. The gym that usually saw preteen basketball players racing up and down the court was now the temporary home of elegantly clad men and women.

Rory cheered with everyone else when the dancers took the floor. All of the male contestants wore suits while the women dressed in elegant gowns in a variety of colors that sparkled under the lights and revealed more skin than Rory would have felt comfortable showing. She almost didn't recognize Brandy in her rhinestone studded dress in a shimmering red. The diagonal fringing on the outfit gently swayed as she walked gracefully across the floor.

Rory swept all her cares to the back of her mind and concentrated on enjoying watching the couples compete in the Argentine tango portion of the program. She crossed her fingers when Peter and Brandy started their routine. Other than an infinitesimal moment of stiffness at the beginning of their first dance, the couple sailed through the competition.

The ten minutes it took for the judges to deliberate seemed like forever. Rory stood up and clapped enthusiastically with the rest of the audience when the winners were announced. A man dressed in tails and his partner, a woman in a revealing blue gown with black lace sleeves and a side thigh opening, came in first, with Peter and Brandy a close second.

After the program was over, Rory milled around in the gym with the crowd, waiting for her friends to come out of the dressing area. When most of the competitors had changed and they still hadn't appeared, she went in search of them, navigating the halls of the elementary school looking for the rooms set aside for costume changes. She peeked in the classrooms as she walked past, but all she saw were empty rooms with tot-sized desks and cubbyholes for backpacks. She was turning a corner to go down the corridor that led to the principal's office when she spotted a man and a woman in a passionate embrace. She started to back away to give them privacy, then involuntarily gasped when she recognized them.

Peter and Brandy broke apart and turned in her direction.

Stunned, Rory stared at her two friends who, open-mouthed and wide-eyed, silently stared back. She felt rooted to the linoleum in the hallway. Finally, her brain got through to her legs and, without saying a word, Rory turned around and walked down the hall and around the corner.

Chapter 15

"Rory, wait!" Brandy's frantic voice echoed down the hallway.

Rory stopped and took a deep breath, then turned around and waited for her friend to catch up. "What was that? She's not even buried yet."

"It wasn't Peter's fault. I can explain."

"How could you? You were friends."

"We didn't plan it! It just happened. You have to believe me." Brandy pleaded for understanding with her eyes.

"Couldn't you wait? Or was this," Rory waved her hand in the air, "*thing* going on under Jasmine's nose?"

"We would never! I need you to believe me."

Rory looked down the hallway where Peter had suddenly appeared and was silently watching them, then returned her attention to the woman standing before her. "Do you have feelings for each other?"

Brandy looked uncomfortable under Rory's steady gaze. "Neither of us have acted on them until now. And we wouldn't have if Jasmine hadn't...you know..."

Rory wondered if Jasmine suspected that her best friend and husband were having an affair. Maybe that was what she'd wanted to talk to Rory about after class. "Did she know how you both felt?"

Brandy gazed at the floor, considering the question, then looked up again. "I'm not sure." In a more defiant tone, she said, "Don't be so high and mighty. The way you look at that detective, you must understand."

"I don't know what you're talking about."

"If you don't want to admit you're attracted to him, that's up to you. But I bet you'd kiss him too, if the opportunity arose, even though he has a girlfriend. At least I'm honest with myself."

Rory's mouth opened and closed a few times as she searched for something to say. "I can't deal with this right now. I'll talk to you later."

She hurried out of the school as fast as she could, ignoring Brandy's repeated pleas for understanding.

As Rory walked back to the hotel, she called Liz's number, but it went straight to voicemail. Unsure what to say, she hung up without leaving a message.

When she entered the Akaw's lobby a short time later, a whirlwind in leopard print flannel pajamas rushed toward her. Her feet encased in matching slippers with leopard heads, Liz skidded to a halt in front of Rory. "What's wrong?"

For a moment, Rory wondered why her friend was wearing pjs, then remembered Liz was helping out at the evening's pajama painting party where everyone wore pjs and worked on unfinished projects. "Why do you think something's wrong?"

"You called, but didn't leave a message. You never do that," Liz said. "How was the dance contest? Did you see Peter and Brandy? Did they win?"

"Came in second, but that's not the problem." Rory tried, but she couldn't keep the bitterness out of her voice.

Liz gestured toward two empty chairs. At this late hour, the bar was busy, but the lobby area was empty except for a man reading a newspaper far enough away that they were in no danger of his overhearing them.

Rory sat down on one chair while Liz shed her slippers and hopped onto another, crossing both legs under her.

"Something happened," Liz said. "Spill the beans."

"I caught them...together."

"Peter and Brandy?" Liz leaned forward in her chair. "Do you think it's been going on long? The affair?"

"I'm not sure affair is the right word. Brandy said it was the first time, that the kiss just happened."

"Do you believe her?"

Rory considered the question. "I want to," she said softly.

They sat in silence for a few moments, each mulling over the conversation. Finally, Liz said in an apologetic voice, "You don't think...I mean I know she's your friend, but...Could she have been responsible for...?"

Rory cocked her head in thought. The Peter and Brandy she knew years ago would never have betrayed Jasmine by having an affair, let alone plotting to kill her. But Rory had been out of touch with them, only seeing her friends half a dozen times in the year since she moved to Vista Beach. They hadn't even told her about Jasmine's suicide attempt. "They both could have taken some of her medicine out of the bottle when she had it at home. No one would have noticed. But they would have had to administer the medicine, somehow, and that means being in the hotel that day."

Liz frowned. "You said before that Hulbert saw Peter going into a ballroom. What about Brandy?"

"We don't know for sure he was in the hotel. Hulbert wasn't positive it was him he saw, and I haven't had a chance to ask Peter about it. Brandy said she didn't see Jasmine that day."

"But was she in the hotel?"

Rory shrugged her shoulders. "I don't know." She pounded her fist on the arm of the chair. "I don't know, I don't know, I don't know."

A cock-a-doodle-doo interrupted their conversation. Rory glanced down at her cell, then turned it off.

"Who was that?" Liz said.

"Peter."

Liz uncrossed her legs, put her slippers back on and stood up. She pulled at Rory's arms, trying to drag her out of the chair. "Come on, come to the party with me. You don't have to paint, just hang around and have fun."

"Thanks, but I'm not in the mood. I think I'll just go home."

"Okay, but you're missing a good time. Call me if you want to talk." Liz waved her phone in the air and skipped down the hallway toward the ballrooms.

Feeling as if she had the weight of the world on her shoulders, Rory headed home.

Chapter 16

The sun had set over the city as Rory rounded the corner onto Seagull Lane. When she pulled into her driveway moments later, her front porch light winked on, reaching out into the darkness, welcoming her home. Looking forward to the healing powers of Canadian bacon and pineapple pizza and an episode or two of "The Big Bang Theory," she parked in front of her detached garage and made her way around the side of the single-story stucco house toward the back door, a route she took every day. She frowned when she spied the pool of darkness where light should have been. As far as she remembered, the back porch light was working the previous evening.

The exterior lights of her neighbor's house cast shadows on her property, but still gave off enough light for her to see the ground in front of her. She picked her way across the lawn toward the back door. As soon as she set foot on the patio, a figure separated itself from a plastic lawn chair that sat on the concrete slab and someone called out her name.

Rory gave a small scream, suppressing it when she recognized the voice. "Peter? What are you doing here?"

"I tried your cell, but you didn't pick up. We need to talk."

She felt for the lock in the darkness, inserted the key and opened the door. "I'm tired. Call me tomorrow."

He grabbed Rory's arm. "Please, I won't keep you long."

She pulled away. This conversation belonged in the privacy of her home, not out here where the neighbors could hear every word. "Okay, fine. You can come inside, but only for a few minutes."

"That's all I need."

Rory turned on the inside light and led the way into the kitchen. She gestured toward the table. "Have a seat."

Peter sat down on one side while Rory took a seat across from him.

Normally, Rory would ask a guest if they wanted something to drink, but tonight she wasn't feeling very hospitable. She rested her elbows on the table and leaned forward. "Okay, talk."

Peter sat back in his chair and played with the wedding ring on his finger, twisting it around and around, then pulling it on and off. Finally, he looked directly into her eyes and said, "Brandy and I are *not* having an affair. That kiss you saw was a one time thing. We got...caught up in the moment."

"But you have feelings for each other. Brandy said so."

Peter looked out the window at the side yard and the darkness beyond. "It's not easy being married to a person with narcolepsy. There are things I had to give up. She wouldn't go to a play or ballet with me because she usually fell asleep. We rarely went out to dinner or to a party."

"It didn't have to be that way, did it?"

He shrugged. "Maybe not, but that's the way it turned out." He paused as if choosing his words carefully. "Brandy's different. I can do all those things with her. It's such a relief to spend time with her. No drama. No worries."

"Why are you telling me this?"

"I want you to understand. What you think matters to me, to us. We've all known each other a long time. We don't want to lose that friendship."

Rory studied his face, trying to decide if he was telling the truth. Lord help her, but she had to wonder if his earnest expression was only a facade, and he was merely saying these things to cover up his involvement in his wife's death. "Are you going to get together now that Jasmine's gone?"

"I don't know. Would it bother you if we did?"

"You should at least wait until her killer's found."

"She overdosed. That's what the police said," Peter said. "Unless you know something I don't?"

"I can't believe she'd take her medicine in the middle of the day. She was too careful about following doctor's orders. And from everything I read and what the ER doctor told me, she would have had to take it not long before she returned to class. What happened to your believing it wasn't an accident? That she couldn't have overdosed?"

"I changed my mind. That detective convinced me there's nothing suspicious about her death. You've barely seen her in the last few months. How can *you* be so sure it wasn't one?"

"I just am. Where were you when Jasmine died?"

"So now I killed my wife, did I? You know me better than that."

"Do I? I'm not so sure anymore. Someone saw you going into the Zuma ballroom during the alarm, dressed in coveralls."

"What? Who told you that? I was nowhere near the hotel. I was at work. Why would I be wearing coveralls? I'm an accountant, not a janitor."

"So you haven't taken a second job?"

"There's no need. We're doing fine."

"You say you were working. I thought you had the week off?"

"I was called in to talk to a client at the last minute." Peter threw up his hands. "Why am I even justifying myself to you?"

"Someone killed your wife. Her medicine wasn't in her purse and, like I said, she had to have taken it a short time before she collapsed."

"So she went up to her room before she returned to class," he said, echoing Detective Green's thoughts. "Check the hotel security footage."

"There isn't any security footage. No cameras on the guest room floors."

"So you can't say she didn't go up there."

"Who had keys to her room?"

"The one I gave you was the one Jaz had in her purse. I know she requested another one, but I don't know who she gave it to."

"Could it have been Brandy?"

"Now you're accusing her?" Peter stood up. "I've had enough of this."

"Wait, before you go. I heard you're under investigation at work. What's going on?"

"What are you talking about?" He stared at her in disbelief.

"Rumor has it—"

"Rumors. You of all people should know rumors don't equal truth. Look at everything you went through in the last few months."

After Peter left the way he came in and she locked the door behind him, Rory sat at the table and buried her head in her hands. She didn't know whether to trust him or not. He could have killed Jasmine with or without Brandy's help. She wondered if he'd merely been playing the part of the concerned spouse when he asked Rory to talk to the police.

Whatever the truth was, she'd lost her appetite. She got up from the table and headed straight to bed.

Rory woke up early the next morning, changed the bulb in the back porch light, and drove to the convention without eating breakfast. When she couldn't find Nixie in the office, she headed to the El Porto ballroom. Rory scanned the dozen tables set up around the room, spotting Liz at a table by herself.

Rory sat down and pinched a piece off the blueberry muffin her friend was eating.

Liz reached over and touched Rory's hand. "How are you this morning? Did you get a good night's rest?"

"Peter came to see me last night."

"He did? What did he say?"

"He was trying to convince me he and Brandy weren't having an affair."

"Did he? Convince you, that is?"

"I'm not sure my opinion matters. I asked him about other keys to Jasmine's hotel room. He thought she'd given one to someone, but he didn't know who."

"Might not make all that much difference. Veronica didn't have any problem getting in the room without a key."

"That's true."

When Stella approached the table moments later, Rory invited her to join them.

"How's everything going, Stella?" Rory nodded toward the camera the woman had placed on the table. "How's your project going? Are you getting a lot of interesting footage?"

"It's turning out better than I expected. I don't record everything, of course. I'm just doing a sampling of events. So far I've filmed two classes and did a tour of the hotel. I'll edit it down before I show it to the chapter. Do you want to see some of it?"

"Sure, I'd like that." Rory expected Stella to pick up the camera but, instead, the woman took out her cell and pressed its screen a few times. "The camera comes with this great app," she said. "I transferred the footage I've taken so far to my phone so I can share it. Here, take a look at this." She showed the two other women the list of short video clips she'd downloaded to her smartphone.

Rory checked out each one, fast-forwarding through most of the clips, occasionally stopping at an item of interest. Whenever she spotted Jasmine, Rory stopped the video and replayed it from the beginning. In one, Ian and a man she didn't recognize were arguing in the side courtyard. Jasmine entered the frame, concealing herself behind a plant as the two men talked. As the unknown man was leaving through the side gate, he spotted Jasmine and briefly spoke with her before heading toward the exit, alerting the hotel manager to the woman's presence. Ian confronted her. They talked for several minutes, the camera panning to the inside of the hotel in the middle of their conversation.

Rory showed the footage to Stella and Liz. "Do either of you recognize the man talking with Ian?"

The two of them looked at the clip, but neither one had ever seen him before.

"Stella, do you know anything about this? Do you know when it was taken?" Rory asked.

A few taps on the screen and the woman had the answer. "Let's see. The time on the file says five-twenty p.m. Looks like it was taken Tuesday. I was taking video of the hotel then. I stopped to talk to one of the staff. I didn't realize I'd left the camera on."

That would explain the sudden change in the clip, Rory thought. She cast her mind back to the day and time indicated. That was forty minutes before the opening of the trade show floor for the early shopping opportunity. Rory remembered seeing Jasmine working at the VivEco booth that evening. They'd both been so busy, the two of them only had a chance to talk once or twice. She hadn't thought anything was wrong at the time, but now that she thought about it, her friend had seemed a bit uneasy.

"Can I have a copy of this video?" she said to Stella after they watched the footage of Ian and the unknown man a half dozen times without coming to any conclusions.

The woman nodded her head. "Sure. I'll email it to you. Just give me your address."

Once she had the video clip on her own cell phone, Rory said goodbye to the two women and headed into the lobby in search of Ian Blalock, hoping to discover what he and Jasmine had been talking about the day before she died.

Chapter 17

Rory found Ian in the lobby, speaking with a guest. She waited until the hotel manager finished his conversation before approaching him.

He frowned when he saw her. "Just the person I wanted to see. I didn't appreciate the comment you made about the Akaw on Facebook."

"I didn't say that to anyone. I don't hold the hotel responsible for my friend's death at all. I took the comment down as soon as I saw it."

Ian nodded, seeming to accept her apology.

Rory took a deep breath and plunged in. "Speaking of Jasmine, I was wondering if you could help me with something."

A quizzical look on his face, Ian nodded his agreement.

"Would you mind looking at some footage I have? I'm tracing Jasmine's movements in the days before she died. Her husband, Peter, hadn't seen her much during that period and, well, he wants to know as much as possible. You can imagine how distraught he is. I told him I'd help out."

In a soft voice, the hotel manager said, "It's hard to lose a spouse, especially in such an...ugly way. I'll do whatever I can to help."

On her smartphone, Rory played the footage Stella had sent her showing Ian arguing with the unknown man and his talk with Jasmine afterwards.

As he watched, his face darkened. After they viewed the entire video, Ian stared off into space for a moment, then looked at Rory and said, "What do you want to know?" There was an edge to his voice that hadn't been there before.

"What did you talk with Jasmine about?"

"I don't remember. I have conversations with dozens of people every day. She was probably asking where something was in the hotel. Or maybe it had something to do with the convention. Whatever it was, it wasn't important or unusual enough to stick in my mind."

"Who's the man you were arguing with?"

"Why do you want to know?"

Rory crossed her fingers behind her back and said in a hushed tone of voice, "He ran into my car in a parking lot and just drove away without leaving a note."

"Not the hotel's lot, I hope?"

"No, no, a grocery store parking lot down the block."

"I'm sorry to hear that. He's a former employee. Not the most responsible type. I fired him recently. He wasn't exactly happy about it."

"The hotel's only been open a couple weeks, I wouldn't think you'd have time to fire anyone."

"Sometimes it doesn't take long to figure out an employee is not going to work out. Besides..." Ian lowered his voice so Rory could barely catch the words. "I caught him talking with those protesters. There were other problems, but I can't discuss them with you. Legal reasons."

"Do you think this man had something to do with the recent sabotage, then?" Rory asked.

Ian sighed. "You heard me in the bar, didn't you? Talking with Detective Green?"

"Did you tell the detective about Mr....?" Rory waited for the hotel manager to supply the unknown man's name, but he ignored the implicit request.

"To tell you the truth, I'd forgotten about him until you

showed me that video. I'll be sure to contact the police and let them know as soon as possible." The hotel manager glanced at the gold watch on his wrist. "Now, if you'll excuse me, I have an appointment."

Rory sensed the man was holding something back. For some reason she couldn't define, his account of his conversation with Jasmine didn't ring true. They'd talked too long for it to have been a simple request for directions. And, besides, he was the one who'd approached Jasmine, not the other way around.

She was heading to the El Porto ballroom to report back when Liz walked down the hallway toward her.

"Did you find Ian?"

Rory nodded her head. "The conversation was...interesting."

"I need some fresh air and sunshine," Liz said. "Let's take a walk and you can give me the details."

The two headed out the door and soon found themselves on a stone bench north of the pier, facing the ocean. Rory stared at a waist-high concrete wall that separated the path reserved for joggers and walkers from the one slightly below them that bikers and skaters used. The two paths converged in front of the pier, merging into a single trail shared by everyone. With all the beachgoers moving every which way, the area was ripe for potential collisions. She thought back to the time, just two months before, when she witnessed a minor biking accident between Detective Green and an inline skater at the same spot. She hadn't been able to prevent the accident, but she felt good about being there to help him bandage his scrapes.

"What are you smiling about?" Liz looked down at the bike path. "Do you recognize someone?"

Rory felt her face heat up. "It's nothing."

"Wait. This is where Dashing D had his bike accident, isn't it? That's what's got you all flustered."

Rory shrugged her shoulders in a noncommittal gesture.

"Bikers have good bodies, don't they? All that exercise gives them muscular legs and tushes." Liz grinned.

Rory rolled her eyes.

"Don't look at me like that. I've seen you checking out his butt. Don't deny it," Liz said. "Now, tell me about your conversation with Ian."

After Rory related every detail she could remember, Liz said, "What was that about your car? When did it get hit?"

"My car's fine. That was just a little white lie. It's the only reason I could come up with for wanting the man's name."

"Not a bad idea, but it didn't help. He still didn't give it to you."

"He didn't, did he?" Rory stared at the ocean thoughtfully.

"What about his body language? Did you get anything from that?"

"He tensed up when I asked about the man, but if he's a disgruntled employee, I can understand why."

Liz nodded in agreement. "You hear about people going on rampages after getting fired all the time these days. Or, at least, that's what makes the news."

"You know what we need to do? Verify his story." Rory thought about the problem for a moment. "You know lots of people. Do you know anyone who could tell us if the man really was a hotel employee? Maybe someone who works there."

Liz thought for a moment, then her face brightened. "I know, Nevada Nellie!"

"Nevada Nellie?"

"Sorry, Nell Fremont. She moved here from Nevada. She works at the Akaw. I found renters for her parents' house here in town. If the man worked at the hotel, maybe she knows his name. Let's go see if she's here today."

They returned to the hotel and were walking up to the front desk when a young woman wearing a dress in a Hawaiian-style print came out of a back room. Liz put on her best meet-the-client face and walked over to her. "Nell, so nice to see you. How are those tenants working out for your parents? Are they enjoying their retirement home in Palm Springs?"

Nell's face brightened. "They're wonderful. Mom and Dad wanted me to tell you how grateful they are to you for finding them. You're here for the painting convention, right? I was sorry to hear about the woman who passed away."

"Thank you." Liz cleared her throat. "We were wondering if you could help us with something."

"Anything I can do."

Rory cued up the video on her cell phone, stopping at the frame showing the face of the man in question.

"Do you know this man's name? He worked here and was fired."

Nell looked at the frame carefully, then shook her head. "I don't think he was ever an employee. At least not as long as I've been here. But there's something..." She frowned. "I feel like I've seen him before, I just can't remember where. When was this taken?"

"Tuesday evening, five-twenty or so."

They stood in silence for a moment while Nell stared off into space and thought. "Can I see that again?"

Rory held her phone up and the hotel employee looked intently at its display for several minutes. For a moment, Rory thought she saw a glimmer of recognition in the woman's eyes, but decided she must have been mistaken when Nell denied knowing who the man was once again. Before they could ask anything else, someone called Nell's name. The young woman looked toward the front desk where another employee was motioning to her. "I'd better go. Sorry I couldn't be more help. Let me know if you need anything else."

Rory stared after the hotel employee. She had a feeling the woman had been about to say something, but thought better of it. "I wonder why Ian lied about the man working here."

"Maybe he didn't. Nell might not have met him before he was fired." Liz glanced at her watch. "I'd better get going. Your mom's expecting me at the booth."

Rory waved goodbye and headed to the Manhattan ballroom

to see Nixie. Inside, she found the convention organizer sitting by herself behind a table in the office, chewing mint gum.

"Just wanted to let you know Gordon gave me the check. Thanks," Rory said.

"I'm so sorry it was late. Won't happen again."

Rory nodded her understanding, then played with a stack of aprons on the desk, unsure how to bring up the subject of embezzlement. She'd just decided on her approach when one of the convention attendees poked her head around the door.

"Sorry to interrupt," the woman said. "But we have a problem. Our instructor hasn't shown up for class and it's already fifteen minutes in."

"Which class is it?" Armed with the information, Nixie called the AWOL instructor's cell phone, but it went straight to voicemail. "I guess I'm going to have to hunt her down." She hesitated. "Rory, I hate to ask you, but could you look after the office for a few minutes? I'd rather not close it."

"Sure," Rory said, even though she wanted to pound her head against the wall in frustration. With all these interruptions, she was never going to get to ask the woman about Tempest's accusations.

After explaining where everything was, Nixie headed out the door to track down the missing instructor.

Rory settled down in the chair behind the table and tried to keep herself busy. She straightened the pile of aprons and picked up some brochures that had fallen to the floor. As she was looking around to see if there was anything else she could do to be helpful, she realized now might be her only chance to search the office. She had no idea what she would find, or even what she was looking for, but felt it important to try. Nixie wouldn't be gone long. She had to act fast.

Rory walked over to the door and looked out. People milled around in the hallway, but no one seemed interested in the office. She closed the ballroom door enough so no one walking by would see what she was doing and began her search. She looked through everything on the table, straightening up as she went, but found nothing secreted among the aprons, brochures and the half-dozen envelopes convention attendees hadn't picked up.

When she spotted Jasmine's roller bag off to one side, she made a mental note to remind Peter it was there and ask him what he wanted them to do with it. She looked under the table and searched the boxes, flipping through the papers in a yellow folder secreted under a stack of extra conference brochures. The numbers on the page made little sense to her and the writing on the folder's tab, "Financials," was too generic to tell her much. She put the folder back and continued her search, hesitating when she came across Nixie's large shoulder bag. She briefly debated with herself before quickly going through its contents.

Inside she found an e-reader, wallet, perfume, makeup, mint gum, and miscellaneous other items normally found in the average woman's purse. When she unscrewed the top of a water bottle, a whiff of alcohol escaped. She returned everything to its place, then checked the rest of the office, finding nothing of interest, not even the laptop Nixie had been using earlier.

Rory was refolding the aprons on the table when the convention organizer returned.

"That's the last time I work with that woman," Nixie said before Rory could ask about her quest. "She fell asleep in her room. Thought the time had been changed on her class. Said I'd called her and told her it was switched to evening. I never did that. She made it up, I'm sure. Just trying to cover up her own mistake. She's teaching now, but not all the students wanted to stay, so I'm going to have to refund some money." The two exchanged places. As Nixie settled down in the chair behind the table, she said, "Thanks for looking after the office while I was gone."

"No problem. I wanted to ask you about something. I was wondering where you worked before you started your own business and put together the convention."

Nixie sat back in her chair and stared at the young woman for what must have been at least twenty seconds. "She got to you, didn't she?"

Rory plastered what she hoped was an innocent expression on her face. "Who are you talking about?"

"You know who." The convention organizer sat back in her chair and sighed. "Poor misguided child. Her mother and I were friends." She produced the wrinkled photograph Rory had seen earlier and placed it on the table. "This is me and Tempest's mother. I was as shocked as everyone else when the theft came to light. And even more shocked to discover my friend was the one who'd done it. I feel for the girl. She insists I let her mother take the blame." She looked down at her hands. "No one wants to think ill of their parents, but even mothers are human."

Before Rory could ask anything else, a half dozen students entered the office seeking class refunds. Rory slipped out the door. As she passed by the bulletin board set up on an easel outside the office, she spotted a notice pinned to it. Sunday morning a short service was to be held in one of the ballrooms for Jasmine. She noted the time and location in her phone's calendar before heading to the trade show floor.

Chapter 18

When Rory arrived at the Scrap 'n Paint booth, the line at the register was so long it stretched down the aisle past the next two exhibitors. She stowed her bag under a table and pitched in. With her help, the checkout line soon dwindled to a more manageable length.

After the booth quieted down, Arika thumbed through the stack of credit card receipts, nodding her head in satisfaction. "This is the busiest we've been all convention."

Rory's gaze swept the booth, taking in the greatly depleted shelves. "Do you want me to run down to the store and get more stock?"

"That's very thoughtful of you." Arika eyed the displays, grabbed a pad of paper, and wrote down a dozen items. As she handed the list to her daughter, she said, "Have you talked to Peter today?"

Rory's face heated up. "We had a bit of a...misunderstanding. I'm not sure he wants to hear from me."

Arika's gaze dwelled on her daughter's face for a moment. "Call him. Good friends are hard to come by. And congratulate him for me on the dance contest."

Rory gathered her things, drove the short distance to Arika's Scrap 'n Paint, and picked up the items on the list. Before she headed back to the hotel, she sat in her car and dialed Peter's number. The call went straight to voicemail. She drummed her fingers against the steering wheel, checked the time, then put her car in gear and headed to his house.

When she pulled into his driveway a few minutes later, Peter was pulling open the door of the detached garage.

"What do you want? Have you found something else to accuse me of?" he asked her when she got out of her car.

Rory stepped forward. "Let's not fight. I just want to get to the bottom of Jasmine's death."

"I wish you'd let it go, but you always were stubborn."

An awkward silence fell over the two of them as Rory tried to find the right words to say. She gave up attempting to justify her actions and said instead, "My mother wanted me to congratulate you on the tango competition. And I wanted to make sure you know about the memorial at the hotel for Jasmine on Sunday."

Peter studied her for a moment, then his face softened. "I've been working with Nixie on it. I was going to ask if you had any pictures of Jaz at the convention, before...you know. We're going to use them in a slideshow."

"I haven't taken any, but I know people who have." She gave him several names and, after a few more minutes of polite conversation, she headed back to the hotel.

After dropping off the merchandise at her mother's booth, Rory found a quiet spot in the lobby, away from the hustle and bustle of the convention, and checked out the hotel and convention websites. Relief washed over her when she found everything functioning properly. She was examining the convention's Facebook page when Liz sank down on the chair next to hers.

"What are you looking at?"

Rory turned her phone's display around so her friend could see. "Just making sure no one's said anything else about me on the convention page."

"Ooh, are there any new photos?" Liz whipped out her own phone and began reading the most recent post.

The two sat next to each other, gazes trained on their own phones, and continued to view photos from various social media sites, occasionally sharing ones they thought were particularly interesting.

"Here's one of Dashing D and Mel. They're a cute couple." Liz looked over her phone at Rory. "You missed the boat on that one."

"I'm not really on the market right now. I'm happy by myself. Besides, he's shorter than I am."

"Excuses, excuses." A few minutes of silence, then Liz said, "This one reminds me of someone I went to high school with. No, it's not her. Sure looks a lot like her, though."

As soon as her friend said the words, a light went on in Rory's mind. "Oh."

"What is it?" Liz looked up from her phone.

"I just realized how we could figure out who the man in the video is. High school yearbooks. The VB Library has a slew of them."

"We don't know how old he is. How do we know where to start?"

"We could guess." Rory didn't relish digging through countless yearbooks on the off chance they would find a picture of the man. Assuming, of course, they would actually recognize a teenage version of him.

"Plus, we don't even know if he went to school here. He might have moved to town like you did," Liz continued.

"We have to start some place." Rory stared at the surfboard that hung on the wall opposite her, looking for inspiration. "I have an idea. Let's go find Maybelline." The woman had been a fixture in the city for more years than Rory had been alive. She'd probably seen a lot of its residents pass through the high school. If the mystery man in the video had grown up in Vista Beach, the former high school principal was sure to know.

After asking around, they found Maybelline on the trade show floor in the HennaMe booth, where customers could get a temporary tattoo applied to a hand or arm or, for the do-it-yourselfers, buy henna kits and supplies. Dressed in a purple suit with matching fedora, the older woman was talking with the artist who was applying the henna paste to the back of her hand, freestyling a design of flowers and squiggly lines.

After Rory got over the surprise of seeing the octogenarian getting any kind of tattoo, she showed the clip to her. "Maybelline, I was wondering if you knew who this is."

The woman peered at the phone's screen and said with little hesitation, "That's Oscar Carlton. Not one of my best students."

"Are you sure?" Rory asked.

"I'd never forget him, believe me."

"What do you remember about him?"

"Horrible grades. Always had some scheme going. He was in my office more than once. I remember him being a very convincing liar, but I didn't have any problem seeing right through him. From what I hear, he hasn't improved much since high school."

"I've heard that name," Liz said. "He's a private investigator. One of my clients hired him. Nasty divorce."

"Somehow I'm not surprised he digs into people's private lives for a living." Maybelline returned her attention to her hand. "This is shaping up very nicely."

As the tattoo artist made each stroke, Rory wondered why the hotel manager had been talking to a private investigator, and if it had something to do with Jasmine's death.

Rory and Liz watched until the last flower was painted, then waved goodbye to Maybelline and took a tour of the floor, occasionally pausing when something caught their attention.

"How much do you know about this Oscar Carlton?" Rory asked Liz as they rummaged through boxes of discounted pattern books.

"Not much. I've never met or even seen him. Just had that one client who hired him."

"We should see if we can find out more about him. You ask your client, and I'll ask around. Maybe my dad knows something. He might have run across him in his legal work," Rory said.

"I'll see what I can do."

Chapter 19

Rory left Liz on the trade show floor, found a quiet spot outside and called her father at his law office to see what he could tell her about the private investigator Ian had been talking to. He told her Oscar didn't have the best reputation and related a few stories he'd heard about the man's questionable practices, then ended the call by warning her to stay away from the man.

After promising her father she'd be careful, Rory went back inside the Akaw. As soon as she entered the lobby, she spotted Nell at the concierge's desk.

Remembering how she'd thought the hotel employee was keeping something back, Rory walked up to the desk and said, "I wanted to ask you about the man on the video again. I got the feeling when we spoke before there was something you wanted to say."

"I have no idea what you're talking about."

Rory settled her face into an earnest expression and lowered her voice. "I won't tell anyone you talked to me, but it's important. It might help me find out who killed my friend."

Nell studied Rory's face for a moment, then looked around and said in a whisper, "Not here. Meet me outside in five minutes." The hotel employee smiled at Rory and said in a normal tone of voice, "The hotel restaurant has a number of gluten-free options. I'm sure you'll find something that will please you."

Keeping up the pretense, Rory thanked the woman for the information and studied the menu posted next to a statue of a surfer by the entrance to the restaurant. After she felt she'd spent enough time reading the menu, she exited the hotel and settled down on a wrought iron bench in the courtyard in front of the Akaw and waited for the woman to arrive. The only people in the area were a couple sitting on the other side of the courtyard, too absorbed in each other to care about anything anyone else was doing. Right on time, Nell sat down on the bench beside her.

Rory peered around the courtyard, but didn't see anything resembling a security camera. Unless one was hidden in a planter, the area appeared to be free of surveillance. "No cameras here, right?"

Nell nodded. "That's why I chose it." She looked straight ahead as she talked. "You asked about the man in the video. If I was holding something back." She cleared her throat. "I saw Mr. Blalock, the hotel manager, talking to him the day after it was taken," she said in a whisper.

"Are you sure it wasn't the same day?" Rory asked.

"Positive. It was Wednesday, after the fire alarm sounded. On my breaks I sit on one of the benches near the ocean, watching the waves and the families on the beach. I find it very calming after dealing with people all day. Mr. Blalock and this man were standing on the path below me. My boss handed him a long, white envelope filled with something. I think it was cash."

"Do you know why Ian gave him the money?"

"No. There was something odd about it, though. Mr. Blalock glanced up and saw me on the bench. He seemed startled to see me, so I just pretended I didn't notice anything."

"Did he ask you about it?"

"When I got back to the hotel, he made conversation, fishing around to see if I'd seen anything. I just pretended I didn't know what he was talking about. He hasn't mentioned it since. That's all I know. Now, I have to get back to work." Nell was halfway out of her seat when Rory touched the woman's arm. "Wait. Why are you telling me all this?"

For the first time, Nell looked directly into Rory's eyes. "You mean why should you believe me? I have nothing to gain by telling on my boss and everything to lose. There's something...not right about it. It's been bothering me ever since I saw Mr. Blalock and that man together, that's all."

"If it bothers you that much, why don't you talk to the owner?"

"I don't even know who that is. Hides behind some company called Blue Wave Investments. He's never set foot in the hotel. I hear he lives back east somewhere. He's given Mr. Blalock carte blanche when it comes to everything to do with the Akaw. He put up the money, but doesn't seem to want to know anything about what's going on."

"I thought he lived up north."

"All I know is he's not around." After Rory assured the woman she wouldn't tell anyone Nell had squealed on her boss, the hotel employee headed back inside.

Rory leaned back on the bench and thought about what she'd learned. The exchange of money confirmed Ian had hired the PI, although she still didn't know why. Plus, she found it odd that he'd said the man was a disgruntled employee. Instead of coming up with an elaborate lie, he could have insisted it was none of anyone's business. No one could force him to talk. And where did Jasmine fit in? From the video, they could tell the woman had overheard the conversation between Ian and Oscar Carlton. Plus, Jasmine had her own conversation with the PI. As the Akaw's manager, Ian did have access to all of the rooms, and could have easily taken some of Jasmine's medicine.

Deep in thought, Rory headed toward the front door. She'd barely stepped inside when someone grabbed her arm.

"We need to go," Liz said, excitement dancing in her eyes.

Rory stared down at her friend. "Why? What's going on?"

Liz dropped her voice down to a whisper so low Rory could hardly hear her. All she could make out were the words "car" and "ton." She bent down and asked her friend to repeat what she'd said.

"We have a meeting with a CI about that PI, Oscar Carlton."

Rory raised an eyebrow. "CI?"

"You know, Confidential Informant. Like the police have on TV."

"You don't work for the police, and this isn't a TV show."

Liz waved her hand as if dismissing Rory's comments as unimportant. "My *contact*, then, wants to meet us in the underground parking area in..." She consulted her watch. "...ten minutes. But first, we need to get something from your mother's booth."

Rory stared at Liz in complete bewilderment. She wondered what her friend planned on getting at the Scrap 'n Paint booth that would be needed for a clandestine meeting.

On the trade show floor, Liz weaved her way through the crowd of shoppers, Rory close on her heels. When they reached their destination, Liz immediately went to a display of unfinished wood and snatched up two fourteen-inch by twenty-inch trays. "Good, there are still some left."

"What do we need wood trays for?"

"Protection." Liz brought the trays to Lily, the college student manning the cash register, and whipped out her credit card.

"Protection?" The trays *were* heavy. Rory could see using one as an impromptu weapon, bopping someone on the head with it or using it as a shield, but she didn't plan on getting into a situation where that was required. "Why do we need protection? Just who are we going to meet?"

"No one dangerous, but I'd rather be safe than sorry." Liz handed Rory one of the trays. "You can pay me for it later. Let's go."

As they made their way to the parking garage elevator, Rory wondered who they were meeting and what that person could tell them about the private investigator.

She tried to ask questions as they rode down in the parking garage elevator, but Liz jerked her head slightly toward a couple standing beside them, indicating she didn't want to talk about it in front of the car's other occupants. Not until everyone else had gotten off would she give Rory more details.

"We're meeting Carlton's assistant. She has information for us."

"How do you know her?"

"She's a friend of a friend. Agreed to meet as long as we do it somewhere her boss won't see her."

"Why is she even talking to us?"

"There's no love lost between her and her boss. She's studying to be a PI. Really close to getting her license and setting up her own business. I promised to send clients her way when she does."

Liz was well thought of in the city and encountered a boatload of people through her work in real estate. Many of her clients contacted her long after their real estate transactions had been completed, asking for referrals on contractors, gardeners, and a host of other services. Rory could easily imagine some of them wanting recommendations for local investigators.

They continued their ride in silence until they stepped out of the elevator at the bottom level. An eerie quiet enveloped them. Rory glanced around, but didn't see anyone. She imagined a masked man crouched next to an SUV, hidden by its bulk, ready to spring at her as she passed by. She stepped closer to Liz and gripped the wooden tray tightly.

"She's meeting us by her car. Look for a white van," Liz said.

"Whoa!" Rory grabbed her friend's arm. "There's no way I'm getting into someone's van. That's just stupid."

She'd read enough newspaper accounts of people being kidnapped and pushed into nondescript white vans to know how dangerous that could be.

"It'll be okay. We won't get in it, I promise. They use the van for surveillance. She's not on a case right now. She took it in for servicing." Liz pointed to the far end of the lot where a white van with no distinguishing markings and no front plate was backed into a space next to a post, sandwiched between a black SUV and a silver sedan. "I think that's it."

She'd no sooner spoken when the van's lights flashed once, twice, three times.

"That's the signal. Let's go."

Rory held her tray in front of her as they made their way toward the van. They were two car lengths away when a figure slipped out of the driver's side, stepped behind the post, and silently waited for them to approach.

Rory felt like a spy as they walked toward the lone figure who turned out to be a middle-aged woman with bright blue hair styled in a bubble cut and matching eyeshadow. She reminded Rory of a character in an old British sitcom she'd once seen on PBS. Rory half-expected the woman to have a British accent, but what came out of her mouth was more Boston than Bristol.

"Which one of you is Liz?" the woman said.

Liz stepped forward. "Candy?"

A car drove past and Candy stepped further into the shadows between her van and the sedan, motioning for them to follow. Rory raised her tray, prepared to use it to protect herself and Liz if the situation warranted.

Candy nodded her head toward Rory. "Who's that? You didn't say you were bringing anyone with you."

"This is Rory. She's okay, a friend."

Candy gave Rory the onceover as if trying to decide if she could be trusted. Rory must have passed muster because the woman continued. "Okay, I don't have much time. I've got to get back to the office before Oscar misses me. What do you want to know?"

Liz nudged Rory. "Show her the video."

Rory cued the clip of Oscar and Ian up on her cell and played it for the woman, stopping at a two shot of the two men. "Do you know anything about this? That's Ian Blalock, the manager of this hotel, with your boss."

The blue-haired woman mulled over the question for a moment before answering. "Name's not familiar. When was this taken?"

When Rory gave the woman the day and time, she stared at the nearby post for a moment. "Must have something to do with this case Oscar has been working on. All hush-hush. Won't let me in on it. Keeps the file in his personal filing cabinet."

"Is that typical?" Rory asked.

The woman shook her head. "No, I usually see all the cases. For some reason, he decided to keep this one to himself. But this man," she jabbed a stubby finger at Ian's picture, frozen on the phone's screen, "is involved somehow."

"If you haven't seen the file how do you know that?" Rory asked.

"I might have followed Oscar one day. Just for practice. Don't know if Liz told you, but I'm getting my PI license soon." The woman held her head up high and pushed back her shoulders, causing her considerable chest to jut out. "Oscar promised to help me, but he hasn't lifted a finger. Anyway, he met that man outside the hotel. I didn't hear everything they said, but I heard something about Seattle. It sounded like they were talking about a case, and Oscar doesn't have any other cases right now."

"What kind of case is it?" Rory asked.

"A cold one. Criminal, I think, but I'm not sure."

"The day after this was taken, Ian gave Oscar an envelope filled with cash. Do you know why?"

"He gave Oscar money? That son-of-a..." The woman pounded her fist on the side of the van.

Rory clutched her tray tighter. "What's the matter?"

"He owes me two months back pay, two *months*. Said he didn't have the money. Now I hear he's had it for days!"

"Could the money have something to do with the protesters?" Liz asked.

"Protesters?" Candy looked off into the distance as if considering the question. "Nah, I don't think he'd have anything to do with them. This Ian could have hired him, I suppose, and Oscar never told me about it. He's been very secretive lately. Is there more to the video?"

Rory played the rest of the clip.

"I've seen her," the PI's assistant pointed at the screen. "She came to the office Tuesday, no, Wednesday morning. Very nervous, but then, most of our clients are at first. Had all sorts of questions about Oscar."

Rory and Liz exchanged puzzled glances.

"Did she meet with him?" Rory said.

"Scooted out as soon as the boss arrived. Happens more often than not. Lots of people want to hire a PI, but then reality sets in and they lose their nerve." Candy looked at her watch. "I've got to go. I'm trusting you not to tell my boss I talked to you, okay?"

"You can count on us. Thanks for the information." Liz handed the woman one of her business cards. "If you ever need anything from me, give me a call. And let me know when you set up your own shop. I'll send business your way."

As Rory and Liz headed back toward the elevator, Candy hopped into the van and drove off.

"Odd about Jasmine, isn't it?" Liz said as she punched the call button. "Do you think she wanted to hire Oscar because she suspected Peter of cheating?"

"Could be. She talked to him on the video. Maybe he told her to stop by and she lost her nerve."

"Or maybe there's something else going on. Jasmine could have found out something one of them wanted to keep secret."

"I think we need to figure out some way to find out what the cold case is, what Ian hired Oscar to look into, and why the PI is so secretive about it," Rory said. "Somehow I doubt either one of them is going to tell us."

Chapter 20

Five minutes later, the two young women were passing through the Akaw's lobby on their way outside when Rory spotted the hotel manager in the bar, sitting on a stool by himself. His forearms rested against the counter as he stared down at a full glass of whiskey.

Rory indicated Liz should wait for her and walked inside the Wave to talk to Ian. "Everything okay?"

He turned toward her and gestured toward the empty stool next to his. "Join me."

"Some other time. I'm on my way to lunch. Just thought I'd stop and see if there have been any other problems you need me to look at. I've been monitoring the website off and on since the denial-of-service attack. Everything seems fine now."

"Good. I hope nothing like that happens again. These protesters are going to be the death of this hotel." He twirled the glass between his hands.

Rory bent down and lowered her voice. "How do you think Nixie's doing? I was a little worried about her the other day. You know, her drinking."

"I know what you mean. She's been through a lot with her husband dying so suddenly. She's trying to keep it together, but it's not always easy."

"You sound like you know that from personal experience."

Ian gripped his glass tighter. "I lost my wife awhile back. Cancer. You're never prepared for a loved one's death, even when you think you are. When something like that happens, you really learn how you deal with stress. I drank. First it was one drink when I got home from work, then two. Pretty soon I couldn't get up in the morning without a glass of whiskey. It took me a long time before I was able to get out from under alcohol's influence. It's still a constant struggle."

Rory nodded toward the drink on the bar. "Should you have that in front of you, then?"

Ian shoved the glass away. "Don't worry, I haven't had a drop. I like to test myself every once in a while."

"What made you stop?"

"My son. He was sixteen at the time, same age as Gordon, Nixie's son. I didn't want him to lose a father as well as a mother. I got off the booze, and we moved down here from Seattle. Gave me a second chance. Everyone deserves one, don't you think?" Ian pulled a photo of a young man out of his wallet. "He's in college now. Reminds me of his mother."

After she got a good look at the photo, Ian put it back in his wallet and stood up. "I need to get back to work."

Rory cleared her throat. "I know you lied about the man in the video, the one you were arguing with. You said he was a fired employee, but I found out he's a local PI, Oscar Carlton. Why did you hire him?"

The hotel manager turned toward Rory and plastered a rigid smile on his face. "I'm afraid that's none of your business."

"Maybe the police will be interested in seeing the video."

The veins bulged on the man's neck, and Rory could tell his patience was wearing thin. "If you must know, I hired him to find out who was sabotaging the hotel." He raised his hand in the air as if to stave off any questions. "Before you say you'll call the owner of the Akaw to verify my statement, he doesn't know about it. I used my own money. I don't like the idea of someone messing around with *my* hotel. Now, if you'll excuse me, I need to get back to work."

Before Rory could ask anything else, the hotel manager headed out the door.

Rory frowned. She didn't know whether to believe the man or not. His explanation didn't jibe with Candy's description of the matter as a cold case involving Seattle, but the PI's assistant could have been wrong. Some more investigation was necessary before deciding if Ian was telling the truth or not.

Rory rejoined her friend in the lobby and the two of them walked to a popular lunch spot, perched on the hill above the coastline. They sat at a table on the patio and studied their menus.

After they ordered, Liz said, "What did you talk to Ian about?"

Rory quickly brought her friend up to date on what the hotel manager had said about Oscar Carlton.

"Seems reasonable he'd hire someone to find out who's after the hotel. The police haven't had much luck." Liz took a sip of her ice tea and sat back in her chair. "Now, where are we with the investigation?"

"Everything is muddled in my mind. I think we need to take some notes." Rory grabbed a clean paper napkin from the dispenser on the table and started writing down everything they'd learned so far, with Liz providing a suggestion here and there. Before long, a list of suspects and possible motives covered the white rectangle.

After staring at the notes for a few minutes, Rory finally said, "Makes me sad looking at this." She put the napkin down on the table between the two of them.

Liz studied the list. "Peter's still the best bet. He has the most strikes against him. He had easy access to her medication, their marriage was on the rocks, and he was seen in the hotel going into the ballroom during the alarm."

"Assuming Hulbert wasn't mistaken," Rory pointed out. "Peter said he was at work. Let's say Peter *was* in the hotel, he could've taken advantage of the fire alarm. Everything was a bit chaotic. But that's leaving a lot up to chance."

"That fire alarm was awfully convenient."

"Maybe too convenient. Peter could've pulled the alarm to get everyone out of the hotel. He would know what Jasmine's class schedule was."

"Brandy could be involved. If the two of them were having an affair, they could have been in on it together. We can't forget about that," Liz said.

"Good point. Let's move on." Rory stabbed at a line on the napkin with her finger. "Nixie. That girl, Tempest, said she told Jasmine about Nixie having embezzled money in her last job."

"If she's telling the truth, that's a good motive for murder."

"Especially if Jasmine discovered proof when she was doing the books for the convention. She had Nixie's laptop. There might have been something on it."

"We didn't find any evidence of embezzling when we searched Jasmine's hotel room," Liz said.

"Could be on paper, could be on a flash drive. Or Nixie could have retrieved it after Jasmine died." Rory frowned and sat back in her chair. "There might be other motives out there we haven't even heard about. There's still Ian. Something's off with him. I don't believe him when he says he hired Oscar Carlton to investigate the sabotage."

"Ian has access to every room in the hotel. He could have gotten the medication out of Jasmine's room. Plus he knows where all the security cameras are." With her fork, Liz speared the last strawberry in her bowl of fruit and waved it in the air. "But what's his motive?"

"Jasmine overheard that conversation between him and the PI. Who knows what they talked about. Probably something far more incriminating than hiring him to investigate the sabotage."

"Did you ever track all of Jasmine's movements on Wednesday?"

Rory put down her cheeseburger and consulted the list she'd entered in the app on her phone. "Candy said Jasmine went to Oscar's office that morning. That must have been before she worked at the VivEco booth. She went straight to your class after that. She called Peter and told him about the alarm, then she went up in the elevator and got off on her floor before she returned to class. That's all I know."

"Was she drinking or eating anything during class? Do you remember? I was busy teaching and didn't really notice. Then she collapsed..." Liz said between bites.

Rory closed her eyes, trying to picture Jasmine's work area. "A soda. I remember her drinking from a bottle of soda. That must have been what the drug was put in. Any idea where the bottle went? You packed her things up. Did you throw it out?"

Liz scrunched up her face in concentration. "It's all a bit of a haze. I emptied her water basin and shoved everything at her station in her roller bag. I wasn't really thinking straight. I'm pretty sure that included the bottle. Where's the bag now? Did Peter get it from the convention office?"

"It was still there earlier today. We can go find it when we get back to the hotel." Rory pursed her lips in thought. "So assuming we're right about how and when she was dosed, who had access to the bottle?"

"Pretty much everyone. Anyone could have slipped into the ballroom after the alarm sounded."

Rory cast her mind back to the day of the fire alarm and tried to remember what she had seen in the chaos that had ensued after the alarm went off. "I remember Ian at the front desk. He could have walked around and gone into all the ballrooms. No one would think twice about the hotel manager checking to make sure they were all empty. The same goes for Nixie. She must have been around there somewhere, but I don't remember seeing her."

"With everyone out of the room, how did the killer know what station was Jasmine's?"

"Good question." Rory tried to picture Jasmine's workspace again to see if there was anything distinctive about it. "Her roller bag. She painted a design on it that included her name, remember? Find the place with the roller bag and you'd find her things."

Liz nodded her head in agreement. "So what do we do now?"

Rory stared at the waves rolling onto the beach and gathered her thoughts. "Let's start with the roller bag and Ian. We'll take care of the bag when we get to the hotel. As for Ian...we need to find out more about this case the PI was working on. Do you have Candy's phone number? I think we should talk to her again."

"I'll make the call." Liz took her cell phone out of her purse and dialed the woman's number.

When they got back to the hotel, the two split up in the lobby. Rory headed to the convention office to retrieve Jasmine's roller bag, but when she got to her destination the bag was no longer there and no one knew where it went. She continued her search, taking the elevator to the top floor of the hotel in case someone had brought it to Jasmine's room. She was walking down the hallway when she noticed a familiar figure knocking at a door at the end of the hall. She was about to call out Brandy's name when the door opened and the woman slipped inside.

Rory stood stock still. Brandy had never mentioned staying at the hotel. She lived with her aunt only two blocks away. There was no need for her to be here, especially at this time of day when she should be caring for her ailing relative. Unless Brandy and Peter *were* having an affair. They could have lied when they told her the kiss was a one-time thing.

Rory wondered if she was mistaken. She'd only seen the woman from the back, plus she had been some distance away. While she was pretty sure it was Brandy, she couldn't be positive. The more she thought about it, the less sure she became. Rory took note of the room number, hoping she would have an opportunity to discover who had booked it later, and unlocked the door to Jasmine's room.

She was heading toward the closet when she saw the elegantly clad body lying on the bed, a washcloth draped across the woman's forehead. Viveca propped herself up on her elbows and said in a weak voice, "Aurora, is that you? What are you doing in here?"

"Sorry, I didn't realize anyone was using the room. Are you all right?"

"Jasmine gave me a key in case she needed me to get her up. I have such a headache, I came up for a short nap. Did you need something?"

At least now she knew who had the second key to the room, Rory thought. Though she wasn't sure what difference that made to her investigation. She couldn't picture Viveca harming her favorite niece. "Jasmine borrowed a brush from me the other day. I think she put it in her painting bag. Have you seen it?"

Viveca waved her hand in the general direction of the closet. "It's in there. A bellhop just brought it up."

"Thanks. I'll just be a minute."

Jasmine's aunt lay back down and closed her eyes, placing the washcloth over her forehead once again.

Rory slid the closet door open and rummaged through the roller bag's contents, moving aside palette paper, the project from Liz's class, and various other odds and ends until she found the plastic soda bottle tucked among the painting supplies. What looked to her to be about a teaspoon of liquid covered the bottom of the bottle. From everything she'd read, that should be more than enough for the police to test for the presence of GHB.

Rory reached inside the bag to pick the bottle up and take it with her when she thought better of the idea. She'd leave it in the room and tell the police where to find it. That way no one could say she'd contaminated the evidence. Instead, she picked up a mop brush and held it up so Viveca could see it. "Got it. Sorry to disturb you. Hope your headache is better soon."

Rory was turning toward the door when Viveca held up a hand. "Wait. Aurora, could I ask you to do something for me? With me up here, Hully's shorthanded in the booth again. He didn't want to impose on you, but could you help him out? Just for an hour or so?"

Rory went over her schedule in her mind. "I'm working at my mom's booth soon. I can help out at VivEco until then."

"Whatever time you can spare."

After promising to get to the booth as soon as she could, Rory headed down to the lobby. When the elevator stopped at the next floor, a bellhop who looked to be about college age, dressed in an Aloha shirt and khakis, entered, smiled at her and pressed the "close door" button.

She stared at him thoughtfully. "Excuse me," she said. "Can I ask you a question?"

"Yes, ma'am. What can I do for you?"

"Do you know how I can find out who's in a particular room?"

"I'm afraid the front desk won't allow us to reveal that information, but you can call the room on one of the hotel phones. They'll be happy to connect you."

"Is there any other way?" She sidled closer to him and batted her eyelashes.

The bellhop was so short he had to crane his neck to look at her.

Rory stared down into his eyes, and said in her sultriest voice, "Can't *you* help me?"

"Um, well, um, I don't know." He gulped and, plastering a nervous smile on his face, pressed the lobby button several times, mumbling something about the elevator usually not taking so long.

Rory leaned against the back of the car. She should have known her efforts at charming information out of the bellhop wouldn't work. She was trying to come up with another approach when the doors opened and a couple in their eighties walked in, holding hands.

Forgetting about her quest for a moment, Rory smiled at the couple and wondered if she would ever find someone she could grow old with. She pictured a gray-haired version of herself, walking along the beach hand in hand with her husband, enjoying one of many sunsets. Her companion turned toward her. She almost gasped out loud as she recognized Detective Green's ruggedly handsome face. She was shaking her head, trying to clear the image from her mind, when the bellhop said to the couple, "How's the honeymoon going?"

The question brought Rory out of her reverie. Her mouth involuntarily dropped open, and the bellhop winked at her. For the rest of the ride down to the lobby, the couple discussed the best restaurants within walking distance of the hotel with the employee. The bellhop pocketed the tip the husband handed him and glanced over at Rory, a thoughtful expression on his face.

When they all exited the elevator on the lobby level, the bellhop drew her aside and looked shyly up at her. "I, uh, thought about what you asked. I can get you that information if you want me to."

Rory wondered what had caused him to reconsider. "That would be great." She told him the room number and waited for him to go somewhere to access the information, but he just stood there and stared at her pointedly.

Only when he held out his hand did she realize what he wanted. Wondering what the going rate for information was these days, she drew her wallet out of the pocket of her jeans and pulled a five into view. The bellhop frowned and gave an almost imperceptible shake of the head. She pulled up another five, then a ten. It wasn't until she pulled out a Jackson that he smiled his approval.

After she gave him the money, he said, "Wait right here."

Rory didn't know how private investigators did it. She hoped she didn't have to pay anyone else for information. Otherwise, it was going to cost her a small fortune. She studied the picture on a nearby wall, pretending to be fascinated by every detail, while she waited for the bellhop to return. She'd almost decided he'd taken her money without any intention of giving her the information she wanted when he walked toward her and pressed a slip of paper into the palm of her hand.

On a yellow Post-it note was written a name in an almost illegible hand. "Kym Hough. Are you sure this is right?"

"Yes, ma'am."

As the man left, Rory studied the unfamiliar name. She must have been mistaken about Brandy entering the room, after all. She continued to puzzle over it as she walked toward the trade show floor. She was halfway to the Hermosa ballroom when Rory spotted

Detective Green heading into the management offices. She tried to flag him down to tell him about the bottle, but he waved her away. Afraid she'd forget to tell the detective later, Rory left a message with an officer at the police station, giving him all of the details about the bottle. Satisfied she'd done everything she could, she headed to work at the VivEco booth.

Chapter 21

The rest of the afternoon, Rory split her time between the Scrap 'n Paint and VivEco booths. She was waiting in the lobby for Liz when her friend raced over to her.

"Dinner will have to wait," Liz said. "We have to go *now*."

Minutes later, the two young women stood in a narrow alley behind Oscar Carlton's office, hidden by a dumpster, waiting for their contact to signal the coast was clear.

Rory wrinkled her nose at the smell of rotting garbage that assailed her nostrils. She stepped as far away from the metal container as possible while still remaining hidden. She longed to get out of the alley before eau de garbage once again became her cologne.

"Are you sure she's coming?" Rory whispered.

"Don't worry. She'll be here," Liz whispered back.

"Why does she keep helping us? She must have some sense of loyalty to her boss."

"I think that flew out the window when she discovered he had money, but still didn't pay her. Besides, once her own PI office is set up, she'll be getting lots of referrals from me and every real estate agent I know. That's worth a lot."

They waited in the shadows, not saying a word, their gazes riveted on the single-story building where the PI's office was located. They both jumped at a mouse that emerged from behind a dumpster farther down the alley and scurried away. When Rory felt she couldn't take the faint rustles and squeaks coming from nearby any longer, Oscar Carlton's assistant poked her head out of the alley door. "Psst! Are you there?"

Rory and Liz emerged from the shadows and walked as quietly as possible toward the doorway where Candy stood waiting for them.

The woman opened the door wider and ushered them inside. "Come on, you have to hurry. Oscar left, but I don't know how long he'll be gone."

Rory and Liz stepped into the back room of the PI's office, a small storage area that doubled as a kitchenette. A single bulb hung overhead, giving off little light. Rory could make out a small refrigerator and coffeepot as well as various bankers boxes that she assumed contained files of cases long closed, given up on, or forgotten.

"Okay. Oscar's office is around the corner. What you're looking for is in there somewhere. Here." Candy pressed a key into Rory's palm. "This opens Oscar's desk."

"Won't he miss it?"

"Doesn't even know I have it. I made a copy. Just stick it under the phone on my desk when you're done."

"Wait, aren't you going to stay and be our lookout?" Rory asked.

"It's more than my job is worth. Just close this door when you're done." Candy gestured toward the entrance they'd come in through. "It'll lock behind you. Good luck."

After the assistant left, Rory and Liz peeked around the corner into the main area. Candy's desk sat in the middle of the small room, facing a picture window which gave a view of the street. A bathroom was on the far side of the room opposite the PI's office. After making sure the coast was clear, the two of them tiptoed across the floor. They entered Oscar's windowless office, closed the door behind them, and turned on the overhead light.

"We need to be as fast as possible. I'll set the alarm for ten minutes. We'll see where we are after that." Rory set the timer on her cell phone and placed it on the desk. She surveyed the room which seemed to be a typical office with its computer, phone, file cabinets, and desk.

"Where do we start?" Liz said.

"You take the file cabinets. I'll check out the computer and desk. Look for anything that has Ian's name on it," Rory said.

Liz started to examine the files in the cabinet against the far wall while Rory settled down in front of the computer. As she expected, it was password protected. Unlike on television, she didn't have any magical way to get through the login screen. She could sit there for years and never guess the password, so she turned to the desk drawers, hoping the man was careless enough to write it down on a piece of paper.

Rory inserted the key Candy had given her into the topmost drawer. Excitement coursed through her as the lock clicked and the drawer slid open, but all she found inside were a log book, a pile of flash drives, and other odds and ends.

"None of the folders in these cabinets has Ian's name on it," Liz whispered. "It'll take too long to read each of them and this other cabinet's locked."

Rory rifled through the rest of the desk drawers. "I don't see any other keys."

"Let me try something." Liz grabbed two paper clips out of a bowl on the desk and went back to work on the locked file cabinet.

Rory returned her attention to the log book. On the back page, she found columns of random strings of letters and numbers with no indication of what they were for. She checked the countdown on her phone. Half the time had passed, and they still had nothing to show for their search. Guessing the items on the list were passwords, she tried the first two on the login screen. When neither of them panned out, she gave up on the computer and tackled the rest of the log book.

The heading on each page consisted of a three-letter code followed by a number. Underneath were a list of dates and expenses. When she looked at the most recent page, headed SEA, something tickled at Rory's brain.

A click told her Liz had picked the lock on the file cabinet.

"Where'd you learn to do that?" Rory said.

"Online video. Thought it might come in handy someday."

"I think I found something," Rory said. "Didn't Ian say he was from Seattle? I have an entry here labeled SEA. That could stand for Seattle. See if you can find a file with SEA and this number on it." She rattled off the digits written on the log book page.

"Bingo!" Liz said as she drew out a file. She spread it out on the desk and the two of them glanced through it. Inside were a police report on a hit-and-run and some gruesome photos of the elderly victim splayed out in a crosswalk. A bup-bup-bup-bup sounded, startling Rory until she realized it was her phone telling her the timer had ended. She tapped a spot on its display to stop the noise. "That's ten minutes."

Rory peeked out the door into the main office. She could see pedestrians passing by on the sidewalk outside, but inside it was still quiet. She returned to the desk and turned the photos over so she wouldn't have to see them, then started skimming through the report. She was trying to decipher Oscar's crabbed handwriting on various Post-it notes stuck to the back of the folder when she heard a sound coming from the outer office.

Rory signaled for Liz to be quiet and tiptoed over to the door. One peek around its corner and she could see Oscar Carlton through the partially open front door. Through the window, she spotted a man talking with the PI. "Oscar's here!"

Liz stuffed the file folder back in the cabinet and relocked it while Rory returned the desk to its original state.

Head down and heart pounding, Rory followed Liz out of Oscar's office toward the storage room. As they crept crab-like across the floor, she hazarded a glance toward the front door. The PI had finished his conversation with the man and was halfway through the doorway. She jerked her head toward the storage room, indicating they needed to move faster. Liz ran the short distance to the back room. Rory was about to follow when she heard the front door close. She peeked over the desk she was hiding behind to find Oscar standing less than three feet away, staring down at his cell phone. She held her breath and twisted herself into as small a shape as possible. When she thought she couldn't stay in that position a minute longer, she heard footsteps moving away from her. She peeked over the desk once again and saw him heading into the bathroom.

As soon as he disappeared through the door, Rory tiptoed across the room. She breathed a sigh of relief when she joined Liz outside. Not until the alley door started to close behind them did she realize she'd left her cell phone on the PI's desk.

Rory caught the door before it latched, crept back inside, and peeked into the outer office. The light was now on in the PI's inner sanctum and music was playing. Silently cursing herself for leaving her phone behind, she looked around for something to get the man out of his office. She tiptoed to the outer door and stuck her head outside.

"Psst," she said to Liz. "I need a distraction."

Liz gave her the thumbs up. Rory crept back inside and waited. Moments later, a chorus of car alarms sounded, so many that the PI left his office and walked over to look out the front door to see what all the fuss was about.

As soon as his back was to her, she raced across the floor, grabbed the phone off the desk, and dashed back into the storage room. As she ran, her hand brushed against Candy's desk, dislodging a cup full of pens. They fell to the floor, making a sound so loud Rory was sure it could be heard miles away. She was slipping out the back door when she heard a "Who's there?" coming from the outer office.

The two young women ran down the alley, not taking time to catch their breath until they reached the street. Then, as nonchalantly as possible, they headed back to the Akaw, not saying a word until they were two blocks away from the PI's office.

"That was close. Nice touch with the car alarms," Rory said.

"Did you see Ian's name on that file? I didn't. Wouldn't it be there if he hired Oscar?"

"Didn't see his name anywhere, but I didn't get a chance to read all of it."

"I should've taken pictures of the file with my cell phone. I'll know better next time."

The information fresh in their minds, they compared notes and put together the basics of the hit-and-run case. A car had barrelled through an intersection, hitting an octogenarian, and sped off without a backward glance. The police had conducted an extensive search, but the car and its driver had never been found. One of the witnesses had moved to Vista Beach not long after the accident. A PI in Seattle had hired Oscar to locate and re-interview that witness.

"Maybe Oscar found him and he told him something of interest," Liz said.

"Did you see the name of the witness?" Rory asked.

"Only the address. It's right next door to a house that's on the market. Guess who's representing the sellers?"

"Maybe we should check it out. See if that witness is home and willing to talk to us," Rory said thoughtfully. "Find out what Oscar discovered."

Liz glanced at her watch. "Too late now. It'll have to wait until tomorrow."

"First thing tomorrow, then."

The next morning, Liz picked up Rory at her house and drove to the witness's address on the southern end of Vista Beach.

"You can do the talking," Rory said. "I'll be your assistant. You're taking me around with you, showing me the ropes."

"I can do that." Liz's eyes twinkled. "How are we going to find out about the hit-and-run? We can't just say to whoever answers the door 'Did you witness an old woman get mowed down a few years ago?' We don't even know the name of the witness, or if that person still lives at the address."

"We'll play it by ear. I'm sure something will come up. Maybe we'll get lucky."

Before long, Liz reached the address on Oberg Lane and pulled up in front of a one-story stucco house dwarfed by the monster next door. "That's the one that's for sale." She pointed to the two-story mansion that filled the entire lot.

"Have you had any offers?" Rory asked.

"Not yet. It's the most expensive house on the block and the sellers are very picky." The petite real estate agent grabbed a few flyers out of her backseat and headed toward the smaller house, Rory following closely behind.

They walked through the gate of the fenced-in yard toward the front door, passing a tricycle and a stroller along the way. When Liz rang the bell, they heard a faint yipping coming from inside, followed by footsteps approaching the door. A very pregnant woman who Rory guessed was in her thirties answered the bell.

In her most professional voice, Liz introduced herself, explaining she was handling the sale of the house next door, and handed the tired-looking woman a flyer for the property.

"I'm just out here seeing if you or any of your neighbors are thinking of buying or selling anytime soon. If you're looking to upgrade, I know of several properties suitable for a growing family."

The woman leaned against the doorjamb. "I wish. We could certainly use some more space." She patted her swollen belly. "Twins this time."

"Congratulations," Rory and Liz choroused.

The woman glanced down at the flyer Liz had given her. "Wish we could afford this one, but I suppose it's not really suitable for young children. Do you know why they're selling? They didn't move in that long ago. There's no problem, is there?"

"None at all," Liz hastened to reassure the woman. "The place is in tip-top shape and they love the neighborhood. He was transferred out of state so they're selling sooner than expected."

"Oh really? Do you know where they're going?" the woman asked.

Liz pursed her lips as if trying to remember what her client had told her. "Somewhere up the coast." She turned to Rory. "Do you remember where?"

Rory took the hint and said, "Seattle, I think, or somewhere near there."

"That's where I'm from!" the woman said.

"It's a small world." Rory nodded her head. "I've heard the Seattle area is nice. A friend of my mother's lives there, or should I say, lived there." She lowered her voice. "She was killed in a hit-and-run a few years back. Sad case. Just minding her own business, walking across the street. Never found the driver."

The woman shuddered. "I saw one of those myself. Not something I ever want to see again. I still have nightmares about it."

Relief washed over Rory when she realized they'd found the witness they were looking for. She tried to keep her expression neutral as she listened to what the woman had to say.

"That must have been horrible," Liz said sympathetically. "I'd have been so shocked I wouldn't have been any use to the police."

"I wasn't able to tell them much at the time," the woman admitted. "They never found the driver. I guess they're still looking into it. Some investigator came around asking me about it a couple weeks ago. Wanted to know if I remembered anything else."

"Did you?" Rory did her best to appear only mildly interested, but inside she was hanging on the woman's every word.

"I didn't get a good look at the driver, but it was a man. I'm sure of that. He had a beard. I thought I'd seen him somewhere but, until recently, I couldn't place him. Then I remembered seeing him at a hotel near where the accident occurred. I think he works there. That's what I told the investigator, anyway. Later, he came back and showed me a picture of someone who I'm pretty sure was the man."

Rory stored the name of the hotel she gave them and its location in her memory.

Before they could ask any more questions, cries of "Mommy! Mommy!" came from inside the house.

"Guess Juliette's up from her nap. I'd better get going. Nice talking with you. I'll let you know if I hear of anyone who's interested in the house."

The woman closed the door, and Rory and Liz headed back to the car.

"That description sounded like Ian. Do you think he was driving that car?" Liz said.

"I'd say it's a safe bet. He lived in the area at the time. We can easily verify that he worked at that hotel." Rory brought up the Akaw's website on her smartphone. A few taps on its screen and she had the information she wanted. "Here's Ian's bio. He worked at a number of places and, yes, one of them was the hotel the woman mentioned."

"So that's why he gave that money to Oscar, to keep him quiet. That could have been what Jasmine overheard. You'd better call Dashing D and let him know what we found out. He can talk to the witness himself."

While Liz drove them to the hotel, Rory called the detective and told him what they'd learned about the hit-and-run.

"How did you get this information?"

"A little birdy told me," Rory said.

"Cute." The detective gave an exasperated sigh. "Why were you even looking into this cold case? It's not local."

Rory made static noises. "Sorry, you're breaking up. What did you say?"

She could almost hear the detective's eyeballs rolling in his head. "Fine, I'll look into it. In the meantime, stop investigating."

The two young women spent the rest of the morning in class. After lunch, Rory started a shift on the trade show floor. She was helping out in the VivEco booth when Nixie and Ian stopped by to remind everyone how the breakdown process would work.

"The floor closes at noon tomorrow," Nixie said. "No packing up until after it closes. Just leave the boxes in the booth after you're done and mark them with your company's name. Someone from the hotel will bring them to the loading dock and make sure all of the boxes from your booth are grouped together." She looked down at her clipboard. "I see you have a truck scheduled to pick them up Monday afternoon, Hulbert."

"That's right," he said. "I hope that's not too late. It was the only time I could book the moving company."

Nixie waved away his concern. "Not a problem. We won't be moving the boxes into the loading dock area until Monday morning, anyway. We'll have trucks coming and going all afternoon. Ian's here to answer any questions you might have about the hotel's role in this."

The hotel manager answered the few questions Hulbert had about the process. He and Nixie were about to move on to the next exhibitor when Detective Green walked down the aisle, stopping in front of the VivEco booth. "Mr. Blalock," he said. "I need a word with you. If you could come with me..."

"What's this about?" Ian said, confusion written all over his face.

"I think it would be better to talk about it somewhere more private."

Exhibitors from the neighboring booths started gathering around as word spread the police were on the floor. Liz, who was working in the Scrap 'n Paint booth across the way, joined the group, as curious about the drama playing out before them as everyone else.

"I won't go anywhere until you tell me what it's about. Does it have something to do with the protesters? Whatever they're saying about me, it's not true," Ian said.

"This has nothing to do with the hotel or the protests. Really, we should talk about this somewhere else."

Ian glanced at the crowd that was growing larger by the minute. "Follow me."

Rory looked over at Hulbert who inclined his head, silently urging her to go, apparently as interested in what was going on as she was.

Ian led the detective and Nixie, who insisted on going along, into an empty ballroom nearby. Rory caught Liz's eye and the two of them followed, stationing themselves outside the half-open ballroom door to listen.

"Okay, what's this about?" the hotel manager said.

"It's about a hit-and-run in the Seattle area three years ago. The victim was..." a pause where Rory pictured the detective consulting his notes, "...an Esmerelda Downs. It's come to our attention you might know something about the accident."

"Three years, did you say? That was a long time ago. How do you expect anyone to remember the details of their lives so far back?"

"Let's start with whether or not you were living in Washington state at that time," the detective calmly said.

"Yes, I was living there. I moved to California with my son after my wife died two years ago. Why do you think I know anything about an accident that killed an elderly woman?"

"I didn't say how old the woman was."

"Esmerelda's a rather old-fashioned name. I just assumed..." Ian cleared his throat. "You still haven't told me why you think I was involved."

"New evidence has come to light that indicates you were driving the car that night."

"What kind of evidence?"

"An eyewitness places you in the car."

"After all this time?" Ian's tone of voice conveyed his disbelief.

"She's quite adamant about it."

"You need more proof than that."

"I talked with the police in Seattle. They recently tracked down the car involved. At the time it was registered to you."

Rory cautiously poked her head around the partially open door so she could see inside the ballroom.

Ian's shoulders sagged. He sat down on a nearby chair and buried his head in his hands. Finally, he looked up and said, "I'm done trying to cover this up. It's about time I told the truth. It's been weighing on my mind for a long time now."

"So you're confessing?" Detective Green said.

"That's right. I hit that woman, and I'm prepared to take the consequences. I was drunk and had no business driving. It's no excuse, but my wife had just died and I was upset. At the time, I wasn't even sure I'd hit someone. Then I saw the news the next day and realized what had happened. It's the one thing I never made amends for. It's about time I did." He took a deep breath and stood up.

"Why didn't you go to the police when you realized you were responsible?" the detective asked.

"My son was only sixteen at the time. He'd just lost his mother, I didn't want him to lose his father too. I kept waiting for someone to find me, but no one did. I cleaned up the car, sold it, got help for my drinking problem, then moved us down here for a fresh start."

"Is that what the PI was talking to you about in that video I showed you?" Rory said as she stepped inside the ballroom.

Ian jumped at her sudden appearance, then nodded. "The woman's family hired someone to find out what happened since the police hadn't had any luck. A witness had moved to Vista Beach, so the investigator in Seattle contacted Oscar Carlton to re-interview her in case she remembered something else. Apparently, she did."

"Instead of telling the PI in Seattle, Oscar decided a little blackmail was in order," Rory said. "That's what Jasmine overheard, wasn't it? Him blackmailing you."

"That's right." Ian looked at Nixie then took a deep breath. "And that's why I killed her."

Chapter 22

Rory gaped at the hotel manager, not quite believing the search for Jasmine's killer was over. Liz poked her head around the door and said in a soft voice so only Rory could hear, "Did Ian just confess?"

Nixie stared uncertainly at him. "Ian? What are you talking about?" She touched his arm as if to make sure this was real and not some dream she'd conjured up.

Ian squared his shoulders. "That's right. I killed Jasmine. She knew about the accident and threatened to go to the police. I tried to buy her off like I did that PI, but she refused. So...I killed her." He said the last few words without a trace of emotion. The man appeared to have regretted his being involved in the hit-and-run more than giving an overdose to an innocent person.

"How? How did you kill her?" Detective Green's words challenged the man to prove he was telling the truth, as if the police officer didn't quite believe his confession.

"I'm not saying anything else until I talk to a lawyer." Ian turned to Nixie. "Can you let Nell know what happened and tell her she's in charge now? And call my lawyer. His number is in my office. Nell will show you where to find it." He held out his wrists. "Okay, I'm ready. Cuff me."

As soon as Detective Green led Ian away, Nixie awakened from her shock. "I'd better take care of getting that lawyer. I'll deal with the rest of the booths later. Something tells me we won't be on schedule, anyway." Disbelief radiating from her eyes, the convention organizer headed out the ballroom door.

Rory and Liz made their way back to the trade show floor, each returning to the booth she was in before the commotion started.

When Rory reached her destination, Hulbert pulled her aside. "What was that about?"

"Ian's been arrested for a hit-and-run in Seattle and..." she paused, unsure how to break the news to him. "Jasmine's murder."

"What?" He sank down onto the chair next to the cash register. "He killed our Jasmine?"

"That's what he said. I heard it with my own ears."

Hulbert shook his head and stared down at the floor. Finally, he looked at Rory and said, "I'd better go tell Viveca what happened before she finds out from someone else, but I'm worried about the booth. Aren't you supposed to go over to Arika's Scrap 'n Paint soon?"

"Maybe we can work something out." After consulting with her mother, Rory returned to the VivEco booth and said to Hulbert, "Go. Take care of Viveca. My mom says I can stay here until you get back." He left the floor, and she settled down in the chair next to the cash register. A sudden flurry of customers kept her busy for the next ten minutes.

Once the rush was over, Liz walked across the aisle. "Do you think Ian really did it?" she said.

Rory sat back in her chair and crossed her arms. "It would be nice to have it all over with, but I'm not really convinced. I guess Ian could have set off the alarm so he'd have time to plant the medicine in Jasmine's soda." Her hand flew to her mouth. "The bottle. I don't think Detective Green knows about the bottle yet. I tried earlier, but he was busy. I left him a message."

"You found her bag, then?"

"Someone brought it up to her room. I'd better call him again. He might need it to verify Ian's story."

"If they find his prints on it, that's that, and we'll know for sure."

Rory dialed the detective's number and left a message on his voicemail reminding him about the bottle and where he could find it.

"There, that's done," she said. "I still think the killer dressed in coveralls and set off the alarm so there'd be a chance to dose Jasmine's bottle. I'm not sure Ian could have done it. He was in a suit at the front desk when we were evacuating the hotel. I saw him there. I doubt he would have had time to strip out of the coveralls and get to the lobby before someone missed him."

"He could have paid someone to set it off for him," Liz pointed out. "Or maybe he didn't need to pay anyone. He's the manager. He could have told one of his employees it was a surprise test or something and that no one should know about it."

"Let me get this straight. Ian set off the alarm, or convinced someone to set off the alarm. When he's going through the ballrooms, ostensibly to make sure everyone evacuated, he puts the medicine in Jasmine's soda bottle."

Liz nodded. "He knows which bottle is hers because he recognizes her roller bag. She did have her name painted on it."

"Then he goes about his business and waits for her to collapse in class. But how did he even know she was drinking a soda?"

"Could have seen her buy it in the gift shop. Same is true for everyone else."

"But what if she'd taken the soda with her? What then?" Rory asked.

"He would have simply tried some other time. Did he look surprised when you told him what happened?" Liz said. "You were the one who alerted him to Jasmine's collapse and told him paramedics had been called."

Rory cast her mind back to the moment she'd run down the hall toward the convention office, but couldn't recall many details. She'd been in such a panic, the time was just a blur in her memory. "I really can't remember. I found Ian and Nixie together in the convention office. Beyond that, I don't know." She thought about it some more. "Let's say he's telling the truth. He'd have to have some sort of container to put the medicine in. The bottle was found in her hotel room."

Liz shrugged. "Or he put it back in her room afterwards. He's the hotel manager. He has access to all the rooms. No one would think twice about him going into any one of them. He could've been checking on some problem. But how did he know about Jasmine's medicine in the first place? He knew about her condition, of course. You told me he witnessed that cataplectic attack."

"Peter called the hotel and informed the staff about Jasmine's narcolepsy. He also gave them a list of her medications. Ian mentioned it when I saw him in the lobby Monday evening." Rory screwed up her face in concentration. "Maybe if we looked at that video ourselves we could figure out if he was the one wearing the coveralls."

"He confessed. Why are we even bothering to look into it?"

"Because I'm not sure I believe him. The hit-and-run, that I believe. Killing Jasmine, not so much." Rory looked at her friend. "Did you ever get the name of Veronica's source for the hotel footage?"

"She wouldn't tell me. Something about protecting her sources."

"I'll have a run at her later, see what I can find out."

Liz looked at her watch. "I have to get going. I'm helping with a class. Do you know what we need? Distraction. We don't have anything planned for tonight. How about we get dressed up and go out. Let's meet in the lobby at seven."

Rory nodded her head in agreement. After everything that had happened, she could use some fun. She spent the next two hours splitting her time between the two booths. The hotel manager's confession was the talk of the trade show floor. Since she'd been present when the police arrested him, she spent more time answering questions about what had happened than ringing up purchases.

As soon as she finished work and her last class was over, Rory drove home to change. Wearing a casual summer dress and two-inch heels, she met Liz in the Akaw's lobby precisely at seven. After a quiet dinner at a nearby Italian restaurant, they headed back to the hotel.

"We're all dressed up and it's not that late. We can't waste this." Liz gestured toward the dresses both of them were wearing. Her face turned thoughtful, then burst into a smile. "I know! Let's go to a nightclub. I want to shake my booty!"

"You've had way too much caffeine. And I don't know how to dance."

"You just move your body in time to the music." Liz demonstrated, moving her arms and gyrating her hips to an imaginary song only she could hear.

Rory couldn't help laughing. "I don't think I can do *that*. Isn't there somewhere else we can go?"

Liz furrowed her brow in thought. "I know, how about karaoke? There's a bar near here that has it on Saturday nights. It's right up your alley. You spent all those years in your church choir, so you're used to singing in public."

"That's not quite the same thing. It was a long time ago, and I wasn't particularly good at it."

"No one cares. Come on!" Liz pulled on Rory's arms. "The murderer's in jail. We helped figure out who did it. You can shed all those doubts you have and think about it all again tomorrow. Let's see if anyone at the hotel wants to join us."

"Okay, okay, but I'm not going up by myself. We have to do a duet." Rory followed her friend down the street as she danced her way toward the Akaw. When they reached the hotel lobby, Liz explained their plans to several painting friends who were milling around, looking for some way to spend the rest of the evening. Before long, she'd added a half dozen karaoke converts to the group, including Mel and Stella.

The group streamed out of the front door of the Akaw, and with Liz enthusiastically leading the way, walked the five blocks to a bar on Main Street that had karaoke on Saturday evenings.

By the time they arrived at their destination, Rory was looking forward to sitting down and resting her feet for a minute. She wasn't used to walking in heels, no matter how low they were. Tennis shoes were her footwear of choice. She didn't know how Liz managed to balance on her stilettos, let alone walk and dance in them.

Strains of "Raindrops Keep Falling On My Head" reached their ears as the group entered the bar. The place was packed with people of varying ages, from middle-aged locals to young college students. The painting group snagged two tables together that a large bachelorette party had recently vacated. Half the patrons around them listened to a forty-something man belt out a competent version of the B.J. Thomas hit while the other half carried on their own conversations.

Everyone applauded when the man came to the end of the song. After explaining to the newcomers this was sixties night, the karaoke host called up the next group to the stage. Rory had grown up listening to music from that decade, so she was familiar with most of the songs. A mother and daughter who were part of a birthday celebration began a rendition of "It's My Party," the daughter occasionally messing up the unfamiliar lyrics.

"I'm going to get a glass of wine. Does anyone else want anything?" Rory asked everyone at her table. She took an order from Mel, but the rest of the group opted to get their own drinks. Rory headed to the bar where a number of college-aged students had gathered. She elbowed her way through the crowd to the front and ordered. While she waited for her drinks, she struck up a conversation with a young woman standing beside her, waiting for her own order.

"Riverside?" Rory nodded toward a blue keychain attached to the college student's purse. "I graduated from there."

The girl nodded. "What was your major?"

"Computer Science. What about you?"

"Me too!" They were soon chatting away like old friends, talking about professors and classes. When the student's drink arrived, instead of paying for it and leaving, the girl drew a coaster out of her purse, dipped a finger in her drink, and rubbed it on two spots on the four-inch by four-inch square.

"What's that for?" Rory nodded toward the coaster.

The girl looked around and lowered her voice. "It tests for the presence of GHB and ketamine in drinks. Can't be too careful these days." She nodded to the spots where she'd applied the liquid. "Nothing changed, so the drink's okay. The spots turn dark blue if the liquid you're testing has one of those drugs in it." She looked pointedly at the margarita and glass of Pinot Grigio the bartender had placed on the counter. "You should get some coasters. There's a pharmacy in town here that carries them." She mentioned its name and the street it was on, then left to join her friends who'd moved over to a nearby table.

Rory paid for her drinks and returned to her own table, thinking about what the student had told her. Better to be safe than sorry, she thought, but she felt sad that female students felt the need to test the drinks they ordered in public places.

"What are you looking so serious about?" Liz asked when Rory sat down. "You're not still thinking about the case, are you? You're supposed to be having fun!"

Rory smiled. "Sorry. Did you sign us up to sing?"

"Don't worry, we're on the list. There are several people before us." When the karaoke host called the next name, Liz clapped her hands in delight. "Oh, Mel's up!" During the song, Stella motioned Liz over to her table.

As she listened to Mel's rendition of "It's in His Kiss," Rory couldn't help wondering if the woman was thinking about her good-looking boyfriend while she sang.

After the song was over, Rory joined in on the applause and congratulated Mel on her performance as soon as she sat down. "Too bad your boyfriend wasn't here to see it."

Mel blushed. "I'm not sure I'd have had the courage to sing that in front of him."

"Something tells me he'd enjoy it."

"Thanks for making me feel so welcome here at the

convention. I really appreciate it. I'm glad Martin gave me that gift certificate for your mother's store. I hadn't really thought about taking up painting until he did."

"And I'm glad you were there when Jasmine collapsed. Don't know what we would have done without you," Rory said. "Why did you decide to become a paramedic, anyway?"

"I was in a bad car accident when I was a teenager. My cousin was driving. She was barely eighteen and hadn't had her license for very long. It was raining and dark. She lost control on a curve. Paramedics saved my life, so I decided that's what I wanted to be when I grew up."

"What about your cousin?" Rory asked softly, suspecting what the answer would be.

Mel looked down into her drink. "She wasn't so lucky, but the driver who caused the accident got off without a scratch." For a moment, anger suffused the woman's face.

"I'm sorry." As they listened to the next singer, Rory searched her mind for a more pleasant topic of conversation. "So, was it love at first sight? You and Detective...uh, Martin?" she found herself saying. "Or is that too personal?"

"You're attracted to him, aren't you?" Mel studied her as if searching for the truth in her eyes.

Rory looked down at her drink, avoiding the other woman's steady gaze.

"Don't worry. It's okay. Who wouldn't be? He's a handsome man." Mel laughed. "We're enjoying spending time together. This is the second time around for us, so it's familiar."

"That's right, you mentioned that when we met. If you don't mind my asking, why did you break up?"

"I moved away for a while and we just...drifted apart. We each met other people." Mel took a sip of her margarita. "We'll see what happens this time around. I don't think he's eager to get too serious after, you know, what happened to his wife."

"His *wife*? He was *married*?" She shouldn't be so shocked, Rory thought. She didn't know his exact age, but the detective must be in his thirties. He was bound to have had several serious relationships over the years. But, somehow, she'd never pictured him with a wife.

Mel looked as surprised as Rory felt. "You didn't know?"

Rory shook her head. "News to me. What happened to her?"

"He doesn't really like to talk about it. She passed away. You'll have to ask him the rest."

Before Rory could find out anything else, Liz ran up to the table and grabbed her friend's arm. "Come on, we're up next."

Once the two were on the stage, they enthusiastically belted out "I Got You Babe." Liz took Sonny's part while Rory took Cher's, flinging her long hair in Cher fashion at the appropriate times in the song. As she sang, she forgot all about the detective's love life and her friend's murder.

A couple hours later, the group returned to the hotel. As she walked through the automatic doors into the lobby, Rory glanced toward the Wave. Nixie sat by herself at one of the tables, staring at a glass of white wine in front of her. Rory said goodnight to those who were staying at the hotel, tilted her head toward the bar, and whispered to Liz that she would be right back.

She walked up to the table and gestured toward an empty chair. "Hi, Nixie, can I join you for a moment?"

The woman nodded her agreement, barely looking up from her contemplation of the glass of wine.

"How's Ian? Is he okay?" Rory asked. "Have you been able to see him?"

"He's in jail, how can anything be okay? I got him a lawyer, at least."

"That's good to hear." Rory nodded toward the glass of wine. "Should you be drinking that?"

Nixie wrapped her fingers firmly around the glass as if to make sure no one could take it from her. "What are you, my sponsor? I don't know why everyone wants to stop me from drinking. Ian, you, my own son. I don't know what the big deal is. I don't have a problem."

"I just thought Ian would want—"

"He means well, but sometimes he really doesn't understand how hard it is."

"I'm sure that's not true. He lost a wife to a serious illness. He probably knows exactly what you're going through."

"It's not the same." Nixie banged the glass on the table. Wine splashed onto the polished wood as well as the woman's suit. A few drops landed on Rory who grabbed a cocktail napkin and wiped the liquid off her hand. "I should never have left Seattle," the woman continued. "Nothing good has happened to me in California." She stared morosely at her wine for a moment, then finished it in one gulp.

"I can take you home if you need a ride," Rory said, worried the woman would attempt to drive in her current state.

"No need. I have a room in the hotel for the night." Nixie gingerly stood up and, on unsteady feet, headed toward the exit.

Rory followed her and made sure she took an elevator up to the guest rooms, not down to one of the parking levels.

When she rejoined her friend in the lobby, Liz said, "How's Nixie?"

"Not great. Don't know what she's going to do with Ian in jail. He helped her out a lot."

"I just realized you never told me what Dashing D said about Jasmine's soda bottle. Did he get confirmation that's how Ian drugged her?"

Rory stared at Liz.

"What? Did I say something stupid?"

"No, not at all. I left a message on his cell, but I never heard back from him. I wonder if he picked up the bottle."

"We could go see. You still have the key, right?"

When the two of them entered Jasmine's hotel room a few minutes later, Rory slid open the closet door, took out the roller bag, and set it on the bed.

When she opened it, she found all of the painting supplies she expected, but the bottle was no longer inside.

"He must have taken it," Rory said. "I'll have to ask him about it tomorrow. It shouldn't take the police long to verify it contained GHB." If she had one of those coasters the college student in the bar had, she would have been able to test it herself, she thought. "I wish he'd called me to tell me he had the bottle."

"He's a detective, he's busy on the case. Probably didn't even occur to him."

They returned the roller bag to the closet and parted ways in the lobby.

Before going to bed that night, Rory settled down at her computer to catch up on email. While she was online, she checked Vista Beach Confidential to see what Veronica had been up to since the convention started. The woman had posted photos and daily reports of her experiences at her first painting convention, from the classes she took to the products and people she'd seen on the trade show floor. Rory snickered at the account of the exhibitor who had stuffed receipts in her bra. According to Veronica, business must have been good, because the woman had grown two cup sizes in an hour.

One of the earliest posts was an interview with Jasmine about her struggle with narcolepsy that turned out to be a sensitive portrayal of a condition few people knew anything about. Rory hadn't realized her friend had given the interview, but was glad she had.

Next, she checked out the photo gallery, sifting through the dozen of pictures Veronica had taken during the convention. When she came across a candid shot of Hulbert and Jasmine together, she wondered if he'd seen it. She doubted the man frequented the website or even knew of VBC's existence. Thinking he might appreciate a copy of one of the last photographs taken of his step-niece, she printed the picture out and studied it. Judging by the statue of a surfer in the background, it had been taken in front of the entrance to the hotel restaurant. She could just make out a bottle in Jasmine's hand. Rory wondered if it was the soda she bought before class, though this picture could have been taken another day. She made a mental note to ask Hulbert when she gave the photo to him.

Rory returned her attention to the blog. In her most recent post, Veronica mentioned the arrest of the Akaw's manager and speculated on what that would mean for the hotel. She conjectured the community would finally discover the identity of its mysterious owner, who would be forced to come out from the shadows now that his right-hand man was no longer available to manage the property.

At the bottom of the page was an exclusive interview with Oscar Carlton, who claimed he'd been instrumental in uncovering the identity of the hit-and-run driver. In it, the local PI explained his part in the capture of the hotel manager—how he had re-interviewed the witness and handed the new information over to the local authorities.

Rory snorted and shook her head in disbelief as she read the words. If she hadn't alerted Detective Green to what the witness had told her, Ian would probably never have been found out—unless he stopped paying the PI hush money, that is.

When Veronica asked Oscar about the alleged blackmail attempt, the man claimed that for his entire life, people had been after him, accusing him of things he'd never done. So he'd learned to protect himself. That's why he'd installed hidden cameras in his office that even his assistant didn't know existed.

Rory stared at the words on the screen, reading them over and over again. Hidden cameras. Office. She gulped. If what he said was true and he wasn't just spouting off, they were in trouble. Big, big trouble. She didn't want to know what such a man would do once he discovered they'd searched his office. It wouldn't be difficult for him to find out who either of them were. He was a private investigator, after all. Plus, Liz's face was plastered around town in real estate ads on benches and shopping carts and, by this time, Rory's was almost as well-known.

Even though midnight had come and gone, she called her friend to warn her about the perceived threat.

Liz yawned into the phone. "How do we even know he's telling the truth? Maybelline told us he lied a lot."

"I don't see why he'd lie about this."

"We don't know for sure he has any cameras. I didn't see any. Did you?"

"That's the point. They were hidden." Rory wondered if she was making a mountain out of the proverbial molehill, and they had nothing to worry about. "He's probably mad we eliminated his cash cow. I'm worried about what he might do."

"If the cameras actually existed, why would he mention them in an interview? Wouldn't he want to keep them secret?"

"Not if he wanted to warn people not to mess with him."

"Go to bed. A good night's sleep will put it all in perspective. Big day tomorrow. It's the last day of the convention, plus we have the meet and greet and Jasmine's tribute." Liz yawned into the phone once again and hung up.

Rory placed the phone in its charger, then walked around the house straightening, trying to expend enough energy so she could fall asleep. As she put away the painting supplies she bought at the trade show, she wondered if she was worrying for nothing. She couldn't get the picture of her being led to jail in handcuffs out of her head. She wondered if the PI would even bother with the police or decide to take justice into his own hands. Rory didn't want to know what Oscar Carlton considered acceptable punishment for their invasion of his privacy.

Chapter 23

After attending an early church service the next morning, Rory headed toward the Akaw for the final day of the painting convention. She was driving past the offices of the *Vista Beach View* when she spotted Veronica going inside. Remembering she hadn't yet asked the reporter about the hotel security footage, Rory found a parking spot nearby and went in search of the woman.

As soon as Rory stepped inside the newspaper offices, her gaze swept the dozen desks scattered throughout the large room until it landed on one in the far corner where a woman with black hair sat, her back to the entrance, attention focused on something in her hand.

Rory wended her way around the desks toward her prey, not stopping until she reached Veronica's side. She peered over the woman's shoulder at a smartphone, catching a glimpse on its screen of a Facebook page that didn't have the reporter's name on it.

"So this is what you do at work," she said right next to the woman's left ear. "Who is Jennifer—" Before she could read the rest of the name, Veronica turned off her phone.

"Don't creep up on me like that!" The reporter frowned. "You're always startling me."

"Sorry." Rory sat down on the chair next to Veronica's desk, facing her. "How come you're not at the convention?"

"Work. Why aren't you there?"

Rory rolled her chair closer to Veronica. "I'm looking for information."

The woman's eyes narrowed. "What kind of information?"

"I need to know who your source is for the hotel footage. The anonymous one you mentioned in the paper."

"Why?"

Rory rolled a little closer, her knees coming within inches of the other woman's chair. "I need to look at the footage. It's important."

Veronica backed up her chair until it hit the desk behind her. "Can't. Journalism. Protecting sources. You know the drill. I wouldn't tell the police when they asked, why should I tell you?"

"You'd be helping to verify Ian's confession."

"So you want the name of my contact so you can look at the footage and verify that it's Ian who set off the alarm? What if it's not him?"

"Could be an accomplice. Either way it'll be a coup for you. You can write about it in the paper or on your blog."

Veronica stared at the wall opposite her. A smile flitted across her face.

"So you'll do it? Give me his name?" Rory said.

"No, sorry."

"Why not? Don't you want the scoop?"

"I don't need to give you his name. I have the information right here." Veronica patted her keyboard. "But I'm not going to show the footage to you. I think I'll keep it to myself."

Rory stared straight ahead without seeing what was in front of her, trying to come up with some way to ferret the information out of the reporter.

"Stop staring at me. You're making me nervous."

"Sorry, didn't realize I was." Rory leaned forward in her chair and placed her elbows on her knees. "What if Ian's innocent? Do you want that on your conscience?"

"The police have the footage. If he didn't do it, they'll figure it out."

"I don't know, he confessed. They might not look too hard. And you just said it yourself, the police have the footage. Why keep it from me? If you show it to me, I'll let you in on anything I find out."

"You do seem to be friendly with Detective Green's girlfriend." Veronica drummed her fingers on her desk as she considered the proposal. "Okay." She typed on the keyboard and brought up the hotel security footage on the display.

They watched over and over again as someone dressed in coveralls with a ball cap obscuring their face pulled the fire alarm.

"Could be a man, could be a woman. Average build and height from what I can tell. The coveralls are pretty shapeless so I could be off on the build," Rory finally said after reviewing the footage at least ten times. "Can't see much of the face, but I'd say it's not Ian. No beard."

Veronica nodded her head. "So we're talking an accomplice, then."

Or Ian had nothing to do with it, Rory thought. And someone else entirely was responsible.

Veronica glanced at her watch. "Isn't the memorial service soon? We should get over to the hotel. Can you give me a ride?"

The two headed out the door, and less than ten minutes later, were walking into the lobby of the Akaw. They followed the handwritten signs to the Huntington ballroom where the tribute to Jasmine was being held. When they reached their destination, Veronica joined the throng going into the room while Rory stopped to talk to Peter who was standing in front of a poster size photo of his wife displayed on an easel just outside the entrance. She placed her hand on his shoulder. "That's a lovely photograph of her."

"Isn't it? It was her favorite," Peter said.

"Have you seen Brandy?" Rory asked.

He motioned toward the ballroom. "I think she's inside, helping Nixie set up the slideshow. Thanks for suggesting we ask Veronica and Stella for pictures. They both had several good ones of Jasmine taken during the convention."

"I'm looking forward to seeing them."

As people arrived, they gathered around the recent widower, forming an impromptu receiving line.

Rory patted Peter on the arm and said, "I'll see you inside."

As she squeezed her way between people, she spotted Detective Green off to one side, scanning the crowd as they entered the ballroom.

"Sorry for your loss," he said as soon as he saw her.

"Thanks." She cleared her throat. "I'm glad to see you here. I wanted to ask you about the soda bottle. Were you able to test its contents?"

"I don't have it."

"What are you talking about? The soda bottle Jasmine was drinking from right before she collapsed was in her painting bag in her hotel room. I saw it there myself. That's how the killer drugged her. Didn't you pick it up last night?"

He shook his head. "I went up to her room after I got your message. I looked through the roller bag and the suitcase, but didn't find it. Tell me what you know about this bottle, from the beginning."

Rory quickly recounted how she'd seen Jasmine drinking from the plastic soda bottle the day she died, how Rory had found the bottle in her friend's painting bag and called him as soon as she realized its significance.

Detective Green held her shoulders and looked straight into her eyes. In a quiet voice, he said, "I know you and Liz went to see the witness from the hit-and-run. I don't know how you got her name, maybe I don't want to know, but you two shouldn't have been investigating. It's not safe. This is not a game. It's serious business. I don't want to have to worry about either of you. I lost someone dear to me once, I don't want to have that happen again." She nodded. He removed his hands from her shoulders. "Now, we need to set some ground rules. No investigating. If you come across information you think I need, call me right away. Anytime, day or night. Do nothing about it, absolutely nothing, okay?"

Rory silently nodded her agreement, then headed into the ballroom where rows of white folding chairs were set up facing a raised dais with a podium. On an easel next to the dais was a still life Jasmine had painted in oils.

She spotted Hulbert guiding his wife into a seat in the front row and headed down the aisle toward them. She drew him aside and handed him the candid photo she'd printed from Vista Beach Confidential. "Here. I thought you might like a copy of this picture of you and Jasmine. I found it on a website. Looks like it was taken somewhere in the hotel." Her gaze zeroed in on the clothes Jasmine was wearing in the picture. "Probably the day she...you know."

Hulbert stared at the photograph and cleared his throat. "Thanks. I haven't seen this one. That must have been one of our last conversations. I didn't even know anyone was taking our picture." He looked up at Rory and said, "Where did you say you got this photograph?"

Rory was about to explain about VBC when Viveca waved her hand and he hurried to her side.

Rory made her way back down the aisle and settled into a seat between Liz and her mother. "I have news," she whispered to Liz. "About the bottle. He didn't pick it up. I'll tell you all about it later."

A constant stream of attendees entered the ballroom and sat down. Peter and Brandy took seats in the front, while Mel and Stella Nygaard, who had become fast friends, found places in a row behind them. Half the chairs were filled by the time Maybelline settled down into a seat nearby. Rory glanced to the back of the room where Detective Green was leaning against the back wall. A hush fell over the crowd when Nixie stepped to the podium and started the tribute.

After she thanked everyone for coming, the lights in the ballroom dimmed and Nixie began the slideshow. Baby pictures of Jasmine appeared on the screen followed by others of her through the years. Rory smiled at one of the four of them in their Halloween costumes. Rory had been a witch, Brandy a ballerina, and Jasmine and Peter had been Ginger Rogers and Fred Astaire. Nixie rounded out the presentation with pictures taken during the OPS convention.

Liz nudged Rory's arm as a photo of Brandy and Jasmine appeared on the screen. The two stood in a hallway with heads close together, deep in conversation. "That's a nice one. Looks pretty recent."

"Jasmine was wearing that outfit the day she died," Rory whispered. "I saw another picture of her taken the same day."

As the slideshow wound to an end, Rory cast her mind back to the other day when she'd seen Brandy on the beach. She frowned. Even though Brandy had said she hadn't seen Jasmine on Wednesday, the slideshow provided visual evidence to the contrary.

After all the pictures had been shown, Viveca stepped up to the podium. Dressed in a short-sleeved black dress and black pumps, she thanked everyone for coming, then related a few stories about her niece. She was halfway through one when she broke down in tears and was unable to continue. As Hulbert led her to her seat, Peter took her spot at the podium followed by a number of other people who had met Jasmine at painting events.

When Arika took the floor representing her family, Rory's eyes welled up with tears as her mother told of meeting Jasmine and seeing her grow up with her own daughter. By the time she finished, there wasn't a dry eye in the ballroom.

At the end of the service, while everyone filed out, Rory remained in her seat. Once she'd brought her emotions under control, she slipped out the door to join the receiving line.

When she gave Peter a hug, he said to her, "You still have the key to Jasmine's room, don't you?"

"I figured you might need it so I brought it. Sorry I've had it so long." She drew it out of the pocket of her khakis and handed it to him.

"No, that's okay. I was wondering if you'd do me another favor. We need to vacate the room. Could you pick her things up and drive them over to the house later? I'd do it, but I have an appointment I can't be late for and the hotel wants me to check out soon."

Rory wondered if he really had somewhere to be, or if he was making an excuse for not going inside the room. He'd found the idea too upsetting a couple days ago. She had the feeling it wouldn't be any easier for him now. "Sure, I'll bring them over to your place after the event at the store. Do you want me to return the key to the front desk?"

After she'd worked out the hotel room logistics with Peter, Rory mingled with the other guests for what she considered an appropriate period of time, then slipped away and took the now familiar elevator ride up to the sixth floor. She was almost at her destination when she spotted Brandy going into the room at the end of the hall. This time there was no mistake. She was absolutely sure her friend had entered the hotel room. She wondered if a scheduled tryst was the reason Peter was unable to pick up his wife's things, but as soon as the thought entered her mind, she dismissed it. Jasmine's room was only a few doors down. If he were joining Brandy, he wouldn't have bothered to ask for Rory's help. He would have picked up the luggage himself or asked Brandy to do it for him.

Determined to find out what was going on, Rory marched down the hallway and knocked on the door, which remained stubbornly closed. When she heard movement on the other side of the door, she put her eye to the peephole, trying unsuccessfully to see inside the room. She waited, then knocked on the door again, this time calling out, "Brandy, I know you're in there. Open up."

Slowly, the door opened. Dressed in gray coveralls, Brandy stood in the doorway and motioned Rory inside. "We need to talk."

Chapter 24

"Quick, come in." Brandy grabbed Rory's arm and pulled her into the hotel room.

Rory's gaze swept the area from the hallway to the bed all the way to the open bathroom door. She listened for any tell-tale sounds, but couldn't hear anything unusual. Unless someone was hiding underneath the bed or standing statue still in the shower, the two of them were the only occupants of the room.

"You were expecting Peter, weren't you? You still think we're having an affair."

Rory gestured toward the coveralls her friend was wearing. "I wasn't expecting this. What's going on?" She thought back to the alarm that had been set off and the footage she'd seen of the culprit. Put a cap over Brandy's closely cropped hair and it could have been her in the video. "Are you working with the protesters? Did you set off that alarm?"

Brandy sat down on the edge of the bed. "I'm not just working with them, I'm one of them."

"But why? Why would you do that?"

"They deserve it. Every bit of it." Brandy cast a defiant look in Rory's direction, challenging her friend to contradict her.

"Who are you talking about?"

"The people who built this place. And everyone who allowed it to be built. No one will take responsibility for the damage it caused."

"You mean the houses near here? Oh. Your aunt owns one of those, doesn't she? I get it now."

"Do you? I'm not sure you really understand. She's not well. Alzheimer's. My mom and I have it covered for now, but she'll need specialized care soon. And that takes money, a lot of it. We thought we'd be able to sell the house, but now no one will buy it unless we fix it first."

"And you can't afford to repair it," Rory finished the thought for her friend.

Brandy nodded.

"What about the alarm? You didn't answer my question. Did you set it off?" Rory said.

"That wasn't me. All I've done is mess around with the convention a bit. I took the water buckets out of the ballrooms. Called one of the instructors and told her that her class time had been moved. Stuff like that."

Poor Nixie, Rory thought. The first convention she'd put together and it had to be during a time when these protests were going on. "What about the eggs and the rocks?"

"That wasn't us, either, but those city council members deserved it. Allowing this place to be built. Not making sure the city's residents were protected."

"Did I deserve it too? The rock through my window?"

Surprise shown on Brandy's face. "Someone threw a rock through your window?"

"That's right. The same night those council members' houses were egged."

Brandy rubbed her neck. "I don't know anything about that."

"Why should I believe you? You lied before."

"Not about Peter, I didn't. We're not having an affair."

"I wasn't talking about Peter. I'm talking about Jasmine. On the beach, you said you didn't see her the day she died, but there's a picture of the two of you together. Did you think I wouldn't notice?"

Brandy frowned. "What picture? Oh, the one in the slideshow. How do you know it was taken that day?"

"She's wearing the same outfit she wore in class the day she died. If that's not enough, I can always get the files and check the timestamp."

"Oh." Brandy shrank under Rory's steady gaze. "That picture was taken around eight Wednesday morning, long before she was...gone."

"Why did you lie, then?"

"I didn't want you to know I was in the hotel because of...something else. She saw me go into this room and we talked. She thought Peter and I were having an affair, but when I told her about the protests, she was okay with it and headed back to class."

So that's where Jasmine went when she came up in the elevator. Rory frowned. "I'm confused. You saw her in the morning, then later on in this hallway when everyone re-entered the hotel after the false alarm. But before she went to class."

"That's right."

Rory cast her mind back to Wednesday. She couldn't remember exactly when Jasmine returned to class after the alarm, but at least fifteen minutes had passed between the all-clear and when Liz started teaching again. That could be enough time for Jasmine and Brandy to have a quick conversation. "Does Peter know? About what you've done?"

Brandy folded her hands in her lap and stared down at them. "No, but Jasmine supported me wholeheartedly once I told her all about our cause. She was even planning on helping me with some...things." Her gaze shifted to the bed behind her where a package wrapped in brown paper lay.

"What's that?" Rory looked at her friend who stared back defiantly. She moved around the bed and felt the package, but couldn't tell what was inside. "What is this?" By Brandy's attitude, Rory suspected this had something to do with sabotaging the hotel, but she couldn't figure out what it could be. Unless..."Is it another stink bomb? Were you the one who planted the one in the men's room? Is that why you're wearing coveralls? You're going to plant another one?"

Brandy pursed her lips. "Like I said, they deserve it."

Rory leaned down and sniffed the coveralls her friend was wearing. They didn't smell like they'd been in a dumpster. Of course, it had been several days, and they could have been washed.

Brandy pushed Rory away. "What are you doing?"

"Seeing if you were the one who hit me over the head and shoved me in the dumpster the other day."

"I have no idea what you're talking about, but I would never attack you."

"You know I can't let you set off another stink bomb, don't you? It's just not right." Rory sat down on the bed next to her friend. "I'm going to have to take it away from you."

"Do what you have to do, but that won't stop us for long. We can always make another one."

Rory took the package and headed toward the hallway door. She paused with her hand on the doorknob. "What are you going to do now?"

"Whatever I have to do to protect my family."

"One last question. Who's Kym Hough? Why did you use that name when you booked the room?" Rory said.

"You don't recognize it? Hint. Dancing. Stars. I combined a couple names of the pros on the show."

She should have figured that out, Rory thought. Brandy had been a ballroom dancing fanatic for as long as she could remember.

Rory walked out the door and headed down the hallway to Jasmine's room. Once inside, she sank down onto the bed and thought about what she'd learned. She pieced together Jasmine's last day in her mind. Her friend saw Brandy in the hotel lobby at eight, went over to the PI's office, then worked on the trade show floor. Then came class, followed by the alarm and the trip up to the hotel room.

Rory didn't know who to believe anymore. Maybe Jasmine wasn't as supportive of the protesters as Brandy had claimed and had caught her friend planning the act of sabotage. If she'd threatened to reveal the information to someone at the hotel or to the police, maybe Brandy or even the protest leader had silenced Jasmine permanently.

Brandy could have been lying about setting off the alarm. That could have been her in the video. The build was similar and, with the cap, you couldn't tell if it was a man or a woman. She could have used her involvement with the protesters to set it off and put the medicine in Jasmine's soda. By killing Jasmine, Brandy would not only get rid of a threat, but also clear a path to Peter, her heart's desire.

If caught, she could always claim she'd set the alarm off as part of the protest. Even if the other members of her group told the police that wasn't part of their agenda, she could say she'd gone rogue and thought of it all by herself.

Juggling the package, suitcase, carry-on and roller bag, Rory rode down in the elevator to the lobby. She didn't know what to do with the stink bomb she'd taken away from Brandy. She knew she should hand it over to the police, but she didn't know if she could do that without telling them where she found it.

She was standing in the lobby, trying to decide what to do, when Detective Green came out of the hallway leading to the management offices with two hotel employees. Taking his appearance as a sign, Rory waited until he was alone before approaching him.

She handed the detective the package wrapped in brown paper. "I found this. I think it might be another stink bomb. Thought the police should have it."

He took the package out of her hands and examined it. "What makes you think it's a stink bomb?"

"Just a hunch."

"Where did you say you found it?"

"I didn't." She started to wheel the luggage toward the parking garage elevator.

Detective Green walked beside her. "Let me help you with that."

She let him take charge of the suitcase while she slung the

carry-on over her shoulder and wheeled the roller bag full of painting supplies across the lobby into the elevator.

They didn't say a word until they reached Rory's car in the underground parking structure. After stowing the luggage in her trunk, he leaned against her car and said, "Are you going to tell me where you got this package from?"

"I can't."

He studied her face. "Friend?"

Rory stared at a nearby post, trying to come up with the right words. "What would you do if you knew someone had done something...wrong? Would you tell on them?"

"Illegal?"

"Maybe. But no one got hurt, physically anyway."

"Is this a good friend?"

"Does it matter?" she said.

"Not to me, but I suspect it does to you."

"You're ducking the question. What would *you* do?"

The detective paused before answering, considering his words carefully. "I'm a police officer, sworn to uphold the law. I take that oath very seriously. But I'm not you. I can't tell you what to do. I can't force you to talk, but here's my advice to you. Tell your friend to knock it off."

In silence, they rode up in the elevator together, parting ways in the lobby. Rory was on her way to the Scrap 'n Paint booth when she received a text asking her to see Nell in the hotel's office. She retraced her steps and asked someone at the front desk where she could find the acting manager. They directed her to the nearby hallway. In the office at the end, she found the woman sitting in a chair, staring at a computer screen.

Nell looked up as Rory knocked on the open door. "Rory, thank goodness you're here. Ian told me to contact you if there were any more problems with the website."

"What's wrong?"

Rory took Nell's place in front of the computer. While Nell explained the problem, Rory grabbed a Post-it and, clearing a space on the desk, took notes. The acting manager left Rory alone in the office and headed to the front desk to help a guest. Fifteen minutes later, Rory had resolved the issue. When she tried to return the desk to its original state, she noticed a folder peeking out from under a pile of papers. The label on it said "Blue Wave Investments," the name of the company Nell said the owner hid behind.

Rory glanced over at the partially open door to make sure no one was nearby and put the folder on her lap. A quick glance told her the papers inside were a real estate partnership agreement between Ian and several other people.

The document contained too much text for her to absorb so she took photos of each page with her cell phone, periodically glancing up to make sure no one was coming down the hall toward the office. Once she was done, she stuffed the folder back under the stack of papers. By the time Nell entered the room, Rory was out of the chair and ready to head out the door.

"All fixed," she told the woman. "Text me if you have any more problems."

They discussed the solution to the website problem as Nell escorted Rory to the lobby.

As soon as she was alone, Rory headed outside to the courtyard and settled down on a wrought iron bench in the shade. She studied the photos she'd taken of the real estate partnership agreement. Dated less than two years ago, the agreement designated Ian as the managing partner. Three other names were mentioned, none of which she recognized. He'd also contributed the majority of the money for whatever real estate endeavor the group was involved in. With her finger, she swiped across the screen, flipping through the photos, finally coming across one page titled "Property Description," where the address of the Akaw hotel was listed.

Rory set her cell phone in her lap and thought about Ian's investment in the hotel. With this new information, she wondered if she should rethink her opinion about his guilt. He had a lot more to lose than she'd originally thought. If it became public that Ian was responsible for a hit-and-run, his partners wouldn't be happy about it. She didn't know the legalities of the situation, but she suspected he would lose his position as managing partner and might even lose all the money he'd sunk into the Akaw. Given that, Rory understood how Ian might want to silence Jasmine, but none of this explained his sudden confession.

Chapter 25

As soon as the trade show floor closed at noon, Rory and her mother headed to Arika's Scrap 'n Paint to set up for the meet and greet, putting off packing up the booth until later that afternoon. After Jasmine's untimely death, the store owner asked Viveca if she should cancel the two-hour event, but the guest of honor insisted her niece would have wanted them to continue. While Rory stacked pattern books and packets on the signing table, Arika worked on the refreshments, laying out a cheese platter next to bottles of champagne and sparkling cider on a card table near the back of the sales floor.

After everything was set up, Arika surveyed the store with a critical eye, her gaze traveling over the event tables and racks of merchandise, before nodding her approval and unlocking the door. Not long after she flipped the sign from closed to open, the bell over the front door tinkled, signaling the arrival of the first customers. Women began trickling in as convention attendees took the ten-minute walk from the Akaw to the painting supply store. The trickle soon became a flood and, before long, the store was at capacity.

Head cam strapped on, Stella moved around the store, filming the event for her painting chapter. As people milled around, waiting for the guest of honor to arrive, Rory handed a raffle ticket to each person while her mother mingled with the crowd, welcoming everyone and speaking to as many people as possible.

"What's this for?" Mel asked when Rory handed her a ticket from the roll around her arm.

"We're raffling off a basket of Viveca's patterns and a certificate for a class she'll be teaching, as well as some other painting supplies."

"How much?" Mel reached into her purse for her wallet.

"No charge," Rory said. "Just keep half and put the other half in the bowl over there." She waved her hand in the direction of the table where Veronica was snapping a photo of Arika with the raffle items. In front of the basket stood a fishbowl where customers could drop in their tickets.

Moments later, a ball of energy burst through the front door.

"Did I miss anything?" Liz said, a little breathlessly.

Rory smiled at her friend. "She's not here yet. What did you do, run all the way from the hotel?" She looked down at the pumps Liz wore with her black pants, marveling at how fast the woman could travel in heels.

"Just about. I thought for sure I was going to be late." Liz held up a pattern book. "I almost forgot the book I want Viveca to sign."

Mel stared at the front cover of the book, a puzzled expression on her face. "That says Viveca Campbell. I thought her last name was Forster."

"That's a pattern book she published years ago under her maiden name. She got married recently, so she uses Forster now," Rory said before moving on to the next person.

A short time later, Rory was holding the door open for Maybelline when a red Ferrari rounded the corner and whipped into a parking space in front of the store, almost clipping the car in back of it. Viveca emerged from the driver's side of the sports car and waved her sunglasses at the group now crowded around the doorway.

"She always did know how to make an entrance," the older woman said.

"She could've caused an accident," someone said from behind Rory.

"She almost ran into my car the other day. At the time, I didn't know she was the one driving. She hogged both lanes. I had to

swerve to avoid her. I came really close to hitting a parked car."
Rory shuddered at the memory of the red menace bearing down on
her.

Everyone moved aside as Viveca, who had changed into a
colorful dress, entered the store, creating an impromptu tunnel
similar to ones Rory often saw at football games for the home team
to run through onto the field. She half expected cheers to erupt as
the painting teacher walked between the two lines and headed
toward the front counter where Arika waited to greet her. Everyone
was so focused on the guest of honor, few people seemed to notice
Hulbert as he followed his wife inside.

Five minutes later, Arika stood next to the front counter and
rang a hand bell. Veronica made her way to the front, holding her
voice recorder at arm's length so she could capture every word. As
soon as the crowd quieted down, the store owner started her short
speech. "Thanks, everyone, for coming. I'm happy to be hosting this
event honoring Viveca Forster and celebrating her return to
teaching."

"Hear, hear," someone at the back of the crowd shouted. A
smattering of applause approved the sentiment.

Arika waited for the hubbub to die down before continuing.
"Just a few words about the event. All of Viveca's pattern packets
and books are available for purchase. These include the ones she's
reissued as well as several new designs." She pointed toward the
nearby table where the items were laid out in stacks. "Viveca will be
happy to sign them, of course, as well as anything else you brought
with you. Please purchase the books and packets first. Now, I'm
very excited about this next announcement."

She held up two pattern packets, pausing for dramatic effect.
"This is the first time these two new designs will be available for
sale. You couldn't get these at the convention. Be sure to check
them out. We'll also be raffling off a basket filled with an
assortment of Viveca's designs, as well as a certificate that gives the
bearer a spot in a class she'll be teaching in the future." Excited
murmurs ran through the crowd. "Yes, that's right, a weekend class.

Each of you should have a ticket. If you didn't get one, see my daughter. Rory, could you raise your hand, please?"

Rory waved her hand in the air.

"We'll be drawing the raffle tickets a little later. One last thing." The store owner's gaze swept the room. "I see some of you have glasses of champagne or cider already. If you don't have one, now's the time to get one. We'll be making a toast shortly."

The crowd surged toward the refreshment table. People handed filled glasses to their neighbors. Someone thrust a glass of champagne into Rory's hands. Not wanting to drink alcohol at this early hour, she placed the glass on a nearby table and made her way through the crowd to the food area where she snagged a glass of cider for herself and one for Nixie, who was standing nearby. The convention organizer smiled her thanks, then headed toward the front where Viveca stood with her own glass of champagne.

The bell over the front door tinkled, and Detective Green slipped inside the store. Other than Viveca's husband the only man present, he made his way through the crowd to stand beside his girlfriend, who took his hand and smiled up at him. Rory felt a twinge of jealousy, which she quickly pushed to the back of her mind.

As soon as everyone had a glass and had settled down, Arika raised her own. "Here's to Viveca. To your career in tole painting. To everything you've accomplished in the past. To everything you will accomplish in the future. May you have continued success in the years to come."

After everyone raised their glasses and took a sip, the store owner turned to the guest of honor. "Viveca, would you like to say a few words?"

The woman stepped forward. "Thank you, Arika, for hosting this event. I'm so happy to be here. I only wish my niece could have seen the wonderful turnout." She cleared her throat. "I hate to put a damper on such a lovely event, but I'd like to take time to honor Jasmine. A moment of silence, please." She bowed her head. Everyone followed her lead and waited for her to continue. "Thank you." Her gaze swept the room as she raised her glass. "To old friends and new ones. And to my husband, Hulbert Forster, for convincing me to return to painting."

Beaming from ear to ear, Hulbert raised his glass, and along with everyone else, took a sip in celebration.

"Now," Arika continued, "mingle, have fun. Viveca will be at the table over there." She pointed to the table covered with the painter's books and pattern packets. "And don't forget about the raffle."

Rory was kept busy giving out tickets to the handful of people who hadn't received one. A line formed at the register while another began at the table where Viveca had settled down. Before long, the autograph line snaked around the edge of the store. Rory waved at Liz who stood near its front, a pattern book clutched to her chest.

Rory mingled with the other attendees, talking with those she hadn't had a chance to see at the convention. Every so often, she checked with Viveca to see if the woman needed anything. At one point, she motioned for Rory to bend down. "Could we have a chat after this? It's about Jasmine," she whispered. Rory nodded in agreement, wondering what the woman wanted to talk about.

"Does she seem okay to you?" she asked Liz after her friend had gotten her pattern book signed.

"A little tired, I think," Liz said. "A lot of people were asking her about Jasmine. That's probably taken its toll on her."

Rory nodded. She wouldn't be surprised to see the woman collapse from exhaustion after the event was over.

As she moved around the store, she occasionally caught sight of a twentysomething woman with white blonde hair and glasses handing a goldenrod piece of paper to attendees. Some of the woman's targets waved her away while others took the paper and listened politely to what she had to say.

Rory grabbed a discarded flyer out of the trash can. On it was a harangue against the Akaw, detailing how the newly built hotel had ruined the lives of locals and should be boycotted until the hotel's owner fixed all of the problems they were responsible for creating.

When she showed her mother the flyer, Arika frowned. "I don't want anyone spouting propaganda here today. This is supposed to be a fun event, not a political meeting. Who's handing these out?"

After Rory pointed out the culprit, her mother stormed across the sales floor toward the woman, who was trying to shove a flyer in Maybelline's hands. The eighty-year-old refused, stomping her cane on the floor, narrowly missing the other woman's foot. She jumped back, almost running into Rory's mother. Fire in her eyes, Arika thrust out her hand and, in her sweetest voice, said, "Hello, I'm Arika, the owner of this store. Who might you be?"

Uh-oh, Rory thought. Nothing good ever happened when her mother used that tone of voice. You found yourself grounded or doing something you never expected to do, like cleaning out the garage.

"Blondie's in trouble," Liz whispered in a sing-song voice so only her friend could hear.

Rory nodded her head in total agreement.

The blonde-haired woman mumbled something and pushed back her shoulders, trying to look brave, but before she knew what was happening, Arika guided the woman out the door with the rest of her flyers and returned to her invited guests.

"Your mother hasn't lost the touch," Liz said.

Rory silently agreed and went back to talking with people on the floor.

Half an hour remained in the two-hour event when Rory met Nixie at the refreshment table. Somewhere along the way, the woman had switched from cider to champagne.

"How's Ian doing?" Rory asked. "Have you been able to see him?"

"They let me visit him this morning. I think I told you last night, he has a lawyer now. That's a relief. There's talk of extraditing him to Washington state. I don't know what's going to happen to the hotel without him there."

"He and his partners will have to hire another manager," Rory said. "Though I suppose it might cause problems to have one of the owners in jail."

Nixie looked at her, a peculiar expression on her face.

"I know he owns the Akaw with several other people," Rory said. "You didn't know?"

Nixie shook her head. "No, he never told me."

"What about his confession for, you know...?" Rory asked.

"I still don't believe he killed her. I'm not sure the police do, either. He won't tell them any details about how he did it and what he has told them doesn't seem to jibe with the evidence. I know he confessed but, for the life of me, I don't understand why he would tell the police he killed her if he didn't do it."

Rory looked at Nixie with sympathy. She wondered if Ian knew about the embezzlement accusations that Tempest had been flinging around, and if he'd told the police he committed the crime because he thought Nixie killed Jasmine.

"You two are close, right?"

"We've been out a few times recently. We knew each other when we both lived in the Seattle area. I was good friends with his wife. My husband and I convinced him to move down here when she died. He's really helped me out the last six months. I don't know what I'll do with him in jail."

Before she could say anything else, Arika rang the hand bell again. "Could I have your attention, everyone?" As soon as the crowd was quiet enough, she continued, "We're going to be raffling off those items now. Viveca, could you come over here, please?"

Viveca stood up and, a bit unsteadily, headed toward the front of the room where Arika waited for her. Rory watched with concern as the woman made her way through the crowd. The guest of honor had almost reached her destination when she suddenly sank to the floor, unconscious.

Chapter 26

Confusion reigned as everyone talked at once. Hulbert rushed to his wife's side. Mel pushed her way to the front of the crowd while Detective Green held everyone back, clearing a space around the fallen woman so the off-duty paramedic could examine her. While Mel knelt down by Viveca's side, Arika gently guided Hulbert to a stool behind the cash register. The store owner dialed 911 and held the phone up to Mel's face so she could explain the situation to the emergency operator.

Trying to stay out of the way, Rory sank down onto the chair behind the signing table and watched the crowd. She kept her eye on Veronica, afraid she would whip out a camera and start taking pictures. To Rory's great relief, the reporter merely stood to one side and observed the scene before her, occasionally jotting observations down in a spiral-bound notepad.

Rory retrieved a pen and a book that had fallen to the floor. Not until she began straightening the pattern books and packets on the table in front of her did she realize she was sitting in the same chair Viveca had been in right before she collapsed.

After the paramedics came and went with Hulbert accompanying his wife to the hospital, the crowd milled around and talked amongst themselves, no one sure what to do next. People were starting to drift toward the exit when Detective Green held up his hand and called for their attention.

"Before you leave, I'd like to get everyone's name, address, and phone number. Just in case I need to talk with you later," he said.

"Does that mean you think there's something suspicious going on?" someone shouted from the back.

"Not necessarily. It's just a precaution. Thank you all in advance for your cooperation."

"Bit of a cart before the horse, don't you think?" someone behind Rory said. "We don't even know if she's dead yet."

Rory looked around, but couldn't tell who had said the words.

One by one people filed out the front door. The detective pulled out his flip-top notepad and stood next to the exit, writing down each person's name and contact information.

Rory stayed behind the table, straightening and re-straightening the same books and packets as she watched the attendees file out. She was about to throw out the almost empty plastic glass sitting next to the packets when she realized Viveca had probably drunk from it and the police might want to examine it.

Making sure not to touch the glass, Rory used a pattern book to move it closer to her, so she could prevent anyone from contaminating evidence. She motioned Mel over to the table and pointed at the glass. "This is what Viveca was drinking from. Do you think the doctors will want to see it? Would examining the liquid help them figure out how to treat her?"

Before Rory could stop her, Mel picked up the glass and sniffed its contents. "Maybe. You should ask Martin."

The woman returned the glass to the table and joined the exit line. Rory pushed it to the side to make sure no one else touched it. She listened to the conversations going on around her as everyone inched toward the door. Most were talking about Viveca and how sad it was that two people in the same family had collapsed in a similar fashion. Veronica moved down the line, interviewing anyone who would answer her questions as they waited to exit.

A voice, which Rory thought belonged to Mel, mentioned Karma. When she looked around to verify her theory, she spotted the woman halfway down the line, talking with the reporter.

After Detective Green took everyone's information and shooed Veronica out the door, the only people left in the store besides him were Arika, Liz, and Rory.

Rory motioned the detective over to the table. "I think this is the glass Viveca was drinking out of."

"Thanks. Did you touch it?"

"No, but Mel did."

Detective Green raised an eyebrow.

"She was checking it out to see if someone could have drugged it. I asked her to," Rory said.

"I see. Was Viveca drinking champagne or cider?"

"Champagne, I think."

Arika volunteered some paper bags, and the detective packed up the glass as well as the open bottles of cider and champagne for later analysis.

"Do you think her glass was doctored?" Rory asked the detective.

"If it was, we'll find out. Now, tell me what you know about this glass she was drinking from."

"She had it for the toast, I think."

"Did she get it from the refreshment table herself or did someone give it to her?" he continued.

Rory thought back to the presentation and how everyone had rushed to get a drink for the toast. "It was a madhouse. Everyone was trying to get a glass. I have no idea where this one came from."

"Okay. Let me know if you remember more later."

"Wait. There's something else. One of the protesters, a woman with white blonde hair and glasses, left before Viveca collapsed."

"I remember seeing her." Detective Green turned to the store's owner. "Mrs. Anderson, could you keep everything as it is for now? Don't clean up. You can cash out the register. I'd like you to keep the store closed until I know what I'm dealing with."

Arika nodded. "I was planning on closing tomorrow anyway."

As Arika and the detective continued talking, Liz drew Rory aside. "Don't you think it's odd two people from the same family collapsed in similar ways? Maybe there's some family secret you don't know about."

"Maybe," Rory said thoughtfully. "I'll ask Peter when I drop off Jasmine's things. At least we know Ian's not involved. He's in jail."

"That doesn't mean anything. He could have gotten someone else to dose her drink. Nixie was here. They're pretty attached to each other."

"Maybe." Rory thought about the crowd in the store. "Pretty much everyone we thought might have murdered Jasmine was here except Peter and Brandy."

"I guess that lets them off the hook."

"For this, anyway. Unless, of course, they sent someone else like you suggested. But maybe we're getting ahead of ourselves. She could have collapsed from all the stress she was under. She might have simply had a heart attack." Rory looked over at the detective, who was finishing up with her mother. "We'll have to see what the police find out."

With Arika's Scrap 'n Paint temporarily sealed by the police, Rory and her mother headed to the Akaw to pack up the booth and await news about Viveca. Word had spread to the other exhibitors that the painting teacher had collapsed at her meet and greet. As soon as Rory and her mother stepped onto the trade show floor, everyone crowded around them. Talking all at once, they asked questions about the event, some even wanting a blow-by-blow description of everything that happened.

Arika politely waved them all away. As soon as the curious exhibitors realized neither of the two women planned on saying a word, they left the two of them alone to break down the Scrap 'n Paint booth.

Rory brought the empty boxes out from under the tables, and they began the laborious process of packing up the items they hadn't sold during the convention. As Rory stacked wooden plates into a box, she glanced across the aisle. No one appeared to have been in the booth recently. Bottles still stood on the shelves, waiting for someone to pack them up.

"Do you think Hulbert will need help with his booth?" Rory said to her mother.

"We should ask. When we're done here, I'll see what I can find out," Arika said before returning to packing up two-ounce bottles of acrylic paint.

The two worked steadily and, less than an hour later, three-quarters of the booth was repacked. Rory was beginning to take apart and collapse the fixtures when, clipboard in hand, Nixie stopped by.

"Just wanted to let you know about the change of schedule," the convention organizer said. "We've had some personnel...issues in the hotel since Ian was arrested." She was about to say more when another exhibitor drew the woman aside to ask a question.

Rory wondered if "personnel issues" was code for people quitting. Once word spread about Ian's arrest and confession, some of the hotel's employees might no longer want to be associated with the Akaw.

"Sorry about that," Nixie said when she returned. "As I was saying, the hotel is understaffed at the moment. We're going to have to push everything out a day. You can continue packing up, but we won't be able to get the boxes out onto the loading dock until tomorrow afternoon."

Arika opened her mouth to ask a question, but the convention organizer raised a hand to stop her.

"Don't worry, everything will be safe here on the floor. But I'm afraid that means no trucks will be able to pick up your boxes until Tuesday."

Once Nixie answered all her questions, Arika pulled out her phone to inform the moving company she'd hired of the change in plans.

As the convention organizer started to move on to the next booth, Rory asked, "Have you heard anything? About Viveca?"

"Not yet." Nixie nodded toward the VivEco booth, where two employees had arrived and were pulling boxes out from underneath the tables. "Maybe they know something."

When the two women headed across the aisle to inquire after Viveca, the temp employees told them the dreadful, but not unexpected, news that the woman had passed away at the hospital.

After giving her condolences and offering to help them pack up if they needed it, Rory silently prayed for Viveca and her family, then headed back across the aisle to tell her mother the news.

Chapter 27

Once the two booths were all packed up, Rory headed across town to Peter's house to drop off Jasmine's things. As she wheeled the suitcases up the walkway, she wondered if anyone had told Peter about Viveca.

When he opened the door in answer to the bell, one look at his face and she realized he knew.

"You heard?" she said.

"Hulbert called a little while ago." Peter helped her bring the cases inside and set them to one side of the entryway.

"Everything that was in her room is in the suitcase and carry-on." Rory pointed to the roller bag decorated with his wife's name. "And these are Jasmine's painting supplies."

"Thanks for doing this. Let's talk for a minute. Do you want some tea?" He led the way into the kitchen, where Rory sat down on a chair at the island while Peter put the kettle on the stove. "I hope Earl Grey is okay. It's all we have. It's decaffeinated."

"Sounds good. Did Hulbert have any information on how Viveca died?"

"GHB again."

"Can't be Jasmine's medication this time. The police have it. Unless there's another bottle around somewhere?"

Peter leaned against the island. "No, that was the only one. There has to be another source. I did a little research just now, after he told me. Seems like GHB isn't hard to come by. People even make it in their own homes. Looks like water so it's often tinted blue. Did you know some people use it for weight loss and increasing muscle growth? Seems dangerous to me."

Before he could say anything else, the tea kettle sang. They suspended their conversation while he busied himself with the cups and tea bags. He set two cups on the island and sat down next to Rory.

"First Jasmine, now her aunt. I have to wonder if there's some family connection we don't know about. Something that they were both involved with," Rory said. "Can you think of anything the two of them did together that would be a reason someone might want both of them dead?"

Peter stared down into his cup as if looking for answers in the tea. "If there is, I know nothing about it."

"What about some event they both attended where something bad happened? Did they witness anything? An altercation? An accident? That kind of thing."

"Accident." Peter looked up from his tea and turned his head to look into Rory's eyes. "Viveca was involved in an accident years ago. Her fault. You must remember it."

The way the woman had driven that Ferrari around town, Rory wasn't surprised to learn she'd crashed a car at some point in time, but she couldn't recall ever hearing about it. "I don't remember her being hurt in a car accident. Was it a fender bender or something more serious?"

"She wasn't hurt. Only minor damage to her car, but the other driver wasn't so lucky."

"What happened?"

"It was raining. Viveca was driving fast, too fast like she always did. She skidded and caused another car to go off the road and crash." Peter told the story as if he'd recited it many times. "Jaz still occasionally had nightmares about it."

"Why?"

"She was in the passenger seat. Didn't she ever tell you?"

Rory shook her head. "No, I guess she wanted to put it behind her. When and where was this?"

"Somewhere close to home, Riverside area. I don't remember the exact location. Around the time Jaz's mother died."

That's probably why Rory hadn't heard anything about the accident. Everyone was preoccupied with Jasmine's mother's illness. Her friend wouldn't have wanted to worry anyone about a minor accident. Minor for her and her aunt, at least.

"Would the accident have been mentioned in the paper?" she asked.

"I don't remember seeing anything about it, but I wasn't really a newspaper reader when I was a teenager."

They both tried to recall if there was something else from either of the two women's pasts that might be cause for someone to want them both dead, but neither Peter nor Rory could come up with a single thing.

Peter stared down into his cup. "Brandy called me. She's upset at you. I don't know what about. She wouldn't say." He looked at Rory and appealed to her with his eyes. "Whatever it is, you two need to make up. Life's too short."

Rory patted his hand. "Don't worry, I'll call her."

As soon as she settled down in her car, Rory took a deep breath and made the call. After a heartfelt talk, she invited Brandy to have dinner with her and Liz that evening.

On her way home, Rory wondered if the accident could be the key to both deaths. The reemergence of Viveca into the public eye might have stirred up old wounds. She needed to find out more about that accident.

Rory glanced at the clock on her dashboard. She had time before she needed to get ready for dinner. She turned a corner and headed for the library, glad this was the one Sunday in the month when it was open until five.

When she entered the glass building, she walked straight to the reference desk and asked about back issues of Southern California newspapers. The librarian directed her to a service the

Vista Beach library subscribed to where papers across the country could be read and searched. She settled down at a free computer and typed in Viveca's maiden name. Within seconds, half a dozen articles showed up in one of the Riverside papers.

She read the headlines for each of them, discovering most were feature stories that described local charities the woman had been involved with or talked about her career as a designer and painting instructor.

In a story in the news section, a reporter described a horrific accident in which Viveca and a sixteen-year-old relative had come out unscathed, but the female driver of another car had died, leaving the passenger in critical condition. The photo that accompanied the article showed a vehicle mangled beyond recognition. Rory was surprised anyone had come out of the accident alive, but a teenager who was in the passenger seat had somehow managed to survive. She took note of the driver's unfamiliar name.

In a later article, the father of the driver who had been killed railed against the police for not arresting Viveca even though accident reconstruction had shown her actions had been at least partially responsible for the other car spinning out of control. For some reason that wasn't clear to Rory, the authorities declined to prosecute.

She sat back in her seat and thought about what she'd read. Something nudged at her brain. She wondered if a relative of the driver who had been killed could have held a grudge for all these years. Her best bet was to try to find out more about the victim. When a librarian warned everyone the place was closing in five minutes, Rory prepared to finish her research outside of the library. She quickly found the obituary of the woman who had died in the accident and printed it out along with the two other articles.

A short time later, she was pulling her car into a spot in the Akaw's underground parking structure when she spotted Hulbert slumped against the trunk of Viveca's red Ferrari a few spaces away, looking like a man whose entire world had been shattered.

Rory's heart went out to him. She locked her own sedan and hurried over to see what she could do to help.

"Hulbert," she said. "How are you doing? Do you need any help?"

When he heard his name, the man came out of his fog and looked up at her. His face seemed to have aged ten years since she last saw him. "Aurora, I didn't expect to see you here."

"I didn't expect to see you, either. I'm so sorry about Viveca. She was always very nice to me."

The man blinked furiously as if fighting back tears. In a voice choked with emotion, he said, "She was a lovely woman. I felt so lucky I'd found her so late in life. I miss her already."

"What are you doing here?" Rory asked. "I thought you'd be home."

"I was upstairs, checking to make sure the booth got packed up properly. Someone had to do it. It's just me running things now. My workers tell me you helped them out. I appreciate that." He laid a hand on the Ferrari. "This was Viveca's pride and joy. I wish I didn't have to part with it."

Rory was wondering why he couldn't keep it when the man looked at her, a fierce expression on his face. "This is the worst day of my life. Mark my words, I'm going to get back at the person who's responsible for my lovely Viveca's death."

"I'll do anything I can to help."

He smiled and patted her on the arm. "You've done enough already."

While Hulbert settled into the driver's seat of the Ferrari, she headed to the elevator.

Rory sat in the lobby of the Akaw, waiting for Liz to finish teaching her final class of the painting convention, and reviewed the printouts of the newspaper articles she'd found at the library. She read the obituary, not finding anything interesting until she reached the end where it listed all of the deceased's surviving relatives. One name stood out: Melosia Ortega, described as a sixteen-year-old cousin.

Rory did a quick calculation in her head. The cousin would be about twenty-eight now. She'd never asked the Melosia she knew how old she was but, if Rory had to guess, she'd have said they were about the same age. That fit with the time frame of the accident.

Rory laid the paper on her lap and stared off into space, thinking back to the conversation she'd had with Mel at the karaoke bar. The woman had mentioned an accident she was in when she was young that had inspired her to become a paramedic. Plus, Detective Green had said his girlfriend had relatives in the Riverside area. She didn't know how common the name Melosia Ortega was, but this couldn't be a coincidence. They had to be the same person.

For a moment, Rory was too shocked to consider the implications of what she'd learned. She didn't want to believe the woman she was starting to consider a friend could have killed Viveca. But she had motive. From their conversation the previous evening, Rory knew the woman still harbored anger at the driver who had killed her beloved cousin. As for opportunity, anyone could have spiked the painting teacher's drink at the meet and greet, including Mel. The woman had even touched Viveca's glass after her collapse. If she were guilty, she might have planned that to cover up any fingerprints already on the glass. Mel might even have targeted Jasmine because she was in the car with her aunt, blaming her for distracting Viveca while she was driving. And, as someone in the medical field, Mel would probably be more likely to know where to get GHB than anyone else.

Rory tried to picture the event and remember where Mel had been throughout the meet and greet, but she couldn't say for sure how close the woman had been to Viveca at any particular point in time. The store had been too crowded, and Rory had been busy making sure everything was running okay.

Rory hugged her sweatshirt, feeling a coldness invading her soul. She wished a pill existed that she could take to unthink the thoughts she was having. She couldn't tell Detective Green what she discovered, but she didn't want Viveca's murderer to go free either.

Her only hope was that she would find out her suspicions were wrong.

She was trying to figure out how she could determine if Mel was involved in Viveca's death when Detective Green walked across the lobby toward her. She leaned over and, as unobtrusively as possible, stuck the papers on the cushion, then settled back down on top of them and stared at her phone, pretending to be engrossed with something on its display.

The detective smiled and indicated the spot next to her on the sofa. "May I?"

Rory nodded, even though what she really wanted to say was "no, no, no!"

"Mel told me she had fun at karaoke and that you're getting together for dinner tomorrow night. Thanks for making her feel so welcome."

Rory nodded, not trusting herself to speak.

The detective's eyes narrowed. "Are you okay? What's going on?"

She wished he could stop being a detective for one minute. "Just sitting here, waiting for Liz, reading some email. That's it."

"Uh-huh." He studied her from head to toe. She suspected he was analyzing her body language. At that moment, she knew she was sunk. He nodded at the sofa. "What are you sitting on?"

Rory glanced down at the cushion. A corner of one of the printouts peeked out from under her butt. Her face reddened. She shifted her position so her body covered the paper completely.

"Have you been investigating when I told you not to?" The detective held out his hand. "Come on. Hand it over. Let me see what you've been up to."

Silently, she stood up and retrieved the papers. Once they were in the detective's hands, she studied his face, dreading his reaction when he recognized his girlfriend's name. The seconds seemed like hours as he carefully read each article, starting with the one on the top, the obituary of Mel's cousin.

She could tell when he got to Mel's name. A puzzled look came over his face. He looked up at her and said, "Why do you have an obituary for one of my girlfriend's relatives?"

When she didn't say anything, he studied the other articles, frowning as he read. After he finished all of them, he sat back in his seat and stared into space. She could almost hear the wheels turning in his head as he digested and analyzed the articles with his detective's brain.

Finally, he said without looking at her, "Let me get this straight. You think my girlfriend's a murderer, do you? And these articles are the proof?"

Her mouth opened and closed several times, but she couldn't think of anything to say.

A steely look in his eyes, he stared at her and said in a quiet tone of voice, "Answer me, please."

She almost wished he would yell at her. Anything was better than this quiet disapproval.

"I was looking into the accident Viveca was in years ago. I didn't know until I read the articles that Mel was in the other car. It's not like I set out to investigate her. I like Mel, but you have to admit she's a pretty good suspect. If she weren't your girlfriend, you'd see that."

Detective Green's lips tightened. "I see." He folded the printouts and set them aside. "I'm taking these with me. You really need to stop investigating. Leave that to the professionals." He drew a flip-top notepad and a pen out of an inside jacket pocket. "Now, I need to ask you some questions."

"Okay," Rory said. The sudden coldness in the man's demeanor disturbed her more than she cared to let on. "What do you need to know?"

"The glass Viveca was drinking from at the event today. Are you sure you didn't touch it? It was on the table in front of you."

"I'm sure. As soon as I realized whose glass it was, I made sure no one touched it, including me. Well, except Mel, of course." Rory closed her eyes and pictured the meet and greet, once again trying to remember everything she'd done during the event, from the moment she arrived at the store to the moment she left. "I'm positive I never touched the glass," she said in a firmer tone of voice.

"Are you sure? You didn't pour glasses of champagne and hand them out to people?"

"My mom set up the refreshment table. I took care of the signing table. Everyone got their own glasses. Why do you ask?"

"I'm just wondering why your fingerprints are on the glass Viveca was drinking from."

Rory's mouth fell open. "I have no idea. Was the GHB in the bottle of champagne?"

"Just in the glass. You said before you didn't know who gave it to her. Have you remembered anything new?"

"No." Rory considered the problem for a minute. "But I think I know how we can find out. Stella Nygaard was filming at least part of the event for her painting chapter. Some of the footage may show where the glass came from. I can call her and see if she's available."

After Detective Green nodded his head in approval, Rory called Stella and relayed their request. Ten minutes later, the woman joined them in the lobby.

"These three videos are the ones I took at Viveca's event." Stella played each of them on her smartphone, one after the other. The first one showed the event from the moment Viveca arrived to right before Arika started her speech. Rory saw the woman with white blonde hair mingling with the other attendees.

They scoured the footage to see if Viveca was drinking from a glass during this period, but her hands were empty. The second video started with Arika's initial remarks. When it reached the spot where she encouraged everyone to get something to drink for the toast, they watched carefully to see where the guest of honor got her glass.

"Right there." Rory pointed at the phone's display. "She has one now."

"Let's go back and see if we can spot where it came from," Detective Green said.

Stella backed up the footage until they saw the moment the woman picked up the glass off the signing table. She paused the video at the spot.

"Rewind some more. See who put it there," the detective directed.

Rory's mouth dropped open when she saw her own hand place the glass on the table. "That was my glass."

Detective Green stared at the frame, then at Rory. "Why did you put it on the table? Were you putting it there for Viveca to take? That is where she sat during most of the event."

Rory shook her head vigorously. "No. I just didn't want alcohol that early in the day so I set it down and went to get a glass of sparkling cider instead." She stared in horror at the man. "It was meant for me, wasn't it? The GHB."

"Certainly looks that way." He motioned to Stella. "Back it up a bit more. Let's see if we can see where Rory got that glass."

As they watched that section of the video again, Rory looked for the moment when she first held the glass in her hand. While they could see when she had it in her hand, they couldn't tell where she'd gotten it from.

"Do you remember where you got it?" Detective Green asked.

Rory replayed the moment in her mind. "Someone handed it to me." She looked him straight in the eyes. "But I don't remember who."

"Are you sure?"

"Yes," Rory said, her voice becoming fainter as the implications of the revelation finally sunk in. "There were too many people around."

As Stella played the last clip, Rory's mind wasn't on the actions in the video, but on what would have happened if she'd drunk from the glass. *Someone wanted her dead* ran over and over in her mind. Jasmine's murderer might not have liked her investigating. Or maybe Oscar Carlton had sent someone to drug her in retaliation for her foiling his blackmail scheme.

After all the footage had been reviewed, Detective Green

thanked Stella for her time. Before the woman left she said to Rory, "Could you take me to the airport tomorrow afternoon? I have a flight from LAX."

After agreeing on a time to meet in the lobby, Stella went on her way.

As soon as the woman was out of earshot, the detective said, "What have you been up to that someone would want you dead? Have you done something you haven't told me about?"

It must have something to do with her investigation into Jasmine's death, Rory thought. She remained silent, unsure what to say.

Detective Green studied her for a moment, then stood up. "Let me know if you think of anything." He stuffed his notepad and the newspaper articles in his pocket and, without looking back, walked out the front door of the hotel.

As the automatic doors closed behind him, all Rory wanted to do was run to her parents' house and feel her mother's comforting arms around her.

When Liz walked into the lobby, tote bag full of painting supplies slung over one shoulder, and carrying a box of extra wood pieces that hadn't been used in her class, she sank down on the couch next to Rory. She took one look at her friend and said, "What happened?"

In halting words, Rory told Liz what she'd discovered about Viveca, the accident, how Jasmine was in the car, and how Mel's cousin was in the other car and had been killed.

"I didn't intend to tell him. I really didn't. I would never have shown him those articles unless I knew, for sure, that Mel had killed Viveca. I tried to hide them from him," Rory insisted. "He was angry. I mean, really, really angry."

"He'll get over it."

But will his girlfriend? Rory wondered. She hadn't intended to hurt the woman. "I don't think he believed me when I said I didn't remember where the glass that had the GHB in it came from, either."

When Liz looked confused, Rory explained what they'd discovered from the video Stella had taken of the event about the glass Viveca drank from.

Liz curled her feet under her. "Wow. Certainly sounds like you were the target. Maybe we should take you to a hypnotist. They can help people remember things they didn't realize they knew."

"I don't think that would work. I'm pretty sure I didn't see anything."

"Pretty sure is not definite."

Rory glanced at the time on her cell phone. "We don't have time for it now. We'd better get going. Brandy's waiting for us to pick her up for dinner. We can talk about this later."

As they headed to the car, Rory vowed to buy some of those test coasters the college student had told her about. From now on, she intended to test every liquid she drank in a public place before taking a single sip.

Chapter 28

After picking up Brandy, the three young women stopped off at a local Chinese takeout place and bought their dinner.

When Rory pulled into her driveway, Brandy peered through the window of the car at the single-story stucco house. "This is where you live?" she said, a note of dismay in her voice.

"What did you expect?" Rory asked.

"I'm not sure. When you said you inherited a house from your grandmother, I thought it would be...Never mind, I don't know what I was thinking, to be honest."

"It's a nice place. I really love it. Very Goldilocks. Not too big, not too small. Just the right size for me."

Brandy looked at Rory, an apology in her eyes. "I didn't mean to hurt your feelings. I'm just not thinking these days, you know."

"Let's go in the front door so Brandy can get the full effect," Rory said to the two other women.

Liz got out of the car and headed toward the porch, carrying the bags of food. Instead of following her, Brandy walked across the lawn and stood in front of the window that had been replaced. Rory went over to join her friend.

"Is this it?" Brandy said. "The one that was damaged?"

"That's right. How did you know?"

Brandy gestured toward the bush obscuring the bottom inch or two of the glass. "Some of the branches are broken. I just figured."

After they studied the window for a few minutes, Rory said, "Let's go inside. The food's getting cold."

Brandy took a last lingering look at the area before heading over to the front door.

The three of them trooped inside and settled down in the living room with their food. Rory sat in a chair while the other two young women shared the couch. Balancing plates on their laps, they served themselves from containers filled with kung pao chicken, beef with broccoli, sweet and sour chicken, and vegetable eggrolls. During dinner, the three of them talked about the convention and Brandy's plans for the future.

After she finished eating, Liz walked over to study the window that had been replaced. "The glass people did a nice job. Doesn't even look like you need to paint. You'll have to give me their name so I can recommend them to my clients." She returned to the living room and curled up on the sofa next to Brandy. "Have the police found out who threw the rock yet?"

Rory set her empty plate on the coffee table and picked up her water glass. "No. I doubt they ever will. The guy I saw outside the Akaw handing out flyers denied that his protest group had anything to do with it."

"He's right," Brandy said. "We're better than that. And any warning messages we'd give out wouldn't be printed on pink paper."

Rory peered at her friend over her glass, studied her face for a minute, then carefully placed the glass down on the coffee table. "What did you say?"

"The note. It was stupid."

Rory did her best to channel Detective Green's steely gaze as she stared at her friend. "How do you know the note was printed, not written, on *pink* paper?"

"It was in the newspaper." Brandy looked from Liz's open mouth to Rory's hard gaze. "Wasn't it?" she finally squeaked out.

"No, it wasn't. So how did you know?" Rory said.

"Lucky guess?"

Rory thought back to junior high and the games of softball she'd endured during P.E. class. Brandy had thrown a ball farther and faster than anyone else, even then. "You threw it, didn't you? You're the one who broke my window."

"I didn't know it was your house, honest. I didn't even know the address of the place we hit. The driver just stopped the car and pointed at your house, told me I should throw the rock through that window. Then I got back in the car and we drove off as fast as we could."

"So when I asked you about it in the hotel room, you were lying. When you found out a rock went through my window, you must have known it was my house you hit."

"No." Brandy vehemently shook her head. "I thought someone else in the group had thrown the rock through your window. A bunch of us went out in pairs, a driver and a thrower, I guess you'd call it. We each had a house to hit, all over town, at the same time. I figured I'd hit someone else's."

"That's just what you wanted to believe," Liz said.

"The man I saw passing out the flyers outside the hotel denied his group did the egging or the rock throwing. He was very adamant about it," Rory said.

"Did he have a goatee and tattoo here?" Brandy touched the right side of her neck.

"That's right."

"He wasn't lying."

Rory threw up her hands in frustration. "What are you talking about? You can't have it both ways. Either the group threw the eggs and the rocks or they didn't. Unless..." She cocked her head. "...are we talking two groups?"

"That's right. Brian, that's the name of the guy with the tattoo, wanted to be all sit-in and peaceful protest. We had a hard time convincing him to plant the stink bomb. He finally agreed when we told him they'd stunk up our lives, so we should stink up theirs. He liked the way that sounded. Anyway, a group of us decided to...branch out."

"Like a rogue element?" Liz asked.

"That's right."

"Whose idea was that?" Rory asked.

Brandy took a deep breath. "Jasmine's."

Rory blinked several times, not quite believing what she'd just heard. "Our Jasmine?"

Brandy nodded.

Rory put her head in her hands. She was having trouble keeping everything straight in her mind. She couldn't keep track of what was a lie and what was the truth. She sat up and looked into Brandy's eyes. "So everything you told me in the hotel room about Jasmine and how she followed you because she thought you and Peter were having an affair was a lie?"

"Not everything. She really did think we were having an affair, which we weren't, but that wasn't the reason she was in the room."

"Tell it to me once again," Rory said. "From the beginning. Don't leave anything out. The whole truth this time."

Brandy stared at the wall opposite her, gathering her thoughts. She took a deep breath before launching into her explanation. "Okay. Where should I start? Jasmine knew about my involvement with the protesters from the beginning. She wanted to support me, so she attended one of our meetings. She understood my concerns better than anyone else about my aunt's health problems. Anyway, when Brian shot down some of our more...aggressive ideas, she suggested branching off."

When Brandy paused for breath, Rory said, "But that still doesn't explain why Jasmine was in the hotel room."

"I'm getting to that. She knew I booked the room for the group so I'd have some place to change after planting the stink bomb. She volunteered her own room, but I didn't want her to be implicated if something went wrong. The alarm wasn't part of the plan, so after the all-clear was given, she came up to the room to see if I knew anything about it. And I didn't, honestly. Then, I assume, she went to class."

Rory mulled over what she'd learned. If Jasmine was involved with this rogue element of the protesters, maybe it had been a factor in her death. One of the group had come into the store during the event, trying to pass out flyers. Maybe she'd planted the GHB in Rory's drink before getting kicked out. And maybe she'd put the Xyrem in Jasmine's soda. Rory didn't remember seeing the woman with white blonde hair in the hotel, but that didn't mean she wasn't there. Though how the woman had gotten access to the medicine, Rory didn't know.

"There was a woman handing out flyers at the meet and greet earlier today. Do you know who that was? White blonde hair, glasses."

"That sounds like Always."

"Always?" Rory raised an eyebrow.

"Don't ask. Hippie parents."

"Is she part of your splinter group?" Liz asked.

"That's right. Why, what do you think she did?"

"She could have spiked my drink," Rory said.

"But why?"

"That's what I want to find out." Rory studied her friend, who squirmed under her steady gaze. "We're going to infiltrate the protesters, and you're going to help us."

"I can't do that." Brandy seemed horror-stricken at the idea. "They'd never allow you in. Besides, they targeted you. Everyone knows who you are."

"Who's this 'they' you're talking about?" Liz said. "You're the one who threw the rock through Rory's window."

Brandy had the grace to blush. "I already told you both, I didn't know it was your house. No one told me you were involved, either. I'd never have done it otherwise."

"You shouldn't have been throwing rocks in the first place." Rory waved her hand as if dismissing the subject. "Doesn't matter now. Anyway, I'm not the one who'll be attending the meeting. She will." She nodded toward Liz, who grinned when the news sunk in.

"How soon can you get her in?" Rory asked.

"There's a meeting tonight," Brandy reluctantly admitted.

"Good," Rory said. "Liz will go to the meeting and I'll listen in on the discussion."

"How?" Brandy asked. "You can't hide in the shrubs. The neighbors will notice."

"Don't need to do that." Rory held up her cell. "Liz will dial my number right before you two go inside and leave the phone on."

"But what do you hope to learn? Do you think the protesters had something to do with Viveca's death? Or Jasmine's?"

Rory leaned forward. "I think it's a possibility. Now, let's talk strategy."

A couple hours later, the three of them drove back to the Akaw. Liz picked up her car and drove herself and Brandy to the meeting at a house three blocks from the hotel. Rory parked her own car on the street down the block. She moved her seat back as far as it would go, pushed the recline lever, and settled in for a long evening.

She'd just made herself comfortable when her cell phone rang. She put the call on speaker and set the phone on her lap.

"Are you there?" Liz whispered.

"I'm here."

"We're going in now. I'm putting the phone in my pocket. I hope this works."

Me too, Rory thought.

Rory relaxed into the seat and closed her eyes, listening to the sound of a door opening and introductions being made. Then came a period where she imagined the group was settling down in the living room or wherever they were conducting the meeting. For a while, all she could hear was the faint rustle from the phone and the regular sound of her own breathing. She was dozing off when someone clapped their hands, startling her awake, and called the meeting to order.

The leader asked the new members to introduce themselves. Liz explained how she was a real estate agent in the city and, after hearing about the problems with selling houses in the affected neighborhood, she became concerned about how little responsibility the owner of the hotel was taking for them.

"Hear, hear," someone said.

Rory's stomach growled. She picked up a candy bar she'd brought with her. When she tried to open the wrapper, the chocolate bar slipped out of her fingers and fell onto the floor. She groped around for it, swearing when she couldn't immediately lay her hand on her snack.

"What was that?" the leader said.

"Sounded like swearing," someone else said.

Rory froze. To her horror, she realized she'd forgotten to mute her phone and the group on the other end of the line could hear everything she did and said. After hastily correcting the problem, she anxiously waited to hear if Liz had been discovered.

After a minute or two, the group resumed their conversation, making no more references to the mysterious noise.

Rory relaxed and continued to listen to the meeting.

At one point, the leader chastised Brandy for failing to plant the second stink bomb. When she explained she'd been discovered, everyone murmured their concern. Rory thought for a minute Brandy was going to mention Rory's name, but her friend told them someone from the hotel staff had interrupted her and, after some fast talking, she'd managed to get away.

The meeting droned on and on. For a splinter group, they're pretty boring, Rory thought.

She was wondering if the battery on her cell would hold out when the meeting finally ended. She despaired of learning anything useful when she heard Liz say, "Didn't I see you at the event at Arika's Scrap 'n Paint today?"

She must be talking to the woman who was handing out the flyers.

"That's right. The harpy who owns the store kicked me out. I'm Always, by the way."

Rory fought the urge to leap out of her car, run down the block, and burst in on the meeting so she could punch Always in the mouth for the name the woman had called her mother. Instead, she took a couple deep breaths and calmed herself down.

"You missed all the excitement. The guest of honor collapsed."

"That really tall woman? Looks like a model?"

"That's her. That's Viveca."

"What was it? A heart attack?" Always sounded almost bored.

"No. Poison in her champagne."

A sharp intake of breath. "Do they know who did it?"

"Not yet. They're looking at everyone who was there. The police will probably call you sometime to ask you some questions."

"It would be just like the cops to try to pin it on me."

"If you can prove you weren't anywhere near Viveca's glass, you shouldn't have a problem."

A pause where Rory imagined the wheels turning in the woman's brain. "There was this woman who had a stupid camera plastered to her forehead. I think she was taking video or something. That can prove where I was."

"Then you have nothing to worry about. Just tell the police that when they talk to you."

"You know that Rory person, don't you? I've seen you talking to her."

Rory held her breath, sure this time that their scheme had been discovered.

"We both attended the painting convention," Liz said in a very casual tone of voice as if she barely knew the person Always had asked about.

"Were you there when she read the post I put on the convention's Facebook page? I bet she was pissed."

"That was you? She actually said that to you?"

"Of course not. I just wanted to rile things up a bit."

Rory stared down at the phone, not believing what she'd just heard. At least now she knew who the mysterious person was who'd posted the comment on the convention's page.

The rest of the call was a mixture of idle chit-chat and the murmurs of indistinguishable voices. It ended with Liz whispering,

"We're coming out now. Brandy's going to the car. Stay in yours. I'll come find you."

A tap on the window moments later, inches away from her head, caused Rory to jump. She looked up to discover Detective Green peering at her. He mimed rolling down the window.

As surreptitiously as possible, Rory set her cell down in the storage bin between the seats. She returned her seat to its upright position and pressed the button for the driver's side window.

The detective leaned casually against the car and peered inside. "Whatcha doin'?"

"Nothing," was Rory's unimaginative answer.

"Open the passenger door for me," he said in his most commanding voice.

Rory obediently unlocked the door. The detective climbed into the front seat and closed the door behind him. She shut her eyes for a moment and drank in the musky scent that wafted toward her. He hadn't smelled this good earlier in the day. She wondered what the special occasion was.

The detective cleared his throat, bringing her back to her senses. He twisted around in the seat to face her. "You've been parked here for some time. So long someone called to complain."

"Do you respond to all calls from nervous neighbors? I would have thought that was a uniformed officer's job."

"An officer did respond. You just didn't see him. They've all been told if they get a call that involves your car to call me and let me deal with it."

"They have?" Rory squeaked out.

"Now, would you care to explain why you're parked here? You don't live anywhere near here and neither do your parents."

She didn't bother to ask how he knew where her parents lived. He'd probably looked that up when he was investigating her a couple months ago. "I ran out of gas?" She didn't really expect him to believe her, but she thought she would give it a try.

"You'll have to do better than that."

Rory was tempted to respond with "Will I?" but thought better of it. "I was on the phone, that's all. Just wanted a quiet place to talk." At least the phone part was true, she thought.

"So you left your house, drove all the way here to park on this street and make a call." He raised an eyebrow.

"I was on the way home when I got a call, okay? You wouldn't want me to talk and drive, would you? That would be against the law." She mentally crossed her fingers, hoping he wouldn't ask why, since she was a programmer and familiar with electronic gadgets, she didn't have a hands-free device.

He stared at her for what seemed like forever before his face relaxed. She was certain she'd convinced him she was telling the truth when a ball of energy sped across the street and poked her head in the driver's side window.

"Did you get all that?" Liz said before noticing the man sitting beside Rory. "Oh, sorry, didn't know you had company."

She started to back away when Detective Green said, "Ms. Dexter, why don't you join us? I think we're about due for a little chat." The commanding tone in his voice and the stern expression on his face indicated he didn't intend to take no for an answer.

Rory nodded at Liz and unlocked the back door. Liz settled down in the seat behind her friend.

The detective gave each of them a stern look. "Now, what have you two been up to *this* time?"

Chapter 29

After a grilling and several warnings, Detective Green let the two of them go. Liz promised to meet back at Rory's place, then returned to her car and took Brandy home while Rory headed back to Seagull Lane.

Half an hour later, Liz settled down on the couch in the living room with a glass of water. "That was fun. Up until Dashing D chewed us out, that is."

"I wasn't happy to have him knocking on my window. Did you know he's told everyone in the police department to call him if my car is involved in a police matter?"

"Ah, he cares." Liz giggled from behind her water glass. "Did you get a whiff of his cologne? The man smells go-o-o-od. I don't remember that from before. Maybe he was on a date with Mel when he got the call."

Rory groaned inwardly. "As if she doesn't have enough reason to dislike me. I hope he hasn't told her about those newspaper articles. Mel and I are supposed to have dinner tomorrow night."

Liz waved her hand in the air in a dismissive gesture. "I'm sure it's fine. Let's get back to the meeting. Nothing really of interest happened except for that conversation I had with Always. She said Stella was filming at the event."

"I've seen the footage. Stella didn't film everything," Rory said. "As far as I remember, Always wasn't anywhere near the signing table or Viveca's glass. But we couldn't tell where the glass originally came from. What reason would the protesters have for going after me, anyway?"

"You're the one who wanted to investigate them."

"I know, I know."

"You think you were the target. Maybe Viveca was the real target after all."

"But it was in the glass someone gave me." Rory pointed a finger at her own chest. "We're not getting anywhere on Viveca's death. How about going back to Jasmine's?"

"Has Miss Snoop posted anything interesting on VBC? I haven't checked in a while."

"Let's take a look." The two of them gathered around the computer. Rory brought up the blog on the screen, and they read Veronica's account of the aborted meet and greet.

In a matter-of-fact reporting style, Veronica described the event and the chaos that had erupted when the guest of honor collapsed. For once, the woman didn't try to embellish. Just a brief description of the efforts to save Viveca followed by a few quotes from some of the shocked attendees.

"Pretty subdued for Veronica," Liz said. "Can I see some of the earlier posts? I haven't had a chance to read the blog lately."

The two switched places. Liz read through the last few entries while Rory looked over her friend's shoulder. When Liz came to the photos that had been posted, she pointed to one. "This candid shot of Hulbert and Jasmine isn't bad. That's the hotel restaurant, right? I recognize that statue. I wonder when it was taken."

"I thought it was nice too. I printed it out and gave a copy to Hulbert. It was taken the day she died, probably right after she left the gift shop. You can see the soda in her hand."

Liz peered at the screen. "That's not a soda bottle."

"It's not? What is it, then?"

"Don't know. Probably something she picked up on the trade show floor." Liz yawned. "It's past my bedtime. Vacation's over. I have to get back to work tomorrow."

Liz left and, after spending half an hour more on the computer, Rory headed to bed.

As soon as Rory settled down to work the next morning, she found an alert from her bank in her inbox, telling her that Nixie's check had bounced. When her call to the convention organizer went straight to voicemail, she put off dealing with the problem until later that afternoon.

Rory worked through lunch, then headed to downtown Vista Beach to run errands before picking up Stella for the short drive to LAX. As she passed Oscar Carlton's office, she saw Hulbert exiting the building. Suspecting he'd hired the PI to look into Viveca's death, she added *talk to Hulbert* to her to-do list, wanting to make sure he knew the police now believed his wife wasn't the killer's intended target.

After parking on a street near the hotel, Rory walked around town, going in and out of stores, occasionally returning to her car to stash her purchases in the trunk. Her final trip was to the pharmacy where she picked up the test coasters she'd vowed to buy the previous day.

On her way back to her car, she took a favorite shortcut between two apartment buildings. Halfway down the passageway, a homeless man leaned against a wall, his eyes closed, apparently sleeping. In front of him was a hat and a hand-lettered sign that read: *Homeless veteran. Spare change welcome.*

Rory was bending down to put a handful of change in the hat when the man's hand closed around her right arm in a viselike grip. She stared into his eyes and gasped when she realized she was looking at Oscar Carlton in disguise. She pulled away, trying to wrest her arm from his grasp, but he held on tight and drew her closer. Soon her face was close enough to his that she could see every pore and individual hair on the man's face.

"I have a video of you. I could call the police and show it to them."

She swatted his arm with the paper bag she held in her left hand, but he merely laughed at her feeble attempts to free herself. She looked around for something she could use to break his hold on her, but all she saw was a discarded ping pong ball and a flyer for a local bar. When she opened her mouth to scream, his fingers dug into her arm.

"I wouldn't do that if I were you."

"That hurts. What do you want from me?"

"Good. You're going to pay for every dime you lost me with that Blalock fellow. And you're going to stop investigating those deaths."

"The police already know everything I've done," Rory said, doing her best to make the words sound convincing.

"You're bluffing."

"Why do you care about what I've been investigating?" she said. "That has nothing to do with you."

"I don't like anyone invading my turf, and you're costing me money." He released her arm and pushed her away. "Now go, and remember what I said. I'll be in touch."

Without looking back, Rory ran down the passageway onto the nearby street.

Once she was sure the PI wasn't following her, she stopped and leaned against a wall to catch her breath. She debated with herself whether or not to report the incident to Detective Green, but decided not to when she realized that would mean explaining about their search of Oscar's office. Even though Candy had let them in the door, they must have broken a number of laws during their little adventure. She wasn't the only one involved. She didn't want to see Liz go to jail.

Rory glanced at the time on her cell phone. She had just enough time to check with Nixie and ask about the bounced check before she needed to leave for the airport. She shoved the disturbing encounter to the back of her mind and headed toward the Akaw.

As soon as Rory passed through the automatic doors, Mel

walked up to her and said, "What's going on? I thought we were becoming friends."

Rory's heart sank at the hurt look on the other woman's face. "We are."

"Then why did you have those newspaper articles? The ones about that crash I was in years ago."

"He showed them to you?"

"Not exactly, but he should have. Out of the blue, Martin starts asking me about my accident, wants to know the details. I was puzzled at first, then I saw the articles on his desk. Had to drag it out of him, but he finally told me he'd gotten them from you. I couldn't believe it. I tell you about my accident, in confidence, and you immediately go off and investigate?"

"I'm sorry I've upset you. Really, I am. It was a coincidence. I was investigating Viveca's death and started looking into her background. I found those articles on that accident she was in. I had absolutely no idea it was the one you told me about."

"Really? I find that hard to believe. Why do you care about that accident anyway? It was a long time ago. What could it possibly have to do with Viveca's death?"

"I don't know, but both Jasmine and Viveca were in it and now they're both dead."

"Wait, do you think I killed them? I didn't even know Viveca was the other driver until Liz showed me that old book with her maiden name on it. At the convention, I only knew her as Viveca Forster. I didn't know her maiden name was Campbell."

"Viveca's not a very common name."

"I didn't do it, okay? My spot in the strokework class was nowhere near Jasmine's. And I can produce half a dozen witnesses that'll verify where I was during the alarm." Mel took a deep breath. "Look, I don't want to spend any more time with you right now. I don't think dinner tonight is a good idea."

"If that's what you want...Later?"

"I don't know." Mel looked at Rory sadly, then headed toward the front entrance.

Rory stared after Mel, feeling as if she'd lost a friendship before it had a chance to begin. Before going to find Nixie, she went into the restroom to collect herself. She sat on a toilet in a stall and put her head in her hands. A week that had started out so fun had turned into a nightmare. She'd lost an old friend and a potential new one. Plus she was no closer to figuring out who had killed Jasmine and her aunt. And now a PI was threatening her as well.

After she composed herself, she exited the bathroom and found Stella in the lobby waiting for her.

"I need a minute. I'll be right back," she said to the woman.

"No problem. I'm early anyway." Stella sat down on a chair next to her luggage while Rory walked down the hallway to the Manhattan ballroom. She found the convention organizer outside the room, packing up the pictures, painted pieces, and cards from the impromptu tribute to Jasmine.

As soon as she spotted Rory, Nixie handed her the heart-shaped necklace Rory had placed on the display. "Here, you should take this."

"How did you know it was mine?"

"Your name's on the back."

Rory turned the necklace over and read the tiny lettering she'd never noticed before: *To Rory, J.* With a lump in her throat, she put on the necklace. "What are you going to do with the rest of it?"

"Give it to Peter. He should decide what to do with it." Nixie put the last tribute item into the box and carried it into the office. She started sorting through the papers on the desk, neatly placing them in a briefcase. "Did you want to talk to me about something?"

"It's about that check you gave me. It bounced."

Nixie paused with a yellow folder in her hand, but didn't look up from her packing. "Did it? I'm sorry about that. I'll have to go through the bank account again. I promise I'll pay you as soon as I have the money."

As Rory watched the folder disappear into the briefcase, something niggled at her brain. She replayed the last week in her mind and came up with the answer. "Wait. That yellow folder. It's

Jasmine's, isn't it? Shouldn't you be putting it into the box you're giving to Peter?"

Nixie froze in the midst of packing. "I don't know what you're talking about."

Rory thought back to her search of the office and the accounting report she'd seen in the yellow folder. She'd only glanced at the columns of figures, not bothering to read the words on the page. At the time, she figured the report had something to do with the convention, but now she wondered. "I saw that same folder in Jasmine's hand. She was putting it into her roller bag. It's proof you embezzled, isn't it?" With a start, Rory realized that was probably what Jasmine had wanted to talk to her about after class, only she'd never gotten the chance.

"You've got quite the imagination. All this investigating you've been doing has got you seeing crime everywhere." The convention organizer shoved the last piece of paper in the briefcase and zipped it shut. "If you'll excuse me, I'm going to start taking all this to the car."

"I know that folder belonged to Jasmine."

"She's not the only one with a yellow folder."

"She's the only with a folder with her handwriting on it. I bet if I compared what's written on the tab with a sample of her handwriting, they'd be the same."

Nixie's face paled. "I know what you're thinking. She gave me the file. So, you see, I had no reason to harm her."

Rory's mouth dropped open in disbelief. "You're going to let that poor woman serve time for something you did?"

Nixie placed her briefcase on top of a box, picked them both up, and brushed past Rory. "Tell your mother everything's set for pick up tomorrow." Without looking back, she headed down the hallway.

Rory shook her head and walked back to the lobby where Stella was waiting for her. "Sorry about that. Ready?"

Stella nodded. As she bent down to pick up a large tote bag, its contents tumbled out. A half dozen bottles of blue-label varnish lay among the clothes and painting supplies the woman had packed.

"That varnish is bad. Hulbert told me about it when I was working the booth."

"I should have known it was too good to be true. It was the Show Special. I guess I know why now," Stella said.

"He didn't find out about the problem until a few people complained. I'm sure he'll take it back and give you a refund."

"Can't do anything about it right now. I have to get to the airport. I don't think he's around now, anyway. I'll contact him about it when I get home. Thanks for letting me know."

In no time, they'd repacked the tote bag and bundled everything into Rory's sedan. On the way to LAX, they talked about everything that had happened in the past week.

"The convention was fun," Stella said. "Got some great footage to show the chapter. I'm so sorry about Jasmine's death. And Viveca's, of course." She laid a hand on Rory's arm. "Makes you wonder if there's a curse on the family."

"Thanks. At least you and Veronica got some good photographs of both of them so Hulbert and Peter have recent ones to remember them by."

"They all got along, didn't they? Though there was one time, the day Jasmine died. I saw Hulbert and her arguing. They were standing near the restaurant."

"What about?" Rory turned off Sepulveda onto the road for the departure level.

"I'm not sure. All I heard was Jasmine say 'I'll tell Aunt Viveca.' Maybe he was having an affair." Stella peered through the windshield at the signs announcing the airlines. "That's my airline, right here."

After dropping the woman off, Rory headed home and settled down at her desk, intending to catch up on work. But she had a hard time getting back into the swing of things. Her mind kept drifting back to the OPS convention and the argument Stella had witnessed between Hulbert and Jasmine. She doubted the man was having an affair. He seemed too devoted to his wife to stray. She wondered what else her friend could have been threatening to tell Viveca about.

Rory examined the print of the photo taken of Hulbert and Jasmine in front of the restaurant when the argument must have occurred. She peered at their faces, trying to discern the reason for the dustup, but soon realized how stupid that was. She went back to work, but gave up after reading a dozen email messages.

Instead, Rory checked out various social media sites for videos and photos convention attendees had posted. A short video of Liz hamming it up at the pajama painting party brought a smile to her face. She wished she'd been in the mood to participate in the event. Everyone seemed to be having a good time. When she replayed the video, something behind Liz caught her eye. Rory backed it up and peered closely at the screen. In the background, Stella poured a capful of varnish into her water bottle, turning the liquid inside blue. Then she shook the bottle up and took a sip.

Rory puzzled over the woman's odd behavior. She sat back in her chair and wondered why anyone would be swigging varnish. It seemed like a dangerous thing to do, even if the product was eco-friendly. Something tugged at her brain. She searched the internet, but didn't find anything that would explain Stella's actions.

Rory dismissed the thought from her mind and ran through the photo gallery in Vista Beach Confidential to see if any new pictures had been added. When she once again came across the photograph of Hulbert and Jasmine, her gaze strayed to the bottle in the young woman's hand. She enlarged the portion she was interested in. A blue label peeked out above her friend's arm.

The same color as the liquid Stella had poured into her water. In all her years of painting, Rory had never seen varnish that color. What if the blue-label varnish wasn't varnish at all?

Rory closed her eyes, going over every conversation she'd had in the last week. When she went over her most recent talk with Peter and recalled what she'd read on the internet, everything fell into place. GHB was often tinted blue.

It all made sense now. Stella having all the bottles of blue-label varnish in her luggage. Her dramatic weight loss. What Peter had told her about people using GHB to lose weight. She knew where the GHB had come from that had killed Viveca. Jasmine must have discovered the truth about the blue-label varnish and been killed to prevent her from telling the world about VivEco's side business.

But Rory had no proof. She couldn't go to the police without it. She needed to get hold of one of the bottles of varnish and test it. She couldn't ask Stella for one of hers. The woman was already on a plane back to Minnesota.

She needed to go to the source, to get a bottle straight from the VivEco booth. She grabbed her bag and ran out the door. On her way back to the Akaw, she rehearsed the cover story she'd give if anyone objected to her presence on the trade show floor: She'd lost her keys somewhere and was retracing her steps.

But, when she reached the Hermosa ballroom, there was no need for the story. No guard manned the entrance, and no one seemed to care who was walking around. She slipped through the door and headed down the aisle toward the VivEco booth, nodding at a burly young man rolling a stack of boxes toward the entrance. Half the booths she passed had already been emptied, the other half were full of boxes waiting to be wheeled away.

When she reached her destination, she stopped and stared in dismay. Except for the banner announcing the name of the booth, the area was completely empty. Every cardboard box had already been taken away. Rory checked under the table where the box she was looking for had been all through the convention, but it was no longer there.

Defeated, she leaned against a table to think. She was too late. Then she remembered what Nixie had told them about the schedule. She found a hotel worker at one of the other booths.

"Everything is going to the loading dock, right?" she said to him.

"That's right."

"Have any trucks picked up boxes yet?"

The man shook his head. "Not until tomorrow."

"That's what I thought. Thanks." Rory headed toward the exit. Assuming Hulbert hadn't taken the box of blue-label varnish with him, she should be able to find what she wanted on the loading dock. But she would have to wait until the ballroom had been completely cleared. She would tackle the loading dock later tonight when it was sure to be deserted. She only hoped she wouldn't be too late.

Chapter 30

Later that evening, after darkness had fallen over the city, Rory returned to the Akaw, looking for the corridor that led to the loading dock and the evidence she needed to prove VivEco was selling a weight loss product containing GHB. Now that the OPS convention was over, few people traversed the hotel's hallways. The area where the convention had been held was virtually deserted. When she peeked in the Hermosa ballroom to make sure no burly men were still at work, the whole place had been dismantled. Even the walls of the booths were gone.

Rory continued her search for the loading dock, smiling at anyone she encountered, pretending to be exploring the hotel. Every once in a while, she felt someone watching her, but after turning around half a dozen times and not seeing anything suspicious, she decided her imagination was working overtime.

After several wrong turns, she finally found the correct hallway which, to her great relief, turned out to be empty. She didn't relish the idea of explaining why she was headed toward an area where no hotel guest should want to go.

Rory entered the loading dock through a gray metal door, far more industrial in appearance than the guest areas of the hotel. With the outside roll-up door closed and no windows, it was too dark to see anything, let alone conduct a search. The only light came from the hallway she'd just left. Not wanting to leave the door open, in case someone from the hotel staff noticed it, she groped around on the wall until she found the light switch. As soon as the lights came on, she closed the hallway door, then set to work.

Rory surveyed the groups of cardboard boxes that covered the concrete floor. Stacked two high in some areas, corridors divided them into sections. The dim light given off by the overhead fixtures provided enough illumination that she could just make out the lettering on the sides of the boxes. She passed over the ones filled with janitorial supplies and gift shop items, moving on to the group closest to the entrance. When she couldn't decipher the handwriting on the side of one of the boxes, she searched the cage near the hallway door where a guard usually sat and found an industrial-sized flashlight.

Training its beam on the sides of the cardboard box nearest her, she read HennaMe written in a cramped hand. She moved from group to group and was almost at the roll-up door before she found the boxes from the VivEco booth, stacked two high.

Rory looked in dismay at the brown packing tape sealing each box. She hadn't expected them to be taped shut. She checked the area where the hotel supplies were kept, relieved to find a roll of packing tape and a box cutter. She searched the top layer of VivEco boxes, taping them shut again after she'd searched each one. Inside she found bottles of paint and green label products, but no blue-label varnish.

Rory put her flashlight on the floor, its beam trained on the boxes, and lifted the top box down onto the concrete floor. Not finding what she wanted in the one underneath, she moved another box down. Soon all of the top boxes were on the ground and, in the final one of the group, she discovered the bottles she'd been searching for.

Rory lifted one of the bottles of blue-label varnish out of the container. When she tried to open it, the cap wouldn't budge. After a number of unsuccessful tries, she was considering using the box cutter to cut the top off the bottle when the cap finally loosened and came off. She placed drops of its contents onto the test spots on one of the coasters she'd bought at the pharmacy, then picked up the flashlight and pointed its beam on the spots. When they both turned bright blue, indicating a positive test for GHB, she felt relieved she'd been right, yet saddened at the same time.

After recapping the bottle, she set it carefully to one side along with the now turned off flashlight while she returned the boxes to their previous configuration. She was lifting the last one into place when a male voice said, "You had to interfere, didn't you?"

Her back to the new arrival, Rory took her cell phone out of the front pocket of her jeans and as surreptitiously as possible called Liz's number. Stuffing the phone back into her pocket and hoping her friend would hear and understand what was going on, she plastered an innocent expression on her face and turned around to confront her adversary.

Hulbert Forster stood five feet away, his face suffused with anger.

"Hi, Hulbert," she said as brightly as she could, hoping to hide the sound of her heart thumping wildly in her chest. "I accidentally packed my keys in one of the Scrap 'n Paint boxes. Had to use my spare ones to get home last night. Didn't want to wait until they delivered everything to the store tomorrow." She held up her keys and jingled them, hoping the light was dim enough he would believe she'd taken them out of one of the boxes and not the pocket of her jeans.

The man shook his head and took a step toward her. "Do you think I'm stupid? I *can* read." He nodded toward the writing on the side of the box she'd just replaced.

Rory backed away from him, hoping to put some distance and a few boxes between them, doing her best to ignore the man's angry face. "What are you doing here in the *hotel's loading dock*, Hulbert? I can call you *Hulbert*, right?" She kept her voice loud, emphasizing certain words, hoping Liz could figure out what was going on from the little she heard. "And why are you so angry? I wasn't stealing any of your supplies. Honest."

When she backed up further, her heel hit something. She glanced down. The bottle of varnish she'd set aside rolled down into the chasm between the edge of the dock and the roll-up door, landing with a soft thud as it hit the ground. The flashlight almost followed it, but she managed to stop it with her foot before it could disappear into the darkness.

"Why didn't you just believe Jasmine overdosed? I never wanted to hurt anyone."

Rory gave up trying to pretend she didn't know what he was referring to. "Why did you, then? Kill Jasmine? Did she find out about your little side business? The weight loss product?"

Hulbert nodded. "And threatened to tell Viveca all about it if I didn't stop. I couldn't let her do that. The money from that part of the business was the only thing keeping VivEco afloat. I couldn't let my wife's dream fall apart. It meant too much to her, and she meant too much to me. So I told Jasmine I'd stop. I wanted to keep her happy until I figured out some way to get rid of her."

"You got the Xyrem out of her medicine bottle, didn't you?"

"She brought her medicine into the booth when she came to work. It was easy for me to take a bit out, only she left for class before I could replace the bottle. So I took the key card out of Viveca's purse and put the medicine back in her room. No one suspected a thing. Not even the police."

"Weren't you afraid someone would see you?"

"People were so enthralled with being able to talk with Viveca and get her autograph, there was little chance anyone would notice anything I did."

"Not even setting off the alarm?"

"Put on a cap and coveralls, no one pays attention to you. And with everyone running around, trying to get out of the hotel, it was easy to slip inside the ballroom and put the medicine in the soda I saw her buy earlier."

"You tried to throw me off by saying you saw Peter dressed in coveralls going into the classroom." Rory's words were more of a statement than a question.

"I figured it wouldn't hurt to cast suspicion on someone else. Admit it, you suspected him for a while, didn't you?"

The two men did have similar builds, Rory thought, even if

they were decades apart in age. Dress them in shapeless clothes and obscure their faces and most people wouldn't be able to tell them apart. "Did Viveca know what you were doing? She wasn't in on it, was she?"

"No, she wasn't. She had no idea the blue-label varnish wasn't varnish at all. I have a feeling she suspected something wasn't right before she died."

Rory wondered if that was what Viveca had wanted to talk to her about after the meet and greet.

"She would have been okay with it. I'm sure of it. She was always into helping people, encouraging them to make the best of themselves. That's what I was doing with this diet aid. Helping those who had tried everything to lose weight and couldn't."

"But it's dangerous."

"Not if you take it correctly. Viveca would have understood." Hulbert wiped a tear from his eye. "It's all your fault she's dead, you know."

"Why do you say that? You're the one who put the GHB in her drink."

"That was meant for you, not her. If you hadn't meddled, my beloved Viveca would be alive now. The police never really considered Jasmine's death a murder, at least not seriously. I made sure of that. I told them about her suicide attempt so they'd focus on that. You should have accepted Jasmine's death as an accidental overdose like the police did, but you kept on pushing, asking questions, rummaging through dumpsters."

"You were the one who hit me over the head and pushed me into the dumpster, weren't you? Why did you go back for the coveralls?"

"You gave me the idea, talking about the police searching the trash for evidence. I didn't know what they might find on them, but I wasn't taking any chances. Only you got there first." Hulbert stepped closer. "You wouldn't even give up after I hired that PI to harass you. He was only too happy to take my money. He has a bit of a beef with you."

So that's why Hulbert had been coming out of Oscar Carlton's office, Rory thought.

"When you gave me that photo of me and Jasmine," Hulbert continued. "I was sure you knew then. I figured you were getting ready to blackmail me."

"I just thought you'd like it. I wasn't threatening you. I didn't even know the photo's significance until later." Rory inched back toward the roll-up door and pushed the flashlight closer to the edge. The man was so angry he didn't seem to notice the slight movement.

"I gave you the champagne. Why didn't you just drink it? Why did you have to set it down and let Viveca pick it up? Why? Why? Why?" Hulbert kicked a nearby box repeatedly.

One swift kick and the flashlight rolled over the edge to join the varnish bottle. When it clattered to the ground, Hulbert's attention turned to the roll-up door.

Taking advantage of the distraction, Rory crouched down, ducking behind the VivEco boxes. Walking crablike, she began the slow progress toward the door into the hallway and safety.

Halfway to her destination, a large gap between sets of boxes opened up in front of her. She peeked over the boxes she was hiding behind to find the man on the other side of the stack only a few feet away from her.

"I see you," Hulbert said as Rory slid back behind a box marked AS&P. She opened it up and discovered thirteen-inch round wooden plates inside. She grabbed three of them and threw them like a Frisbee, one after another, toward Hulbert. He flung his hands in front of his face and danced back and forth, shielding his head from the flying objects. She raced across the floor. She'd almost reached the hallway door when she tripped over a mop handle her opponent had flung out in front of her legs.

Momentarily stunned, she rolled over onto her back. Hulbert jumped on her chest, a bottle of the blue-label varnish in his hand. He tried to force her to drink, but she clamped her mouth shut and moved her head from side to side. When he punched her in the stomach, she gasped and her mouth dropped open for a fraction of a second. Before she could close it again, he poured some of the liquid in her mouth. She tried to spit it out, but felt some of it go down her throat.

She continued to resist as he held her down, but he was too strong for her. She felt herself fading away, getting sleepier and sleepier until she could no longer fight back. In a dreamlike state, she didn't resist as Hulbert supported her, walking her down the hallway and into an elevator.

Rory remembered nothing after that until she found herself in a dark space unsure where she was or how much time had passed. Before long, she became aware she was moving. She patted her pocket and discovered her cell phone was still there, but when she took it out, no bars shown on its display. Using it as a flashlight, she examined the tight space. When the light illuminated two twelve-packs of soda, she realized she was in the trunk of her own car.

She groped with her hand in the area where she remembered the trunk release was and pulled. The latch released and she raised the trunk a fraction of an inch, filling her nostrils with the night air. She peeked out and discovered she was on a winding two-lane road that appeared to be deserted. With the only light coming from the moon and the taillights of her car, she couldn't see much. If she squinted, she could just make out a hillside with scraggly looking vegetation on one side of the road and a sheer drop-off on the other. No signs told her where she was, but she guessed it was somewhere she wouldn't be found for a long time.

Rory groped around in the trunk until she found the roll of paper towels she'd bought earlier that day. She unrolled the towels and shoved the end out of the trunk, anchoring the roll under her body, hoping another car would see the fluttering white paper. When minutes passed and she still hadn't seen any lights, she realized she was on her own.

No houses, no cars, no cell reception, no hope.

Rory opened the trunk wider and considered trying to climb out, but the car was going fast enough and the road was windy enough, she was afraid she'd end up over the cliff instead of on the pavement. She checked for cell service once again and almost crowed in triumph when a single bar appeared on the screen. She was dialing 911 when the car turned off the highway and slowed down. She dropped the phone and felt around for something to use to defend herself. The only things she could find were the twelve-packs and a tote bag filled with painting supplies.

When the car stopped. and she heard footsteps coming toward the back, Rory shook a couple cans as best she could in the tight space. As soon as the trunk opened, she sprayed soda into Hulbert's eyes. While he was clawing at his face, she grabbed the tote bag. Before she could position herself to swing it at him, he hauled her out of the trunk onto the dirt on the side of the road. She lost her grip on the bag and it dropped to the ground beside her.

As Hulbert dragged her toward the edge of a sheer drop-off, she dug in her heels and flung a handful of dirt in his face. He released her long enough for her to kick him in his manly parts. Before he could recover, she snatched up the tote bag and smacked him on the side of the head.

As he fell to the ground, she heard a police siren in the distance. When a patrol car arrived followed by Detective Green in his own vehicle, she was sitting on the dirt, leaning against the side of her car.

"It's about time you got here," Rory said as she looked up at the detective's relieved face.

Chapter 31

Two days later, Rory and Liz sat at a table near the snack shop at the base of the Vista Beach pier, overlooking the sand and the ocean beyond. With the afternoon sun shining down on them, they leaned back in their plastic chairs and watched beachgoers enjoying the beautiful summer day. From their spot on the pier, they could look down at a volleyball game in progress on the beach below.

Rory took a sip of her lime diet Coke and watched a young mother who was introducing her toddler to the ocean. Clinging tightly to his mother's hand, the child stood on the packed sand and giggled as waves splashed gently around his feet. "I wish Jasmine could be here. I miss her."

Liz patted her friend's arm. "At least you found out who killed her. You have the satisfaction of knowing you helped bring her murderer to justice and stopped the sale of a dangerous weight loss product."

"I hear Blue Wave Investments is going to cough up the money to repair all the houses," Rory said. "They decided it was cheaper to fix the ones that were damaged than to continue fighting."

"That's smart, especially with all the bad publicity the Akaw's gotten lately."

"Having the managing partner arrested didn't help the hotel any. Brandy's happy about the settlement. Her aunt's house will be repaired, and they'll be able to sell it to help pay for her care."

"Do you know what she plans on doing afterwards?"

"Once her aunt is squared away, she and Peter are moving back to Riverside. They were happier there." Rory looked over at her friend. "Are you handling the sale of the house?"

"When the repairs are done. I've already got several potential buyers lined up. Do you think the two of them will get together?"

"Eventually, though guilt may keep them apart for a while."

"What about Peter's problems at work? Wasn't he under investigation or something? Will he be able to get another job?" Liz asked.

"He was *never* under investigation. That was just Nixie muddying the waters, trying to take the focus off her and her problems."

"Do you think she really stole that money?"

"I think so. Money was tight after her husband died, and her situation hasn't improved much. She still hasn't paid that last invoice I sent her. But I doubt she'll admit to the embezzlement. At least not until Gordon's old enough to fend for himself. Family's the most important thing to her."

"I suppose there's no proof. Just Tempest's accusations, which no one seems to take seriously."

"We could've had the proof if we'd realized in time. Jasmine found documents on Nixie's laptop and printed them out, but Nixie took them back after Jasmine died. They were in the roller bag, hidden among the supplies, and we didn't know it. I saw the folder in Nixie's hands on Monday."

"Didn't she claim not to know much about finances?"

Rory snorted. "That's what she wanted everyone to think. Did you hear? She's taken in Ian's son. Given him a place to stay on holidays when he's home from college."

"Speaking of Ian, he confessed because he thought Nixie had killed Jasmine, right?"

"That's right. He knew about the embezzlement accusations."

Liz glanced toward the nearby street. "Here comes Miss Snoop." She leaned over and said in a voice barely above a whisper,

"Guess what I heard. You know how Veronica had access to that security footage? Her source was one of the hotel employees. Nell ferreted him out. Cost him his job." She rubbed her thumb over her fingers. "I guess a little moolah can get you anything."

Veronica crossed the bike path and strode toward them, her tote bag bouncing against her hip as she walked. She plunked down in one of the empty seats at the table. "You two are sure hard to find. Your mother told me you might be here, Rory."

"What did you want to see me about?"

"I want to know if you'll give me an exclusive. Talk to me about your ordeal at the hands of Hulbert Forster." When Rory hesitated, Veronica's eyes narrowed. "Have you been talking to another reporter? Did the *Times* call you?"

"No, nothing like that. I'll answer a few questions."

"Good." The reporter pulled a notepad out of her tote bag. "I've heard the basic story. Just want to clear up a few things. So you're on the loading dock with Hulbert. How did he subdue you? What are you, six feet? He's shorter than you are."

"He's stronger than he looks." Rory thought back to the box he'd easily maneuvered out from under the table in the VivEco booth, one that she couldn't even budge. "Then when he forced some GHB down my throat I was pretty easy to control. Don't remember much after that. And then I ended up in the Angeles National Forest."

"LA's favorite body dumping ground," Liz said.

Rory shuddered when she thought of her narrow escape. If Hulbert had succeeded in pushing her over the side, it would probably have been months before her body was found.

"Uh-huh." Veronica jotted something down in her notepad. "So you came to in the trunk of your car. Tell me about that."

Outwardly calm but inwardly roiling, Rory related her ordeal to the reporter as briefly as possible.

Veronica made another entry in her notebook, then turned to Liz. "Where do you come in?"

"Rory called me from the loading dock. All I heard was this

odd conversation she was having with Hulbert. It took me awhile to figure out what was going on, but once I did I immediately called Detective Green and explained what was happening. He used the GPS on Rory's cell phone to find her."

"So Hulbert did all this just to protect his weight loss business?"

"Not just that. He blamed me for Viveca's death. If I hadn't set that glass down, and she hadn't picked it up..."

"Okay, let's talk about Jasmine's murder. It's not clear to me. Did Hulbert use the GHB from his weight loss product or her own medicine to give her the overdose?"

"He used her own medicine," Rory said. "He was trying to make it look like an accident."

"It almost worked," Liz chimed in.

"What about the soda bottle he drugged? Do the police have it?"

Rory shook her head. "Hulbert disposed of it once he realized it could implicate him."

"I see. Viveca's death really was an accident, right? He was gunning for you?" Veronica pointed her pen at Rory.

"That's right," Rory said softly. A pang of guilt stabbed at her. If she hadn't looked into her friend's death, Viveca might still be alive. "He didn't count on my not wanting to drink alcohol. Anyone could have picked up that glass once I set it down."

The reporter closed her notebook. "I think I have everything I need. I'd better get going and write this up."

As Veronica made her way up the hill toward the newspaper offices, she passed Detective Green and Mel coming in the opposite direction.

"Here comes Marosia." Liz cocked her head thoughtfully. "Or should they be Meltin?"

Clad in shorts and t-shirts, the couple strolled toward them, hand in hand.

"I guess they're both off-duty." Liz took a sip of her smoothie. "Is Mel still mad at you?"

"Sort of. I don't think we'll be bosom buddies, but at least she's talking to me now. I'm not sure I'd be quite so forgiving if I were her."

"We had a long talk. I told her you had no intention of telling her boyfriend about the accident and that you'd never suspect her of murder."

"That's not quite true," Rory said.

"She doesn't have to know that."

As soon as the couple reached the snack shop, they bought smoothies and headed over to join Rory and Liz.

"May we?" Detective Green said.

"Go ahead." Rory nodded toward the empty chairs.

After the couple settled into their seats, Rory looked at the detective.

"What's the word on Ian?" she said. "Will he be charged for his false confession?"

"The D.A.'s not going to bother with that. He'll be extradited to Washington state to face charges for that hit-and-run. His fellow investors will have to find a new manager for the Akaw," he said between sips.

"Nell seems to be doing a good job running the hotel," Liz said. "Maybe she'll get a permanent gig. Now that everything's been settled with the protesters, it should be smoother sailing for her."

"I heard Nixie's sticking by him," Mel said. "I hope she'll hold the convention again. I'd like to go to it without all this drama."

"Amen to that," Rory said. "And Hulbert? What's going to happen to him?"

"The D.A.'s office is working out the charges. Hulbert has confessed to everything, even hiring Oscar Carlton to harass you to convince you to stop investigating." The detective looked pointedly in Rory's direction.

"Ian also said the PI blackmailed him, didn't he?" Liz said, trying to keep the focus off of her friend.

"Between Hulbert and Ian we have a pretty good case against Carlton. He'll certainly lose his PI's license," the detective said.

"Has Oscar been arrested, then?" Rory asked. She hoped the PI was in jail. He still made her a little uneasy.

"We tried, but he's nowhere to be found. Fled the state as far as we can tell."

Rory breathed a sigh of relief and prayed the man would never come back.

The four sat and talked about more pleasant things for a while, then Detective Green and Mel rose to go. "I'll see you at your mom's store sometime, right?" Mel said to Rory.

Rory nodded, sensing the question was an olive branch and she was one step closer to mending fences with the woman.

"I'm signed up for that class you're teaching at the end of the month, Liz. The Halloween design," Mel said. "Arika's Scrap 'n Paint always has such interesting classes."

"Isn't it a little too early in the year to be talking ghosts and goblins?" the detective asked.

Mel shook her head as if to say some people would never understand. "If you're going to be painting holiday designs you have to start early."

Rory and Liz nodded their heads in agreement.

As the couple departed, hand in hand, Liz patted Rory's arm sympathetically. "You could have had that, you know, if you'd made up your mind sooner. Dashing D likes you."

"I know," Rory said wistfully. "Bad timing, I guess. I just wasn't ready."

"But you are now?" Liz straightened up in her chair and stared hopefully at her friend.

Rory nodded. Liz picked up her phone from where she'd put it on the table. "Have I got someone for you!"

Author's Note

Narcolepsy. I'd heard the term over the years, but not until I saw a BBC documentary called "Nap Attack," did I begin to understand what it meant.

For those interested in firsthand accounts of the day-to-day challenges faced by people with the condition, I recommend reading *Wide Awake and Dreaming: A Memoir of Narcolepsy* by Julie Flygare and *Narcolepsy: A Funny Disorder That's No Laughing Matter* by Marguerite J. Utley. Julie Flygare also has a website, julieflygare.com, that's worth visiting.

In creating Jasmine, I have tried to treat the condition with respect and understanding. I hope I have succeeded.

Sybil Johnson

Sybil Johnson's love affair with reading began in kindergarten with "The Three Little Pigs." Visits to the library introduced her to Encyclopedia Brown, Mrs. Piggle-Wiggle and a host of other characters. Fast forward to college where she continued reading while studying Computer Science. After a rewarding career in the computer industry, Sybil decided to try her hand at writing mysteries. Her short fiction has appeared in *Mysterical-E* and *Spinetingler Magazine*, among others. Originally from the Pacific Northwest, she now lives in Southern California where she enjoys tole painting, studying ancient languages and spending time with friends and family.

Henery Press Mystery Books

And finally, before you go...
Here are a few other mysteries
you might enjoy:

COUNTERFEIT CONSPIRACIES

Ritter Ames

A Bodies of Art Mystery (#1)

Laurel Beacham may have been born with a silver spoon in her mouth, but she has long since lost it digging herself out of trouble. Her father gambled and womanized his way through the family fortune before skiing off an Alp, leaving her with more tarnish than trust fund. Quick wits and connections have gained her a reputation as one of the world's premier art recovery experts. The police may catch the thief, but she reclaims the missing masterpieces.

The latest assignment, however, may be her undoing. Using every ounce of luck and larceny she possesses, Laurel must locate a priceless art icon and rescue a co-worker (and ex-lover) from a master criminal, all the while matching wits with a charming new nemesis. Unfortunately, he seems to know where the bodies are buried—and she prefers hers isn't next.

Available at booksellers nationwide and online

Visit www.henerypress.com for details

KILLER IMAGE

Wendy Tyson

An Allison Campbell Mystery (#1)

As Philadelphia's premier image consultant, Allison Campbell helps others reinvent themselves, but her most successful transformation was her own after a scandal nearly ruined her. Now she moves in a world of powerful executives, wealthy, eccentric ex-wives and twisted ethics.

When Allison's latest Main Line client, the fifteen-year-old Goth daughter of a White House hopeful, is accused of the ritualistic murder of a local divorce attorney, Allison fights to prove her client's innocence when no one else will. But unraveling the truth brings specters from her own past. And in a place where image is everything, the ability to distinguish what's real from the facade may be the only thing that keeps Allison alive.

Available at booksellers nationwide and online

Visit www.henerypress.com for details

CROPPED TO DEATH

Christina Freeburn

A Faith Hunter Scrap This Mystery (#1)

Former US Army JAG specialist, Faith Hunter, returns to her West Virginia home to work in her grandmothers' scrapbooking store determined to lead an unassuming life after her adventure abroad turned disaster. But her quiet life unravels when her friend is charged with murder – and Faith inadvertently supplied the evidence. So Faith decides to cut through the scrap and piece together what really happened.

With a sexy prosecutor, a determined homicide detective, a handful of sticky suspects and a crop contest gone bad, Faith quickly realizes if she's not careful, she'll be the next one cropped.

Available at booksellers nationwide and online

Visit www.henerypress.com for details

NUN TOO SOON

Alice Loweecey

A Giulia Driscoll Mystery (#1)

Giulia Driscoll has just taken on her first impossible client: The Silk Tie Killer. He's hired Driscoll Investigations to prove his innocence and they have only thirteen days to accomplish it. Talk about being tried in the media. Everyone in town is sure Roger Fitch strangled his girlfriend with one of his silk neckties. And then there's the local TMZ wannabes stalking Giulia and her client for sleazy sound bites.

On top of all that, her assistant's first baby is due any second, her scary smart admin still doesn't relate well to humans, and her police detective husband insists her client is guilty. About this marriage thing—it's unknown territory, but it sure beats ten years of living with 150 nuns.

Giulia's ownership of Driscoll Investigations hasn't changed her passion for justice from her convent years. But the more dirt she digs up, the more she's worried her efforts will help a murderer escape. As the client accuses DI of dragging its heels on purpose, Giulia thinks The Silk Tie Killer might be choosing one of his ties for her own neck.

Available at booksellers nationwide and online

Visit www.henerypress.com for details

CIRCLE OF INFLUENCE

Annette Dashofy

A Zoe Chambers Mystery (#1)

Zoe Chambers, paramedic and deputy coroner in rural Pennsylvania's tight-knit Vance Township, has been privy to a number of local secrets over the years, some of them her own. But secrets become explosive when a dead body is found in the Township Board President's abandoned car.

As a January blizzard rages, Zoe and Police Chief Pete Adams launch a desperate search for the killer, even if it means uncovering secrets that could not only destroy Zoe and Pete, but also those closest to them.

Available at booksellers nationwide and online

Visit www.henerypress.com for details